As the ship lurched, she cried out, certain she was destined to be pulled beneath those terrifying waves. Just when her hysteria reached an unbearable peak, there was a hard knock on the door.

"Come in," she cried in a wavering voice, eager for any human face.

Giles stepped across the threshold, dressed in his sou'wester and slicker. Taking one look at her pale face in the dim light, he tossed aside his streaming coat and hat.

"What a woebegone girl. Where is all that stalwart courage in the face of danger? Come, Gwyneth, don't be frightened," he said gently and took her in his arms. She nestled against his damp shirt.

"I'm frightened," she moaned. "I fear we are all going to be drowned."

"Perhaps, but I doubt it. I have been in worse storms at sea."

"I feel so alone," she whispered, still hiding her tear-stained face in his chest, comforted by the steady beat of his heart beneath her cheek.

"Well, you are not alone now." He raised her head with his hand and looked into her eyes, his own steady and clear.

Gradually Gwyneth's shaking eased, and she felt a warm glow spread through her shivering body. Here was comfort and reassurance.

Hardly aware of what she was doing, she lifted her face imploringly to his. Giles bent his head and kissed her with a sudden passion . . .

# ZEBRA'S REGENCY ROMANCES
# DAZZLE AND DELIGHT

**A BEGUILING INTRIGUE**                    (4441, $3.99)
by Olivia Sumner

Pretty as a picture Justine Riggs cared nothing for propriety. She dressed as a boy, sat on her horse like a jockey, and pondered the stars like a scientist. But when she tried to best the handsome Quenton Fletcher, Marquess of Devon, by proving that she was the better equestrian, he would try to prove Justine's antics were pure folly. The game he had in mind was seduction—never imagining that he might lose his heart in the process!

**AN INCONVENIENT ENGAGEMENT**              (4442, $3.99)
by Joy Reed

Rebecca Wentworth was furious when she saw her betrothed waltzing with another. So she decides to make him jealous by flirting with the handsomest man at the ball, John Collinwood, Earl of Stanford. The "wicked" nobleman knew exactly what the enticing miss was up to—and he was only too happy to play along. But as Rebecca gazed into his magnificent eyes, her errant fiancé was soon utterly forgotten!

**SCANDAL'S LADY**                          (4472, $3.99)
by Mary Kingsley

Cassandra was shocked to learn that the new Earl of Lynton was her childhood friend, Nicholas St. John. After years at sea and mixed feelings Nicholas had come home to take the family title. And although Cassandra knew her place as a governess, she could not help the thrill that went through her each time he was near. Nicholas was pleased to find that his old friend Cassandra was his new next door neighbor, but after being near her, he wondered if mere friendship would be enough . . .

**HIS LORDSHIP'S REWARD**                   (4473, $3.99)
by Carola Dunn

As the daughter of a seasoned soldier, Fanny Ingram was accustomed to the vagaries of military life and cared not a whit about matters of rank and social standing. So she certainly never foresaw her *tendre* for handsome Viscount Roworth of Kent with whom she was forced to share lodgings, while he carried out his clandestine activities on behalf of the British Army. And though good sense told Roworth to keep his distance, he couldn't stop from taking Fanny in his arms for a kiss that made all hearts equal!

*Available wherever paperbacks are sold, or order direct from the Publisher. Send cover price plus 50¢ per copy for mailing and handling to Penguin USA, P.O. Box 999, c/o Dept. 17109, Bergenfield, NJ 07621. Residents of New York and Tennessee must include sales tax. DO NOT SEND CASH.*

# Violet Hamilton
# A Rake's Journey

**ZEBRA BOOKS**
**KENSINGTON PUBLISHING CORP.**

ZEBRA BOOKS are published by

Kensington Publishing Corp.
850 Third Avenue
New York, NY 10022

First Printing: August, 1995

Printed in the United States of America

# *Chapter One*

The guns had been bombarding the town for three days, and the log houses were little protection against the British two hundred pounders blasting away from batteries across the river. Gwyneth had narrowly missed a ball when she had ventured out to buy flour yesterday and had hurriedly retreated to the stifling and dubious comfort of the Sibley home. Most of the inhabitants of the small fort town on the farthest outskirts of the Colonies wondered why Gen. William Hull did not return the fire, but the aging boastful commander had ordered the men to wait. Gwyneth despised him for his cowardice and feared for the fate of Fort Detroit. With the British were hordes of Indians and their impressive chief Tecumseh, of whom frightful savage attacks could be expected.

When Gwyneth had arrived at Detroit four months ago to visit her sister Delia and her brother-in-law

Isaac Sibley, talk of war between Britain and her former colonies had not appeared likely. She had wanted to escape Montreal and her father's new wife, but she had never thought that she might be in danger. Detroit, little more than a fortified village of eight hundred citizens, had enjoyed good relations with its Canadian neighbors across the river at Sandwich and Fort Malden. Of course, there was always trouble with the British allies, the Indians, but neither the Canadians nor the Americans wanted war. For a time it seemed all might be well, but then President Madison and the Congress in faraway Washington had lost patience with Britain's Orders in Council that allowed impressment of American seamen, and war was declared.

Isaac Sibley, a merchant and a militia captain, had gone off reluctantly with his men into the Ohio country and left his pregnant wife with her sister to console her. With Sibley had gone James Brush, a stalwart young man who had shown interest in Gwyneth, leaving the two women with no protection but the little maid Marie, half French, half Indian, who yesterday had deserted them.

Gwyneth flinched from another blast, and a cannonball sailed over the house, landing with a telling thud several yards behind the home. The pewter plates on the cupboard shuddered and two fell to the floor. From upstairs Delia's two-month-old son, Robert, woke and began to cry. Gwyneth picked up the plates and then went upstairs in answer to her sister's call.

The Sibley house, one of the sturdiest and most comfortable in the village, had little elegance. Built of cedar logs, it had a steep roof, dormer windows shuttered inside, roughly plastered walls, and as evidence of its owner's wealth, a front door painted green. Upstairs the master bedroom held a huge fourposter bed, a walnut wardrobe and bureau, and the baby's cradle. When Gwyneth appeared, she found her sister holding the baby and peering fearfully from the one small window.

"Oh, Gwyneth, we will all be murdered," Delia cried.

Probably, Gwyneth thought, but she hurried to reassure her sister.

"Nonsense. Hull's men are well-positioned with their guns just outside the fort. When or if the British land, they will blast them back to the river," she insisted stoutly.

The sisters had a faint family resemblance, sharing wide hazel eyes and chestnut hair, but Delia was plump with a pouting mouth and lacked Gwyneth's fine oval face and height. Of a timid and confiding nature, she found life puzzling, and Gwyneth often wondered why she had chosen Isaac Sibley as a husband, traveling seven hundred miles into the wilderness away from the comfort of family and friends in Montreal. Of course, Isaac was a handsome forceful young man, a flourishing merchant in Detroit, commanding respect. But Gwyneth found Delia's choice amazing, considering that her sister had several wealthy and attractive suitors in Montreal who had offered her less arduous positions. There was no accounting for it except that Delia had been persuaded by Isaac's more powerful personality or perhaps by love, an emotion Gwyneth was apt to view with some suspicion. But the sisters, despite their very different characters, were devoted, bound by the loss of their mother before they had grown to womanhood. Although Delia was the elder by four years, she had always depended on Gwyneth for support and left decisions to her sister.

"Isaac should never have left us here unprotected, at the mercy of soldiers and savages," Delia wailed, her eyes filling with easy tears.

"He had his duty to do. The men depend on him. He had to go."

"And James, too. Don't you miss him?"

"Yes, he was an admirable companion. But I would not think much of a man who shirked his duty in the face of danger," Gwyneth said decisively. Actually, she missed James Brush more than she wanted to admit. From their first meeting, some days after her arrival in May, she had been attracted to the young lawyer who had left New England to establish a career in this frontier village. Not as strikingly handsome as his friend Isaac, he shared that young man's strength of character and ambition, leavened with a cheerful temperament, an engaging smile, and an optimistic view of life. But Gwyneth was not yet prepared to make the commitment he wanted. She was not sure she cared for him enough, and she was wary of marriage. Neither her father's experience nor Delia's had impressed her with the institution. At eighteen she felt she still had time before making a choice.

Another salvo interrupted her thoughts. The shelling had increased in the last few hours, and as yet there was no answer from Detroit's batteries. The August heat added to her uneasiness. However, her first responsibility was to soothe Delia. His mother's fear was affecting little Robert, and he cried protestingly.

"Come, Delia, be sensible. If we stay quietly indoors, nothing can happen to us."

"Well, yesterday Judge Woodward escaped death by mere inches. A shell exploded in his bedroom, where he had been sleeping just minutes before," Delia complained. She continued to peer out the window. "I can see no one on the street. If only we knew what that old fool Hull was doing."

"Very little, I suspect," Gwyneth said dryly. She had little respect for General Hull, who had marched two thousand troops across the river to Amhertsburg a month ago, a much larger force than that of the British defending Fort Malden, but had made no effort to take the fort. Then hearing that the British general, Isaac Brock, was marching from Niagara, he had cravenly trailed back to the dubious shelter of Detroit. Now he was refusing to engage the British attackers.

"Oh, no," Delia moaned from the window, squeezing the baby in her agitation.

Gwyneth went to her side, deftly removed Robert and put him in his cradle, then rejoined her sister.

"What's wrong? Oh, I see." As the sisters watched, they saw General Hull's son, Capt. A. F. Hull, walking down the street carrying a white flag.

"He's surrendering," Gwyneth announced, appalled. From the distance came the steady tramp of men, the British marching into Fort Detroit, preceded by the triumphant peal of fife and drum.

Delia began to cry in earnest, her sobs again awakening the baby, who joined in the lamentation, if not understanding the reason. Gwyneth made no attempt to comfort her sister, too shocked at what was happening beyond the window. Behind the smart redcoats parading down the street, she saw bands of Indians, dressed in war paint, whooping and brandishing tomahawks, a much more fearsome sight than the British soldiers. Until now she had never seen Indians intent on battle. Most of the Indians around Fort Detroit had been traders or loafing bands, often drunk, scrounging rum and handouts. These Indians were far different and she doubted their British allies had much control over them. Where were the American troops? Visions of pillage and murder filled her with apprehension. Who would protect them? And what would be their fate at the hands of such people?

But her first responsibility was Delia. She must calm her sister. Turning from the window, she tried to ignore what lurked beyond the dubious safety of their house. For the first time she realized their vulnerability; two helpless women and a baby cowering behind a fragile door.

"Delia, we must be sensible and prepared. Did Isaac leave any firearms behind?" she asked, endeavoring to talk sensibly.

"Yes. There is a pistol in the top drawer of the bureau. Can you load and fire it?" Delia said, falling down on the bed in despair.

"I think so. Father taught me years ago." Gwyneth burrowed in the bureau and brought out the gun. With it was a bag of powder. She cocked the pistol. It was already primed, and she hefted it, trying to look competent. Just then came a thud from downstairs, filling her with dread. Someone was attempting entrance. No doubt the green door had attracted them. She ran to the window and looked down. Two Indians were hacking at the door with tomahawks, yelling and dancing as they wreaked havoc.

"I'm so frightened," Delia cried, burrowing her head in the bedclothes.

"Well, I'm not staying here like a scared sheep," Gwyneth insisted stoutly, and brandishing the pistol, she moved to the door. Delia continued to shudder and wail. As Gwyneth hesitated, she heard the shattering of wood and the crack of glass below. Taking a deep breath and holding the pistol before her, she walked to the door and opened it, turning to warn her sister.

"Stay here with Robert and be quiet." Marching resolutely into the hall, she went to the top of the stairs, pointing the pistol and waiting for the invaders. As she watched, the two Indians broke through the door and entered the front room. Yelling and whirling their tomahawks, they looked around for loot and, spying the pewter dishes and china, ran to the cupboard. Suddenly as if aware of danger, one looked up and saw Gwyneth descending the stairs.

He growled a warning to his companion, who turned toward her and shouted, twirling his tomahawk as he rushed toward her. Closing her eyes, she fired, but the charge passed harmlessly over his head, shattering into the wall. Glowering, the Indian did not hesitate but threw his weapon. Gwyneth ducked as the hatchet struck the wall to her left. As she waited, certain she was to be killed, a redcoat stepped over the threshold and yelled a guttural command at the two warriors, stopping them in their tracks.

Gwyneth looked wide-eyed at the huge man, who was dark, forbidding, dressed in the uniform of a British officer but obviously of Indian blood. He must have been at least six foot four, but of a different stamp from the two warriors who obeyed him.

"Don't be afraid, ma'am," he said in a perfect, educated voice.

"Who are you?" Gwyneth asked, hoping her voice did not betray her fear.

"Capt. Thomas McKee, 2nd Regiment of Essex

Militia, at your service," he said, bowing as if at a formal reception.

"What do you want?" she asked, dreading the answer.

"Just to see these braves do not injure you. We intend no harm," he insisted gravely.

Before she could reply, another redcoat stepped into the house. This one was entirely different, a tall, haughty, proper British officer, a major, she thought. Ignoring Gwyneth, whom he took in with one raking stare from dark bold eyes, he turned to Captain McKee.

"What are you up to, Tom? You know Brock said there was to be no attack on civilians."

"Just so, Giles. I was reassuring the lady. I am afraid these two villains were frightening her," McKee said with a grin, indicating the two sullen braves who seemed unwilling to abandon their victim.

"She seems prepared to make a fight of it," the officer argued. Both men appeared to find Gwyneth's attempts to defend herself amusing, which infuriated her, banishing her fear.

"Does the British army make war on women, sir?" she asked coolly.

"Certainly not. But you had better give me that pistol. You might hurt someone," the major drawled, walking up the stairs. Gwyneth made no effort to oblige him, now thoroughly annoyed by his cavalier attitude. He looked her over with insulting candor and then, not taking his eyes from her, tossed a remark casually over his shoulder to Captain McKee.

"Get these braves out of here, Tom, and find some soldiers to guard the door."

"And leave you in possession, Giles?" Captain McKee said with a shrug. "You have a reputation with the ladies, I know, and even this angry little American miss might be impressed."

"I'm not American, but Canadian," Gwyneth blurted out, furious at the implication she might find the haughty major of interest.

"Well, then, you have nothing to fear. But this is the home of an American officer, if I am not mistaken," the major insisted.

"Yes, and I hope he has escaped your bloodthirsty crew," Gwyneth stormed, abandoning all caution.

"I wish you luck, Giles, with this spirited lady. Your servant, ma'am," said Captain McKee. Barking some words to the glowering Indians, he pushed them from the house, turning to bow his farewell.

For a moment after the three had left, neither Gwyneth nor her rescuer spoke. Then, realizing she owed the odious British officer some gratitude, Gwyneth mustered her resources and thanked him with reluctance.

"Glad to be of service. I must search the house, you know, and would feel more comfortable if you would surrender that pistol," he said. "Oh, let me introduce myself. Maj. Giles Fitzalen-Hill, aide to Gen. Isaac Brock, who has just accepted General Hull's surrender," he announced gravely.

Gwyneth lowered the pistol and looked at him with loathing.

"I can't stop you from searching the house, but there is no one here but myself, my sister, and her baby."

"I will accept your word, my dear. And who are you?" he answered with a wry glance at her belligerent stance.

"Gwyneth Winwood, of Montreal," she said curtly.

"Well, Miss Winwood, I suggest you reassure your

sister. There is no reason to fear His Majesty's soldiers. We have taken Fort Detroit but women and children are not our enemies.''

If Gwyneth believed him, she would not admit it, although she did let her pistol drop to the ground.

"There will be a guard posted outside to prevent further incursions, but I suggest you remain in the house," the major said in a tone that was more of an order than a request. Gwyneth stubbornly made no reply.

The major sighed as if disgusted with her intransigence. Then he smiled.

"I don't understand why you are so angry. After all, we did save you from possible injury or death. Do try to stay out of trouble now. I may not always be on hand to rescue you." And with a bow he was gone, leaving Gwyneth more furious than ever, although she did not quite know why.

# *Chapter Two*

For the next twenty-four hours, Gwyneth was thoroughly occupied in calming Delia, preparing some food, and trying to catch a few hours' sleep. After the annoying major had left, she had joined Delia in the bedroom, where her sister was still cowering under the blankets.

"Come, Delia, there is nothing to worry about now," she said, throwing back the blankets. A brief glimpse at Robert had shown her he was asleep, exhausted, his small hands clenched and tearstains still on his cheeks.

Her recent confrontation made Gwyneth impatient with her sister, and she snapped.

"Get out of that bed. You can't stay there all day."

"Oh, Gwyneth, how can you be so cruel? Here we are in desperate straits, defeated, and for all we know Isaac and James are wounded, captured even, if not dead, and you behave as if it were nothing."

"I am doing no such thing, but I have just had a

nasty experience with two bloodthirsty Indians. If you
don't believe me, there is still a tomahawk stuck in
the wall on the landing. I have endured ridicule and
arrogance from a British officer, and I am in no mood
to listen to wails from you about our perilous situation,'' she said sharply. Now that the danger had
passed, Gwyneth wanted nothing more than to join
Delia under the bedclothes. She realized that she was
shaking uncontrollably, and she sank down onto a
nearby chair, eyeing her sister with exasperated
affection.

How did Isaac endure Delia's timidity? Living in
this isolated post at the edge of the wilderness for
the past two years, Delia surely must have learned
how to cope with the primitive conditions. Of course,
until just lately Isaac had always been on hand to
reassure her. Delia had always needed a shoulder to
lean upon. Many gentlemen had found that trait of
dependency appealing, including Isaac, and found
Gwyneth's independence unwomanly and unattractive. No doubt that irritating and conceited major
preferred clinging wide-eyed admiring girls who
looked up to him in awe. Remembering the major's
raking stare and patronizing tones restored Gwyneth's poise, banishing her tremors. Really, he had
been impossible. Even Captain McKee had tried to
be kind, but the haughty major, so impressed with
his own consequence, had been almost offhand. As
if encounters with savages were nothing out of the
way for gently bred ladies.

Not that she had behaved as a gently bred lady,
Gwyneth recalled, her good spirits restored. And honesty compelled her to admit she could not have prevailed over the Indians alone. Still, it was Captain

McKee who had really rescued her and deserved her gratitude, not Major Fitzalen-Hill, she decided.

For the next few hours Gwyneth had little time to think of the annoying major. There was a meal to prepare, Delia to calm, the shattered window to block up. Peeking out into the street, Gwyneth was surprised by the lack of activity. Aside from some companies of soldiers on guard, the rutted street appeared quiet. She noticed, too, that whatever the major's faults, he had honored his promise, and a soldier was posted outside their house. Later in the day, as she was peeling potatoes, carrots, and onions to add to the stewing meat for their supper, she heard the sounds of hammering. Hurrying to the front room, she saw a soldier blocking the broken door with two or three stout timbers. She smiled at him and indicated her thanks.

"That should do it, ma'am. Keep any intruders out and you can sleep safely in your beds," the man assured her, giving a final satisfying whack to a nail.

He seemed to want to talk, a young, probably lonely soldier with a broad Irish brogue, miles from home and family and eager for companionship. She offered him some ale that was gratefully accepted after she had steered him to the back door which led into the comfortable kitchen. She was anxious for news and quizzed him about conditions in the fort.

"It's all pretty quiet now. That half-breed officer, Captain McKee, has great power over them Indians. He chivied them out of town and gave them a deal of rum. They are all dead drunk, mostly asleep, and giving no trouble. Nasty creatures, they are," he confided.

"Did they do much harm?" she asked, remembering with a shudder the fearsome intentions of the two who had broken into the house.

"Scalped a few rebels and tried to burn down a house or two, but Captain McKee sorted them out. Your General Hull didn't put up much of a fight— maybe afraid of what the savages might do—but there is a lot of talk that he should have fired them cannon at us, to try to make a battle of it. He could have done a lot of damage, but old Brock would have won, a damned good fighter, General Brock," the soldier, whose name was Sean Malloy, told her.

"What will happen to General Hull and his men now?" Gwyneth asked.

"Shipped off to prison in Montreal. But the general is most mortified. The militia, who your general ordered into the fort, turned tail and fled back to Ohio. Damn smart of them, if you'll excuse me, ma'am," Corporal Malloy said with a grin.

Did that mean that Isaac Sibley and James Brush had eluded capture? Gwyneth hoped so. And she would put the best face on this defeat to Delia, which might cheer her.

At last Corporal Malloy took his leave, reluctantly returning to his duties. Comforted by his news and his visit, Gwyneth was able to settle Delia into a calmer frame of mind and even persuaded her to eat a good supper. After tidying up the kitchen, she lit some lamps in the front room, determined to ignore all thoughts of what might lie ahead, and settled into some sewing. She was making an embroidered dress for little Robert, and Delia read to her while she worked.

Just as the two girls, studiously avoiding any discussion of the fate of Isaac and James, were thinking of retiring, a knock came at the back door. Delia immediately jumped up in fright.

"Oh, who can that be? More Indians?" she asked, beginning to tremble.

"Don't be stupid, Delia. They would scarcely knock politely. It's probably a neighbor with some news. I hope so. I am tired of sulking here, not knowing what is going on," Gwyneth said. "I'll go see." And leaving Delia muttering to herself, she went to admit the caller.

Somehow she was not surprised to discover Major Fitzalen-Hill on the doorstep. She might have pretended that she would be relieved to see the last of that gentleman, but actually she was pleased for any company, even his.

"Good evening, Miss Winwood," Major Fitzalen-Hill said as he stepped into the kitchen and looked around curiously.

Gwyneth wondered what he thought of Delia's home. No doubt he was accustomed to palaces and stately manor houses, she decided meanly, and found Fort Detroit and its citizens beneath his touch.

Since Gwyneth seemed unwelcoming, Giles adopted a conciliatory manner, exerting his most polished address.

"I thought I would just enquire as to your welfare and give you the news of what is going on now that General Brock has established some order," he explained, rather amused at this Colonial's obvious hostility.

"Very kind of you. Do come in and meet my sister," Gwyneth invited, not convinced of his sincerity. Really, he had a strange ability to arouse her anger, which was most unfair. After all, he had proved to be very accommodating, and perhaps he could not help his haughty manner.

"Thank you," he accepted and held open the door for her, following her into the front room.

Delia, startled at the appearance of a British officer, looked at him with some trepidation. But within moments of Gwyneth's introduction, she had accepted his presence with amazing friendliness.

Of course Delia had a great deal of experience with attractive men, and Gwyneth had to concede that the major was both attractive and polite. For his part he had obviously a great deal of experience with women, she decided cynically. Well, her sister might be taken in by the toffee-nosed Major Fitzalen-Hill, but she still viewed him with suspicion and dislike.

Delia offered him wine, which he accepted politely, and they were soon talking easily, as if this were the most relaxed and social of situations. Gwyneth was ignored, Delia taking control with skilled graciousness. If she found it odd to be conversing so calmly with an enemy officer, she concealed it well.

"I must thank you, sir, for rescuing my sister from a frightening ordeal," Delia said, smiling at Giles as he lounged easily in a chair facing her.

"Not at all. Happy to be of service, although most of the credit must go to Captain McKee, my fellow officer. He's a good chap with an uncanny influence over the tribes," he demurred.

"Gwyneth told me of her near death," Delia replied. Gwyneth was irritated, not only at being ignored, but at Delia's enthusiastic reception of the major. Piqued at his casual manipulation of her sister, she interrupted them.

"The corporal who boarded the door told me that

Delia's husband's militia company was not captured,'' she said, reminding her sister of her first priority.

"Yes, and I won't say unfortunately, for I am sure my charming hostess would prefer that her husband escape to fight another day in this stupid war,'' he said, smiling at Delia.

"Stupid, Major? You don't approve of it?'' asked Gwyneth, not believing him.

"Certainly not, and I am sure Mr. Madison and most of the Colonials regret it, too. England's real enemy is Napoleon, not America,'' he said with a conviction which surprised Gwyneth, who had not thought him capable of much enthusiasm on any topic. The pose of a bored aristocrat was inherent in his character, she had believed, not willing to admit he might have any decent human traits. How foolishly she was behaving, she realized, able to see the stupidity of condemning the man wholeheartedly when he had only acted with consideration. If his politeness masked a certain disdain for their frontier life, he hid it well.

"If you disapprove of the war, Major, why are you here?'' Gwyneth asked tartly, ignoring a frown from Delia.

"Duty. Have to go where I am ordered. I would much rather be serving on the Peninsula with Wellington,'' he confided, determined to be pleasant despite Gwyneth's brusqueness. Was his self-conceit so well developed he could not bear to think that any female, much less an unschooled Colonial, could resist him? Every time she reminded herself that she owed him courtesy if not an enthusiastic welcome, his arrogance, his barely suppressed amusement, raised her anger. He probably had called just to wile away a boring evening in this frontier post. What other entertainment was available, after all, if he did not want to join his fellow officers in a drinking session?

Sensing that he had strained Gwyneth's patience long enough, Giles rose, determined to make his escape. He wondered why he had come. The lady did not find his company appealing, which rather piqued his vanity. He was accustomed to flattering obeisance when he honored any of the females of his acquaintance, whether of the respectable variety or otherwise, with his attention. Mrs. Sibley was much more to his taste, more complaisant if not as intelligent as her fiery sister, but probably much too virtuous or careful of her reputation for a flirtation. Giles enjoyed women in all their guises, and if he had to be immured in this isolated, barbaric outpost, he might just as well cultivate the friendship of any passable female who crossed his path. He had rarely been rebuffed. Gwyneth's dislike puzzled him as well as intrigued him. Could it be that she was attached to one of the local citizens, some rude militiaman now safe in the Ohio country? Well, he should be able to overcome any interest she had in that direction. The seduction of such a tempting morsel should prove a challenging distraction while he was languishing in his depressing backwater.

"I have kept you from your rest, I fear. But I wanted to assure you that you have nothing to dread from the English occupation of your town, ladies," he insisted suavely as he made his adieu.

Delia smiled, impressed with this English officer's style and courtesy, far more sophisticated than she had encountered before. She could not understand why her sister found him so annoying. But, then, Gwyneth's standards were so severe, and Delia believed her sister preferred James Brush, an association she encouraged. She wanted Gwyneth to marry James and stay in Detroit. But Gwyneth could be stubborn and unaccountable. Delia did not always understand her.

Gwyneth ushered their visitor to the back door, eager to see the last of him. Amused, he followed her, wondering what she would confront him with next.

"Do present our compliments to Captain McKee," she said when they were alone.

"He's a handsome chap, but I should warn you, Miss Winwood, that he is married to a charming French girl and is a father. Not available," he drawled, hoping for a reaction. He was not disappointed.

"Don't be ridiculous, Major," she bridled.

"You know, my dear, you are quite a termagant. You'll never win a husband with such fierce manners," he mocked.

"Really. I suspect you think every female is panting for your approval, sir. Let me inform you I am not among them," Gwyneth retorted, growing flushed and throwing open the back door to indicate that he should leave.

"So adamant, I cannot resist you," he said, and before she could protest, he took her in his arms and kissed her with a brutal expertise.

Emerging from the embrace that was more of a punishment than a token of affection, she gasped at the unexpected effrontery and responded with a sharp slap to his cheek.

"Oh, my, so belligerent," he responded, rubbing

his cheek ruefully. "I will have to tame you, I think. You are much too pretty to be ignored. Thank you for a most interesting evening."

He strolled away laughing, leaving Gwyneth embarrassed and furious, prey to a welter of emotions.

# Chapter Three

In the days following the English occupation of Detroit, events settled into a wary normality. General Brock left his second in command, Col. Henry Proctor, an overweight and secretive officer, in charge of 250 men and a band of unruly Indians. There were several alarming incidents when the Shawnee demanded ransom for captives and were only dissuaded from violence by their chief, the redoubtable Tecumseh, who managed them adroitly.

Word came to Delia from her husband that he and James Brush were safe, and the two women tried not to worry about the future. Gwyneth had mixed emotions when she learned that Major Fitzalen-Hill had not accompanied his chief to Montreal. On the one hand she was grateful for his protection. He sent men to install a new front door on their house and a glazier to fix the shattered window. They were not bothered by the Indians, although some of their neighbors were not so fortunate.

Mrs. Brush, James's mother, a formidable woman very much on her dignity, had been affronted by two Indians who had broken into her house one afternoon and tried to steal a red cloak and two copper kettles. Both of the braves had drunk deeply from a keg of rum found in the kitchen and were in no condition to defend themselves. Mrs. Brush, more offended by the braves' intrusion than frightened by their behavior, peppered them with shot from an old blunderbuss owned by her late husband. The abrasive Colonel Proctor, learning she was the mother of a militiaman, meant to make an example of her, even had thought of imprisoning her, but was persuaded against that action. Most of the Detroit inhabitants, old men, women, and children, were not hostile to the English troops, only afraid the soldiers could not control the Indians, as experience had taught them.

Gwyneth knew that her sympathies should be with the English. After all she was a Canadian who owed her loyalty to George III's government, but she felt drawn to the audacious pioneers trying to make a life on this inhospitable frontier. Her independent spirit could not accept the arrogance of men like Major Fitzalen-Hill, who did not question his superiority to lesser men, although he hid his attitude beneath a shelf of impeccable courtesy. Of course, in all fairness, Gwyneth had to admit, he might, after generations of privilege, not be conscious of his snobbery, accepting it as a natural inheritance. But that did not excuse him. When Gwyneth compared his manners— condescending, commanding, and false—to the open, sincere, and enthusiastic view of life held by James Brush, she could not but prefer the American. His attempts to attach her interest were so engaging, so flattering, so endearing. Gwyneth could not prevent a sigh at the contrast between the two. Delia, at first suspicious of entertaining the enemy, had been completely won over by the major's charm. She thought his interest in her sister honorable.

Gwyneth knew better. The major was interested in dalliance and seduction, not marriage. High-toned English officers did not wed obscure Canadian lasses. He was bored and needed distraction. There were few women available, and he was probably too fastidious to take up with those who plied their trade near the barracks, and too conscious of his rank and career to set up an Indian mistress. Gwyneth did not consider his lighthearted flirtation serious, nor was she lured into indiscretion by his pretense of devotion. She might be living in a distant frontier, seven hundred miles from Montreal, but rumor and gossip traveled even that distance on mysterious wings. Delia might not object to Major Fitzalen-Hill's attempts to lure her sister into a liaison but the respectable matrons of Montreal would tear her reputation apart. Virtuous girls, even on the frontier, were expected to cling hard to certain standards. Even war and Indian attacks did not excuse untoward behavior.

Gwyneth had every intention of holding fast to her virtue as the summer turned into fall and Detroit hunkered down for one of the fierce border winters the fort's citizens had learned to endure. A cheering prospect blown in by the arctic winds from western Canada across the Great Lakes was the Indians' absence. Sated by vast stores of supplies, the tribes about the fort had begun to drift away into winter camps, deferring their raids until spring.

News from the war front was meager but Detroit had long lived on the outskirts of civilization, so expected little else. Most of the citizens had a family member fighting in the American forces. Many of the men captured with Hull had been paroled on the promise not to take up arms again. Neither Isaac Sibley nor James Brush were among the group, however. They were encamped with Gen. William Henry Harrison in the Ohio country, waiting for a spring march north to engage the English commanding Detroit and the Canadian border. It would be a long, uncomfortable winter.

But it was a fairly mild October afternoon when Giles Fitzalen-Hill arrived to take Gwyneth on a ride down the river toward Grosse Pointe where the French settlers tilled their acres. He found Delia and Gwyneth comforting Mrs. Brush as she complained of the new burden laid upon her.

"It's dreadful enough with James away so long, fighting those pesky Indians and their un-Christian English allies. But I would not want him to neglect his duty. No, it's that Colonel Proctor, making war on poor widows who cannot protect themselves," she informed her audience. Neither Delia nor Gwyneth doubted that Elizabeth Brush could defend herself handily, whether against Indians or redcoats, but they indulged her with their sympathy.

"What has happened, Mrs. Brush?" Gwyneth asked. She was never sure that James's mother approved of her. Pleasant and welcoming whenever they met, Mrs. Brush remained an enigma. She claimed she wanted James to marry, and she smiled on every girl to whom he paid attention, but somehow at twenty-nine, James Brush was still a bachelor. Gwyneth appeared to be the latest threat to Brush's single state, and whatever Mrs. Brush thought of the Montreal visitor she was canny enough to keep to herself.

"That mean-minded Colonel Proctor has billeted

two ensigns and a captain on me, that's what happened. And the captain insists on my best bedroom. All because I shot those two thieving redmen, I suspect. Colonel Proctor is a be grudging, evil-spirited man," she fumed.

"Would you like to come here, Mrs. Brush?" Delia asked hospitably.

"And leave those careless young men in possession of my home! Oh no. Who knows what jinks they might get up to?" Mrs. Brush's sharp brown eyes sparkled at the idea that any enemy officer might escape her surveillance. A woman of some character, forceful but kind, stubborn but courageous, Gwyneth thought. She had a certain admiration if not real affection for her. Before the girls could pursue the matter, there was a knock on the front door.

Gwyneth sprang up uneasily. She did not want Mrs. Brush to know on what intimate terms she and Delia were with Giles. Of course the woman must know he was a constant visitor and might put the worse interpretation on his visits. Well, she must try to remove him as soon as possible and leave Delia to make any explanations necessary.

"Good afternoon, Major," Gwyneth greeted him warily. She was hoping to avoid an introduction to Mrs. Brush.

"We have a lovely day for our ride," Giles said, his mocking manner for once in abeyance, although he lifted a questioning eyebrow at her obvious attempt to hurry him off the premises.

She snatched up a shawl and indicated she was eager to depart. He could not help but see Delia and Mrs. Brush seated before the fireplace conversing in low tones, although Mrs. Brush bristled with curiosity.

"I must just make my addresses to your sister," he

insisted, intrigued by Gwyneth's effort to hurry him away and wondering why she was so intent on not allowing him to meet their guest.

If Mrs. Brush was affronted and wondered at Gwyneth's determination to prevent her from meeting the English officer, she made no move to interfere. She would quiz Delia and have the whole story out of her in no time, Gwyneth was convinced. And what would she make of it?

Handing Gwyneth into the carriage and releasing the reins from the tethering post, Giles leaped nimbly into the driver's seat and whipped up the horses, two spanking chestnuts. Gwyneth wondered where he had found such an elegant equipage. Horses were in short supply in Detroit, all sequestered by the troops.

"This is a fine vehicle, Major," she said, a question in her voice.

"I had it brought over from Fort Malden," he explained, referring to the English post across the river, the bastion General Hull had tried and failed to capture.

Of course, Gwyneth conceded. He was quite capable of finding horses and a carriage where lesser men had to make do with a mule or their own two feet.

"How long will the trip take?" she asked, deciding not to argue or criticize, relieved to be away from the confines of the fort for a few hours.

"About an hour. Are you in a hurry? I hope not as it's such a fine day," he coaxed.

"No, I just wondered." Gwyneth had decided to behave circumspectly. She would not allow him to rouse her temper. He had an uncanny ability to bring out the worst in her, and she was determined to preserve her dignity. By tacit consent neither of them had ever referred to that brutal kiss he had given her some weeks ago. He had never attempted such an assault in the weeks that followed, behaving with courtesy and flattering deference. But Gwyneth had not forgotten the kiss nor her own response. She wondered why he had decided not to pursue his advantage. She felt ashamed at her reaction and the hours she spent remembering that encounter. Today he appeared subdued, not his usual mocking self.

"I have had some tragic news this morning," he confided unexpectedly, frowning as if annoyed at this betrayal of his usual sang-froid.

"Can you tell me?" she asked, startled.

"It will be all over the town shortly. General Brock has been killed during a battle at Queenstown," he informed her curtly.

Gwyneth did not know how to reply. The major had respected and admired the general, and obviously was mourning the loss. Queenstown commanded the heights above the Niagara River on the Canadian side across from New York. Whoever controlled Queenstown controlled Lake Ontario. It was a vital strategic post.

"The Americans won the battle, I suppose," she offered a bit tentatively.

"I am not sure. The reports are confused. At first we had routed their militia, but then they rallied and appear to have taken Queenstown Heights. I should have been there. With Brock gone all of Canada is exposed to the Colonials. And this means Proctor will be in complete command now." His tone was somber, and Gwyneth was impressed. She knew he felt scorn and contempt for Proctor and had believed only Brock could save Canada from a decisive American invasion. She respected the seriousness he displayed toward his military career even if she could not trust or like him.

"And that is not to your liking," she said, referring to his remarks about Proctor.

"It is not what I prefer that matters. Without Brock's skilled hand, I fear Proctor will commit some bêtise. He will wreak revenge for Brock's death on the Detroit citizens. Without Brock behind me, there is little I can do to stop Proctor. He has vicious instincts."

"I am a Canadian and should want the English to win. They are our protectors, but I am afraid my loyalties are mixed," Gwyneth confided. For the first time she glimpsed another, more human man beneath the arrogant facade of the proper English aristocrat. His concern for the people living under Proctor's hard hand did not fit the image she held of him.

"That's understandable. You feel for your sister's position, her concern about her husband and his friends—your friends, too, I suspect." His tone held a hint of inquiry.

"Yes," Gwyneth answered briefly, not willing to reveal her interest in James Brush. Why she felt reluctant to mention James to the major she could not fathom. She could not explain her aversion to the idea, for she did not really understand her feelings.

Realizing that the subject was not one to pursue, Giles threw off his grim mood. "Well, it is too nice a day to brood over Proctor, or Brock's death. Good men are being sacrificed on both sides in this war. Let us try to forget we are involved, whatever our loyalties, and enjoy this day. We may not have many more. But remember, Gwyneth—if I may call you that—I am not your enemy."

Gwyneth was surprised at his sincerity and was tempted to believe him.

"My savior, Delia would say, Major. And I quite agree we should try to forget the war and live just for the moment," she agreed, relegating whatever reservations she might have about both the war and the major to the back of her mind.

"Friends, Gwyneth, and do call me Giles," he appealed, laying a warm hand on hers.

"Of course, Giles." Somehow he had persuaded her to abandon hostile feelings and accept his offer of friendship. She had crossed some sort of line and their relationship had entered a new stage, one in which she could not foresee the outcome.

## *Chapter Four*

As fall deepened into winter, conditions in the strategic outpost on the Great Lakes worsened. Food was in short supply, and relations between Detroit's residents and the occupying force were uneasy. Proctor did little to improve matters, harassing innocent families, often refusing to let them ransom prisoners when the Indians brought them into the fort, and arresting both men and women for spurious breaches of the peace. The commander was well aware of his vulnerable position, far from his supply center, with an insufficient force of regulars, only tepid support from the Canadian militia, and little control over his volatile allies, the Indians.

Disturbing reports drifted into Detroit concerning a large band of Americans massing to the south. Detroit was the key to control of the Great Lakes and the vital traffic that supported the wilderness. Both sides knew this, and the Americans had begun to act on their knowledge. Rumors of frantic shipbuilding on Lake Erie, preparations for a coming battle to win York or Montreal, disturbed Proctor, who realized Detroit must be defended at all costs. Even the most efficient and courageous commander would have had doubts about his ability to hold his post under these ominous conditions. Proctor, stubborn, afraid of losing his prerogatives, and reckless when restraint was needed, refused to listen to advice despite his fears. He preferred to bluster and hide his apprehensions.

Gwyneth had her own doubts about the situation. She had been in Detroit for seven months, and if not exactly yearning for Montreal, she felt insecure and troubled. Her uneasiness was not inspired by the military threat to Detroit, but by Giles Fitzalen-Hill. Despite her misgivings he had become an important part of her life. He had asked for her friendship and she had given it, although she still questioned his sincerity and motives. His charm was insidious. If he still intended seduction, he was pursuing his purpose with care and patience.

Delia believed he was seriously courting her sister. She had said as much to Mrs. Brush, who snorted and spoke her mind vigorously on the unlikelihood of well-born English officers marrying flibbertigibbet Colonial girls of no particular standing. Mrs. Brush was one of Gwyneth's trials, for she had eventually moved in with Delia and Gwyneth, disgusted with the presence of the English officers in her own home. Not that she left them alone. She checked on their depredations daily, much to their annoyance.

Mrs. Brush was another reason Gwyneth thought of returning to Montreal. If she stayed much longer, she might seriously consider accepting whatever Giles suggested from sheer boredom and a reckless disregard of propriety. Without James Brush to counteract

Giles's influence, who knew what indiscretion she
might be tempted to commit. Not that she loved
Giles, she insisted fiercely, but she was flattered by
his interest and soothed by his courtesy and protection. In Montreal, at least, she would be bound by
the rules of a settled society while this wilderness
outpost offered no such security. Of course, Montreal
itself might be invested at any moment in this border
war where the conflict changed from month to
month. And a journey down the St. Lawrence in the
depths of winter might not even be possible and
would surely be dangerous. Gwyneth wavered as
Christmas approached and a heavy snow blanketed
Detroit, further exacerbating her feelings of isolation
and apprehension.

Giles entertained his own confusion about Gwyneth, although he managed to conceal it well. In the
beginning he had thought her just another possible
conquest, an unimportant little Colonial thrown into
his path by the fortunes of war. Never one to refuse
such an opportunity, he had planned to use her gratitude toward him for saving her from the Indians
(although he had not been the real instrument of
that rescue) to lure her into an affair. Giles had a
poor opinion of Colonials. The men made indifferent
soldiers when they could be persuaded to fight at all,
did not respond to orders from their English officers,
and appeared to prefer the company of the crude
Americans to their natural compatriots. The occa-
sional young woman, like Gwyneth, repaid a second
look, but most of them were drab and provincial.
Even in Montreal he had found them graceless and

untutored in sophisticated repartee so usual in London society.

To his surprise, beyond her physical attributes, an abundant crop of gleaming chestnut hair, a piquant oval face, and elegant figure, Gwyneth possessed an unusual cast of mind. She neither flirted nor simpered, the standard ploys of the females Giles had met and conquered in the past. Her resistance to him challenged his well-developed masculine conceit. He was convinced she would eventually succumb and might just possibly be worth the effort he had expended on this conquest. There was no competition in this damnable outpost at the end of the world. He fully expected to triumph. However, as their relationship deepened over the months as they were thrown together both by his design and general circumstances, his attitude began to change, at first imperceptibly.

She had surprised him when he had confided his grief over General Brock's death, and her sympathy and understanding as well as her reaction to this unfortunate war had altered his opinion of her. He was not accustomed to considering women as people of perception and intelligence. He was not prepared to admit defeat and abandon his pursuit of her, but he was content to wait, intrigued by both Gwyneth and the situation, so foreign to his usual relations with women.

Also, Gwyneth might offer a temporary antidote to his ennui, but his chief concern was to return to England to erase the stigma of his disgrace on the Peninsula and regain his place on Wellington's staff. The last letter he had received from his father, who was laboring mightily in his behalf, had been encour-

aging, but that had been in early September, before
Brock's untimely death. Now it was December and
he chafed at the delay and, his distance from the real
theatre of operations. And he found himself at odds
with Colonial Proctor. Neither as a man nor a commander did that choleric officer inspire respect. This
stupid war in a Colonial backwater disgusted him,
and he wanted to leave it behind him. Neither his
military career nor his future would be influenced
by what happened to him in Detroit, nor would the
irrepressible and lovely Miss Winwood ever achieve
a permanent position in his life, he decided.

That did not prevent him from enjoying their duels
with their sexual overtones. But time was not on their
side. Still, he hesitated to make the next move in this
romantic game. As he strode from his quarters on
that crisp winter afternoon, he wondered if tonight
he should put his chances to the test. He was escorting
Gwyneth to an entertainment some of his fellow officers had organized, a theatrical performance including a scene from *Henry IV, Part One,* followed by a
rollicking farce.


Gwyneth, having done the day's meager shopping,
returned to the house, determined to face Delia with
her decision to return to Montreal. Her sister would
protest, she knew. And her reasons would be sound.
It was stupid to think she could escape Detroit and
Giles while the fort was in the grip of winter. However,
a troubled night and the prospect of a confrontation
of some sort with Giles decided her. She could not
wait for spring and the dim possibility that James
Brush might return. Passage down the St. Lawrence
might be even more hazardous then. At least now

the fighting had stopped because of the weather, but she knew that at the first thaw the sides would challenge each other again.

"Delia, I must return to Montreal," she insisted, facing her sister while Delia gave Robert his bath, a difficult procedure as he disliked it intensely. The baby squirmed and made ineffective efforts to elude the soapy cloth, letting his mother know of his unhappiness with mewling cries. Delia, distracted, did not at first take in Gwyneth's announcement.

"Hand me the towel, please, Gwyneth," she asked, wiping a wet hand across her forehead.

Gwyneth, complying, realized she had not chosen the best time to inform her sister of her decision, but she did not want Mrs. Brush to be privy to their conversation, and that lady was hard to evade. She waited impatiently as Delia dressed the baby and settled in the rocker to soothe him before depositing Robert for his afternoon nap.

"But you can't go now, Gwyneth," Delia complained.

"Better now than in the spring when the fighting resumes," Gwyneth argued.

"But James and Isaac will surely be in the force sent to relieve Detroit, and they will be successful. Proctor does not have enough troops to defend it, and the English will have to withdraw. You cannot leave before James comes home," she coaxed.

"Yes, I can. There is no assurance that Detroit will be relieved in the spring. And even if James arrives, it will make little difference to me."

"You mean you do not care for him?" Delias asked, wide-eyed.

"I don't know, and while this wretched war continues, I cannot decide. I will be better off in Montreal.

If James is determined to court me, and if he survives, he can travel to Montreal and argue his case. But I must go home," she insisted desperately. She could not tell Delia that she might succumb to Giles's lures. Her sister would never understand such a shocking admission.

"You will have Mrs. Brush to protect and comfort you, Delia. It is not as if I am leaving you alone. I know how worried you are about Isaac, but he is safe for now and will come home eventually," she said, unwilling to contemplate the idea that either Isaac or James might not survive the next battle.

"It's Major Fitzalen-Hill, isn't it? You want to escape him," Delia offered shrewdly.

"Not exactly, but he is a factor. Your life is here, Delia, and you have managed very bravely, but I do not want to spend the next few months in Detroit under these trying conditions. I have loved being here with you, but when I came I never expected a war. I would have left in September, you know, if we had not been placed in this frightful position, and I am afraid I am not the brave pioneer I thought," Gwyneth admitted, although that was not really true. If she had really cared for James Brush, she would remain.

"Well, I think you are most foolhardy to think about leaving. The river is frozen, and it will mean a nasty trip through the wilderness, hazardous, too. You will have to leave with the next escort train if Colonial Proctor will give you permission, which I doubt," Delia said sensibly.

"I know, I know. All you say is true, but I must go. Somehow I will persuade the authorities to let me travel with the next train. Giles thinks they will be sending men with prisoners and reports within the week.''

"Will he be leaving, too?'' Delia asked, thinking she now understood Gwyneth's eagerness to depart.

"I doubt it, and that doesn't matter. Giles is just a friend, an acquaintance really, and he is of no account.'' Gwyneth hoped she had convinced her sister but realized that Delia had noticed more than she thought.

"Do you care for him?''

"Of course not. It has just been a distraction. Conditions here have not exactly been pleasant these past months. Much as I love being here with you and Robert, it is time for me to go.'' Gwyneth, unable to bear any more probing from her sister, dropped a kiss on Robert's head and left the room.

Gwyneth, dressing for the evening's entertainment, felt restless and dissatisfied. Really, she was a widgeon. She was afraid to go and afraid to stay. No wonder Delia thought she was foolish. But somehow she felt a deep need to return home, despite her tiresome stepmother and the perils of the journey. In Montreal she would have security and be away from Giles's insidious influence. In defiance she put on her best gown, a warm cherry cashmere trimmed in lace, and a small necklace of garnets. She would tell Giles tonight and beg his aid in securing a pass from Colonial Proctor.

Giles, on arriving to collect her, realized immediately that Gwyneth had come to some decision. Whether it concerned him, he could not fathom, but she looked both reckless and militant. What bee had she in her bonnet now?

She said little as they drove to the improvised theater. Despite his best efforts to draw her out, she remained stubbornly noncommittal. Once in the primitive hall which the military had bravely decked out for the performance, she roused herself and chatted inconsequentially about the play, but he was not deceived.

"I am afraid the acting will be a little rough and not up to Montreal standards, much less London, but you have to applaud the troops courage in even attempting it," he said, eyeing her thoughtfully.

"Any distraction from this dreadful war is a relief. And I see Colonial Proctor is honoring us with his presence," she said, noticing the fort's commander had appeared in the front row with some fellow officers. Then girding herself to make her announcement, she laid a hand on Giles's arm and said quickly, "I want to ask him for a pass to accompany the next train to Montreal."

"Do you?" Giles answered calmly as if her sudden desire was not a surprise.

"Yes, it's time for me to go home. I have been here long enough. Do you think he will allow it?" she asked a bit desperately.

"Hard to say. It will be a nasty and arduous trip, not at all suited for respectable females," Giles replied lightly, hiding his astonishment. Why was she in such a hurry to leave? Did she sense that he was about to pounce and lure her into a liaison? Had he waited too long?

"I know that, but I still insist on leaving," Gwyneth said, her lips tightening. "Will you help me?"

"Of course," Giles agreed. But the makeshift curtains parted then and the play began, so no more explanations were possible.

Whether Gwyneth was enthralled with the play or her own thoughts, he could not tell, but she appeared riveted to the stage and not until intermission could he question her further. Then she surprised him again.

"Let's not stay for the farce. I enjoyed the Shakespeare, but somehow I am not in the mood for a humorous offering tonight," she urged.

"Certainly," he said affably, hoping that once they had left the theater he could find out exactly what she was thinking.

Their breath steamed in the cold night as they drove away from the hall. Giles, deciding that he could delay no longer, was determined to chance his luck. Damn the girl, she had teased him and evaded for months. Now she would pay her dues, he thought cynically. If he remembered his kinder thoughts about her, he ruthlessly suppressed them. If she wanted his help in leaving Detroit, she would not get it without a price.

"Would you mind if we stopped by my quarters? I have that book on fashion I promised your sister. Somebody left it in the mess, and I think it might amuse her," he asked casually as they drove along.

"All right, if you insist," she said a bit curtly. For some reason she wanted to get back to Delia as soon as possible, but she had a certain curiosity as to Giles's quarters. No doubt he lived in the greatest possible comfort. He was not a man to deny himself, she thought meanly.

As Gwyneth had suspected, Giles had sought out the best house in Detroit for his quarters, Judge Woodward's, one of the most comfortable billets in the fort. The judge had preferred an English officer of Giles's standing to his irascible commander and had agreed to house him, although reluctantly. If he had to have any enemy within his roof, the judge decided, he would at least choose a civilized one.

"You can't stay here in the cold. Do come in. It won't take long," Giles suggested smoothly, wondering if she would protest.

If Gwyneth wondered at his insistence, she did not demur. Proprieties on the frontier were not observed as they were in Montreal, and accompanying a bachelor of dubious reputation into his lodgings did not seem shocking. At any rate she supposed Judge Woodward would be on hand in case Giles took any liberties. So she clambered out of the vehicle and accepted Giles's escort into the house. The judge's house, to which she had been invited for several social evenings in happier days with James Brush, had been built of logs, but was quite spacious and furnished lavishly with family furniture he had brought with him from the East. Giles's quarters were on the second story, and he shepherded her upstairs coolly. She saw no sign of the judge.

"Is the judge not at home?" she asked as they mounted the stairs.

"This is his night to play chess with Charles Trowbridge," Giles said suavely, ushering her into his rooms, which were indeed the epitome of comfort. She avoided looking at the dominating fourposter bed and walked to the windows while Giles made a long business of searching for the book.

Outside little was to be seen in the dark snow-shrouded street. Most of Detroit citizens kept indoors when night fell, and beyond the window Gwyneth could see nothing but the vague shapes of other houses and a few bare trees. Suddenly she felt a frisson as Giles came up behind her, and she was not totally surprised when he took her in his arms.

"I know you want this as badly as I do, Gwyneth," he said, clasping her strongly and turning her to face him.

Gwyneth was speechless. Not that she was shocked, only amazed at her feeling that this encounter was inevitable. She did not struggle as he pressed kisses on her unresisting lips and his hands roamed intimately over her body. He evoked all sorts of inchoate feelings, and her blood rose clamorously to meet his demands. When his questing hands delved beneath the décolletage of her gown, she shuddered with excitement. She made no effort to stop him, bemused as she was by the warmth of his eager kisses and his murmured demands. He edged her toward the bed, and still she made no attempt to pull away. All these weeks he had been steadily leading up to this, and she acknowledged that he could arouse her to unknown depths of passion. Deftly he began to undo the buttons on the back of her gown, and although she struggled halfheartedly, she knew she would not stop him. What finally brought her to her senses was the slam of a door downstairs. The judge had come home.

Wresting herself away from him and fleeing to the door, she hurriedly fastened the buttons on her gown. Her cheeks flushing, her heart pounding, she faced him.

"I may want this as badly as you say, but I am not going to allow it," she cried in confusion. "You are not going to add me to your conquests."

Giles, frustrated, lost his temper. "Why not? You did not seem to object. What did you expect, coming up here to my bedroom? A cup of tea and some bland words? Do you want me to confess to undying devotion?'' he sneered.

"Yes, I should have refused to come up here, suspected your intentions. I am not a doxy, although you treat me like one. You will just have to understand I am not some gullible little fool, blinded by your expertise in lovemaking,'' she stormed. "Not that lovemaking comes into it, more lust than anything, I vow. You will have to accept that I am not going to become another of your conquests, Major.''

"You would have if Judge Woodward had not come home so inadvertently,'' he insisted, rapidly regaining his composure. "You know, Gwyneth, you cannot subdue those passionate instincts forever. If not me, some other man will get you into his bed and before too long. Perhaps that bucolic militiaman,'' he suggested with contempt, and crossed to a table to pick up the promised book.

"Let us forget this unfortunate incident, and please take me home. I would not want to call on Judge Woodward's assistance. It is embarrassing enough to be caught in such a compromising position,'' Gwyneth said ashamedly, realizing she was as much at fault as Giles. She had been within an ace of losing all restraint and surrendering to him, and she knew it.

"Your servant, ma'am,'' he said dryly and opened the door, indicating that they should leave.

Squaring her shoulders, Gwyneth marched down the stairs, hoping she could face the judge without humiliation.

The judge looked up from the center hall as they descended the stairs.

"Ah, Major and Miss Winwood, good evening. Mr.

Trowbridge had a fever and I cut short our match. I believe you were going to the theater tonight. Was the performance entertaining?'' he asked smoothly, noticing Gwyneth's flushed cheeks and Giles's frown as he helped her into her cloak. If he had interrupted a delicate moment, he gave no sign of it, not appearing to see anything untoward in his lodger and guest sequestered alone in an upstairs bedroom.

Gwyneth, grateful for his tact, hurried into an explanation. ''We were just locating a book for my sister that Major Fitzalen-Hill had promised to loan her.''

''Of course,'' the judge agreed dryly. He was a tall commanding man with a shock of gray hair, a trim beard, and a pair of piercing blue eyes. Not a man to be gulled and not one to be easily shocked.

''I will be driving Miss Winwood home and be back shortly,'' Giles offered, somewhat at a loss.

''Good, then perhaps you will take a glass with me,'' the judge invited, in a tone that brooked no refusal.

''Honored, sir,'' said Giles, accepting that he would probably receive a blistering reproof once he was alone with his host.

Gwyneth smiled tremulously, bid the judge good night, and scurried out the door. Once in the carriage, the cold night air restoring her senses, she turned to Giles and said in the most quelling tones she could muster, ''The judge will think the worst, and no more than I deserve. I think it will be best if we do not see each other again, Major. It is quite apparent to me you only want one thing. I am not prepared to give it to you, so there is little point in our continuing what you so odiously refer to as our friendship.'' She thought she sounded the veriest shrew, but she had to retrieve her position. Giles was not going to lure her into any more indiscretions, and so it would be sensible to stay away from him.

"You refine too much on the situation, my dear. Why not admit you would have submitted, probably enjoyed our love-making? But then, if you want to deceive yourself, I cannot prevent you," Giles said mockingly. If he was disgruntled by her rejection, he would not admit it.

They completed the short trip to Delia's without another word, and once there Gwyneth rushed into the house without waiting for his escort. She was furious with both herself and Giles. Happily Delia and Mrs. Brush had retired, so she did not have to face them with her guilt writ large to their eyes. What a hen-witted ninny she was, allowing a man of Giles's reputation to lure her into that house, almost into that bed. She was honest enough to admit she had done little to depress Giles's intentions. If that was what living in this beleaguered outpost had done to her, the sooner she left the better. Obviously Giles could overcome her judgment and principles if she did not take care. Well, she would not allow him the opportunity again. She had learned a valuable lesson, that she was a victim of unrestrained, unacknowledged passions, and she would not surrender so easily in the future.

# Chapter Five

*Montreal, January 5, 1813*

Gwyneth woke in her bedroom, surrounded by the comfortable memories of her childhood, reluctant to leave the cozy warmth of her quilt for the cold winter morning. She had been home now for two weeks, arriving just before Christmas to a rather tepid welcome from her stepmother Nancy and measured enthusiasm from her father. Gwyneth suspected that they both had hoped she would remain in Detroit, even marry James Brush. Perhaps she was being unfair. Her father understood that the war had vastly altered conditions in the frontier outpost, and he appeared genuinely happy that his younger daughter had escaped. Nancy probably would have preferred Gwyneth to have remained in the fort or even died on the journey home.

Remembering the perils of the trip, Gwyneth thought that Nancy might easily have achieved her

wish. She had traveled in a covered cariole with a
Mrs. Archer and her two children, escorted by a military train bringing prisoners to Montreal. Every night
pickets posted for the English troops, commanded
by a young lieutenant, George Andrews, had expected
raids from unfriendly Indians and even bands of
American rangers.

On arrival, Gwyneth had been surprised to discover
that their neighbors and most of Montreal's citizens
expected an attack at any moment from an American
army. Montreal's ancient fortifications had crumbled
and the city was vulnerable. Hailed as a heroine, she
had been besieged by questions about the prowess
of the enemy and whether she thought the English
regulars could hold Fort Detroit and protect them
from the enemy. Gwyneth suspected that her father
was more concerned at the interruption of trade than
any real danger.

Although she was relieved to be home, to enjoy
the comforts denied her for the past few months, she
did not appreciate Nancy's efforts to estrange her
from her father. Still, Nancy was far less of a challenge
than Giles Fitzalen-Hill. Despite their last tempestuous passage at arms, when Gwyneth had rebuffed his
attempt at seduction, he had not entirely abandoned
her. She doubted if the odious Colonial Proctor
would have allowed her to leave without Giles's influence. But that was all behind her now. Her only regret
was leaving Delia and little Robert. She assured her
father of their well-being with more confidence than
she felt, for if Isaac should not survive the war, Delia's
position would be untenable.

Happy as Gwyneth was to have put Detroit behind
her, she could not recapture her former life in Mon-

treal. Whether that was due to the war, she could not
decide. But she found herself restless and dissatisfied.

Well, cowering here in bed would not improve
matters. She rose and hurriedly washed and dressed
in the chilly room. Walter Winwood did not approve
of his family dawdling abed. He expected both wife
and daughter at the breakfast table. Taking a silent
vow to be as pleasant as possible to her stepmother,
Gwyneth donned a warm cashmere emerald gown,
smoothed her hair into some semblance of neatness,
and prepared to face the day.

"Good morning, Father, Nancy," she greeted the
two seated at the table brightly, dropped a cursory
kiss on Nancy's cheek and a peck on her father's
head.

"Good morning, Gwyneth. We have not waited for
you," he said a bit repressively as he continued to
eat heartily of his ham and kidneys.

"Of course not," she agreed, determined not to
quarrel. Walter Winwood was man of reserved temperament, disliking any overt display of emotion. A
well-built man of fifty years, with a shock of graying
brown hair cut closely to his head, hooded hazel eyes,
and a tight mouth, he was not unattractive but rather
austere. His first wife, Elsabeth, Gwyneth and Delia's
mother, had been able to tease him with impunity
and laugh at his foibles, but Nancy took no such
liberties. Eighteen years younger than her husband,
she was quite attractive in a matronly way, with soft
light blue eyes, a full sensuous mouth, and an ingrati-
ating manner that could turn ugly when she was
thwarted, a mood she seldom allowed Walter to see.
She had married young to a scion of a well-born
Canadian family. Unfortunately her husband had

contracted a fever after a drinking bout, and died after two years of marriage. She had waited twelve years to marry again, and this time had chosen a wealthy sober man who could indulge her and offer the security she craved. That he had two grown daughters annoyed her, but she had her own methods of coping with that situation. Delia had married within a year of her father's remarriage, but Gwyneth, by far the more troublesome of the pair, was still at home. Nancy had encouraged Gwyneth to visit her sister, hoping she, too, would find a frontier husband and be removed from Montreal and Nancy's life, but, as usual, the vexing girl had proved uncooperative.

"I hope you have not forgotten that tonight is the Prevost reception, Gwyneth," Nancy said as she daintily sipped a cup of chocolate. She never ate much and somehow conveyed the idea that Gwyneth's healthy appetite was rather vulgar.

"No, indeed. I am quite looking forward to it. I have not enjoyed much sophisticated company during the past few months," Gwyneth replied smoothly.

"Your sister didn't realize how primitive life would be in Detroit when she married Isaac, I think," her father intervened. He never really approved of his elder and favorite daughter moving so far from Montreal into the wilderness, and allied to an American at that. Despite his trading successes with the Yankees, Walter Winwood was proud of his position as a United Empire Loyalist, coming to Montreal as a young man after the War for American Independence. He did not like the war because it interfered with business, but he had little respect or sympathy for the Americans either, an attitude Gwyneth found disingenuous and unacceptable. She had challenged him once on his sophistry but had received only the curt excuse

that she did not understand such matters that were
better left to men.

"Delia seems quite happy in Detroit, despite this
stupid war, of course. Her house is comfortable and
she has made friends," Gwyneth assured her father,
not for the first time.

"It could not be pleasant living under an occupying
army," he insisted.

"Well, Father, the occupying army is English, so it
could be worse."

"Yes, it could be the French, wretched people. And
Prevost has given the command of Montreal's
defences to Colonial de Salaberry, now that Brock is
gone. Who knows what will happen to us all," he
grumbled.

"Oh, you don't really feel we are in danger, do
you?" Nancy appealed to her husband with a little
squeal.

"It's very possible we may be attacked by the Americans," Walter replied sternly.

"Of course Gwyneth is used to all these alarms
and excursions, aren't you, dear?" Nancy questioned,
implying there was something a bit crude in having
been exposed to enemy fire.

Gwyneth bit her tongue and kept the peace. She
had not told Nancy of her experience with the Indians
and only mentioned it briefly to her father, whose
reaction had been far from sympathetic. He appeared
to think she should have avoided placing herself in
such jeopardy.

"I'm so tired of all this war talk. At least tonight
we will be able to enjoy some civilized society," Nancy
insisted. Turning to Gwyneth and laying down the
piece of toast on which she had been nibbling, she
said brightly, "I suppose Johnny Tremayne has

already requested several dances?'' Nancy approved
of Johnny, the younger son of an English baronet,
who had been dispatched to Canada to make his
fortune, a task that seemed beyond his power.

"Yes, Johnny has asked for some dances. I have
not promised him any,'' Gwyneth replied briefly. She
did not share her stepmother's fondness for that
young man.

"He called several times while you were away, and
we had some lovely chats. He has joined the militia
and looks a treat in his uniform,'' Nancy informed
her, preening a bit as if to imply that Johnny had
found her company attractive.

"He's a worthless young man,'' Walter said, looking
up from his paper. "I hope you are not interested
in him, Gwyneth.''

"Johnny's not a bad sort. The military may be the
making of him,'' Gwyneth replied, more to aggravate
her father than anything. Her father kept a stern eye
on her beaux, looking for a suitable match. His ideas
and Gwyneth's on this matter did not in the least
agree. She suspected he would disapprove of James
Brush, and she smiled to herself as she remembered
Giles Fitzalen-Hill's attempts to lure her from the
virtuous path. Her father would be appalled. He had
very strict ideas about how his daughters should
behave, although he turned a blind eye to his wife's
blatant flirting with Gwyneth's suitors. He considered
Nancy beyond reproach and a credit to his own standing and reputation. To have won such a wife was an
achievement, he believed, a notion Gwyneth found
odd but forgivable. She was far more tolerant of her
parent's failings than he was of hers, she considered.
Finishing her meal in silence, she finally rose and

made for the door. But Nancy was not finished with her yet.

"Lady Prevost has asked for my assistance in arranging the flowers for tonight's party," she said proudly. "Would you like to accompany me? You are so clever with your fingers. I am sure there are myriad details with which you could assist Lady Prevost."

Gwyneth made her excuses. "I have promised to lunch at Sally Maitland's today."

With Walter standing by there was little Nancy could say, although it was evident she felt insulted. She was too clever to criticize Gwyneth in Walter's presence but she lost few opportunities to let her stepdaughter know of her hostility. She looked on Gwyneth as a rival who threatened her own position as the chatelaine of the Winwood household.

"Well, of course, if you have promised, but I do wish you would let me know beforehand of your engagements, Gwyneth," she complained dulcetly.

Gwyneth only gave an inconclusive nod and left the room before Nancy could bring up some other task. When her father had brought Nancy home as a bride, without previously consulting his daughters, both Delia and Gwyneth had tried to adapt to the situation. Delia had been more successful, but had soon left home to accompany Isaac Sibley to Detroit. After that Nancy had made it clear that she resented Gwyneth's efforts to continue directing the household, and slyly suggested to her husband that the girl was much too bold in her manner and needed supervision. Walter, under his wife's thumb, normally would have resented any criticism of his daughter, but his own views on how young females should behave forced him to examine Gwyneth's behavior, and he found it wanting. Gwyneth realized her best defense was to keep quiet about her activities and stay out of Nancy's way as much as possible.

Sometime later she left the house with a sigh of relief. Comfortable as her home was after the deprivations of Detroit, it was hardly worth good meals, warmth, and service to put up with Nancy. But she had little choice. She could not return to Detroit, and there was no other refuge available. Well-brought-up girls did not leave home until they married, and Gwyneth was not quite that desperate yet, although she thought she might yet come to such a pass.

Hurrying from the solid brick house on Sherbrooke Street toward the Maitland home on this bleak January day, she wondered if the war would alter her circumstances. Even an invasion by the Americans would add some excitement to her life, she thought but then derided her foolishness. How ridiculous and even petty to want a war to solve her problems. She knew only too well that war was not a romantic daring adventure but a bloody carnage where good men died and even civilians suffered disasters.

This thinking just illuminated Nancy's effect upon her. She must learn to deal with her domestic troubles and not let her stepmother drive her to recklessness. Shivering in the cold wind that blew off the St. Lawrence, she crossed the cobblestones into St. Catherine Street, where the Maitlands had their home. Sally's father, John Maitland, was a very successful solicitor, handling much government business as well as the affairs of several trading companies. He had a good grasp of French law and spoke the language well, a rarity among the English business community, who were apt to look down on the French enclave and patronize the citizens.

Sally, a statuesque brunette with a rather grave manner, had served as an antidote to Gwyneth's mercurial spirits since the girls had been schoolmates. She welcomed Gwyneth warmly and led her into the sitting room to greet her mother Anne. Gwyneth envied Sally her mother. Mrs. Maitland was a kind, tolerant, yet worldly woman who had been a close friend of Gwyneth's own mother.

"How nice to see you, dear. I want to hear all about your adventures in Detroit," Mrs. Maitland said, patting a seat beside her on the large divan before the fire.

Gwyneth leaned over and gave her a kiss, then sat down beside her. "Some of them were quite horrendous, and I suppose that is why Montreal seems a bit flat," she explained, knowing Mrs. Maitland would understand.

"Well, you will have some excitement tonight at the Prevost party. The Governor has not been here long and wants to make a good impression. Lady Prevost, although up on every suit, is really quite a cozy woman, not at all starched-up!" Mrs. Maitland confided with a grin, knowing Gwyneth would appreciate the description.

"What will you wear at your first formal appearance back among us?" Sally asked.

"I haven't quite decided. I really need some new gowns, but conditions seem a little perilous to be indulging in fashions," Gwyneth answered.

"Nonsense. A new gown is a fillip, and very necessary to keep up the spirits of the troops," Mrs. Maitland insisted.

"I'm afraid they need keeping up. Most of the

young men have resisted joining the militia, but some have been dragooned into it. They really are not happy about this war, feeling it is England's responsibility. They believe the regulars should do most of the fighting . . . and dying,'' Sally explained gravely.

"I understand Johnny Tremayne has joined, and Nancy tells me, he looks splendid in his uniform,'' Gwyneth said a bit wryly.

"Haven't you seen him yet? He was always complaining about your absence and quizzing me about your return, but your letters were so vague, and then you suddenly appeared,'' Sally said.

"And just before Christmas. That occupied me at first, but now I am at your disposal.'' Gwyneth smiled at her friend, thinking what a soothing girl she was. "And you can tell me all the gossip. After seven months away much must have happened.''

"Well, our society has been enlivened by all the English officers. Quite put our poor boys in the shade. And I hear that Sir George has an earl's son on his staff, just arrived, who will no doubt send all the girls into raptures at tonight's festivity.''

"Quite. Well, he will just have to charm you all. I have had enough of English officers, haughty snobs most of them.'' Pressed to tell of her adventures, Gwyneth, feeling comfortable and appreciated, launched into a fuller description of her experience than she had given her own family. If only her own mother had lived to offer the love and counsel that Sally enjoyed, Gwyneth thought longingly. After a good coze the ladies adjourned to the dining room, where they were joined by Mr. Maitland and his son Robert, who was reading law.

Robert, a sturdy young man with a shock of blond hair and the blue eyes of his sister, had long fancied

Gwyneth but felt she was above his touch. Gwyneth quite liked him as a brother, but was afraid to encourage him as she knew she would never feel any deeper emotion. He looked at her with admiration and joined his father in welcoming her back to Montreal.

"Gwyneth has had some amazing and even frightening experiences in Detroit," Mrs. Maitland confided as the little Irish maid passed the roast lamb.

"We must hear all about them, my dear," Mr. Maitland encouraged. He was a distinguished-looking gentleman with a kindly but firm manner who did not suffer fools gladly. He had a great deal of sympathy for Gwyneth, for he knew Walter Winwood and thought him foolish to have married as he had.

"Well, of course when I left to visit Delia I was not expecting a war," Gwyneth said soberly.

"None of us were and a bungled business it has been."

"The Americans appear to be more enthusiastic than any of the Canadians or English I have talked to," Gwyneth admitted.

"Well, I suppose they think they can annex Canada," Robert offered.

"Never," snorted his father. "But they seem about to try and take Montreal. It's very worrying, but we should be safe until spring. And I only hope Governor Prevost is prepared. His predecessor, Craig, had great success in staving off an Indian uprising, and I only hope Prevost has his skills."

"Indians are frightening," Gwyneth remembered with a shudder and gave an edited account of her own confrontation with them. The Maitlands were suitably appalled and applauded her bravery.

"Well, I really owe my rescue to an officer who was half Indian himself. And I do feel a certain sympathy for the wretches, being forced off their land by the American settlers.''

"Yes, we could have dealt more honestly with them, I think,'' Mr. Maitland agreed.

"Enough of this talk of war and atrocities. Let us turn to more pleasant topics. The girls are both looking forward to the festivity tonight. We all need a little distraction from this worry of war and coming battles,'' Mrs. Maitland intervened, taking control of the conversation.

It was late afternoon before Gwyneth left the Maitlands, much cheered by her visit and promising Sally to see her that evening. Stepping along briskly as she walked home, she felt grateful for the Maitlands' friendship and the knowledge that their home offered a refuge from her own. The prospect of the evening party raised her spirits, too. Looking about her at Montreal's solid brick buildings and trim streets bustling with citizens going about their business as if no danger threatened them, she realized how comforting the civilized surroundings of her native city seemed after the rigors of Detroit. She would not leave it so casually in the future and would endure whatever fate the coming months brought to Montreal. In that decision she had not calculated her father and Nancy's reaction to what was to become a distinctly unexpected development.

# Chapter Six

The Governor's home had been built more than a hundred years ago for France's eleventh governor of Montreal. Gen. Sir George Prevost, who had been promoted to that rank for his services against the French in the Caribbean, had only been in his post for a short time but had already proved cautious in military matters, although well-intentioned and honest. Prevost's main task was to engage the Canadians in the war against America and protect this city. He was having great difficulty in accomplishing the former, and the latter job might prove his undoing. But the English-speaking residents of the city were prepared to give him the benefit of the doubt. His wife Catherine, daughter of a general herself, added a cachet to Montreal society which had not been evident under Craig, a peppery bachelor who disliked the French.

Sir George and Lady Prevost greeted their guests at the entrance to the mansion, then sent them into

the drawing room that had been cleared for dancing.
A large and representative crowd had already gathered when the Winwoods arrived. As she passed down
the receiving line, Gwyneth was shocked to be greeted
by the Governor's military attaché, Giles Fitzalen-Hill.
She had never expected to see him again and at first
could not decide whether to be pleased or not. She
was relieved that she looked her best, in a heavy cream
silk gown beaded with seed pearls, and long white
gloves, quite a contrast to her frontier dress, but then
was disgusted at her concern that he see her in a
fashionable mode.

"Good evening, Gwyneth. How nice to see a familiar face in this strange city. I only arrived two days
ago and hoped you would appear. Of course, you will
spare me a dance?" Giles said smoothly, casting a
practiced eye over her and approving of what he saw.

A line of guests was forming behind her, and Gwyneth, too startled to reply, only nodded and walked
on into the improvised ballroom. Nancy had preceded her and turned sharply to quiz her.

"Do you know that attractive aide? Did you meet
him in Detroit? If so it must have been far more
exciting than you led us to believe."

Gwyneth, reluctant to explain matters to her stepmother gave a curt yes and was grateful to be
approached by Johnny Tremayne, looking smart in
his regimentals, who immediately pressed her for several dances. In a daze she allowed him to scribble
his initials on her card, hardly heeding his remarks.
Fortunately several other young men crowded around
her, and she was forced to concentrate on their
demands for her company. Among them was Robert
Maitland, and she agreed to give him the opening
minuet.

The steps of the dance precluded much conversation, which was fortunate, for Gwyneth was distracted by the sudden appearance of Giles. From the corner of her eye, she noticed that he had been relieved of his duties in the receiving line and was now talking with her stepmother. If she could have heard the tenor of their conversation, she would have been even more disturbed. Nancy's preening air suggested that Giles was using his best social techniques on Mrs. Winwood and what that signified she feared would only cause her trouble.

"You look much too young to have a daughter of Gwyneth's age, Mrs. Winwood," Giles was saying, exerting all his considerable charm.

"Oh, Gwyneth is not my daughter, you know. I married her father several years ago, some time after Gwyneth's mother died. Do I take it that you met Gwyneth in Detroit, Major?" she asked, looking at him with admiration.

"Yes, indeed. I was able to give her some assistance during the occupation," he informed her suavely.

"She returned very suddenly. We thought she would remain until spring," Nancy said. Then thinking that did not sound very warm, she added, "Not that we are not happy to have her home."

If Giles doubted her specious assurance, he gave no sign of it.

"I do hope you will allow me to call?" he enquired, giving her one of his best smiles.

"Of course, Major." Nancy was under the impression that she had charmed this elegant gentleman and looked forward to a mild flirtation with him. His interest was apparent, and she had enough conceit to think he found her far more attractive than the *farouche* Gwyneth. That was just the impression Giles hoped to create, for he doubted Gwyneth would invite him herself. He wondered idly as he chatted with Nancy why he was bothering, but his self-esteem had been pricked by Gwyneth's rejection of him and he was determined to change her mind. When General Prevost, with whom he had served in Portsmouth a few years ago, had requested his presence, an outranked Colonial Proctor had to let him go. He was relieved to be out of Detroit but still yearned to return to Wellington's staff now that the Peninsular War appeared to have reached a decisive stage. He feared it might be all over before he could join Wellington again.

Robert Maitland returned Gwyneth to the chaperone's corner after their dance and was introduced to Giles, whom he immediately disliked. Bowing, he made a quick departure, leaving Gwyneth to cope with Nancy and Giles.

"Your stepmother has kindly given me permission to call, Gwyneth, but in the meantime I would like to request a dance," he urged, noting her glowering face with amusement. The girl obviously wanted nothing more to do with him, but he was going to thwart her attempts to put him off. Why he was so anxious to renew their battle, he could not understand, but her hostility only whetted his interest.

"Surely you will oblige the major?" Nancy cooed.

"I believe my card is full," Gwyneth insisted shortly.

But Giles was having none of her protests. In a masterful fashion he commandeered her card and found an empty square just after the supper dance. He scrawled his initials and then, before either Nancy or Gwyneth could protest, made his adieux.

"Really, Gwyneth, you were quite rude to that charming major. You must tell me all about how you met," Nancy quizzed, her interest aroused.

"He was on General Brock's staff when the English took Detroit," Gwyneth obliged briefly.

"He has such a manner. Obviously he is a man of some consequence," Nancy observed. She intended to get his whole pedigree from Catherine Prevost at the first opportunity.

Gwyneth's next partner, Johnny Tremayne, had now appeared, and she thankfully escaped on his arm before Nancy could probe any deeper into her relationship with Giles.

"Didn't like the looks of that major," Johnny muttered as they took the floor.

Neither did Gwyneth, but she did not intend to confide in Johnny Tremayne, a devil-may-care youth who made a good companion but lacked stability. He looked most dashing in his uniform, but Gwyneth had known him for years and had long ago decided he was a fribble. Attractive enough, of a good height, with a crooked merry smile and bold blue eyes and brown hair, he had more than his fair share of charm, but little else. Still, he might serve to warn Giles off, so she smiled and encouraged him in his fulsome compliments.

For the rest of the evening she tried to ignore Giles's presence. His effect on the females of Montreal society from the oldest dowager to the youngest belle was evident. But she refused to follow their example. The man was haughty, conceited, and too sure of his ability to lure women. She would not be one of his victims.

When Giles came to claim his dance, Gwyneth had just enjoyed a cheerful supper with Johnny Tremayne,

Sally Maitland, and her beau, Denzil Harte, a young man of lively spirits who acted a fine foil for Sally's sobriety. To Gwyneth's disgust she noticed that Sally, whom she had always admired for her good sense, seemed as enthralled by Giles as the rest of her sex. Even Denzil viewed the experienced major with awe. Only Johnny remained truculent and defiant, an attitude that Giles took in stride.

"Your cavalier doesn't like me," Giles admitted to Gwyneth as they left the supper room.

"Should he?" Gwyneth asked tartly, conscious that she was behaving badly but unable to help herself.

"Well, no, of course, you are right. He views me as a rival for your affections," Giles riposted with outrageous aplomb.

"I will soon disabuse him," Gwyneth snapped and then separated from him in the intricacies of the dance. She was slightly ashamed of herself for acting so ill-tempered. Her proper attitude should be one of cool scorn, unwilling to rise to Giles's taunts, but she had never been a good dissembler.

"You know, Gwyneth, you are good for me. You depress my pretensions. I missed you when you left Detroit," Giles mocked, which did nothing to strengthen her good intentions.

She made no reply beyond a speaking glance, and they separated again. Finally the dance came to an end, and Giles escorted her to a secluded alcove, rather than returning her to Nancy as was proper.

"Can I get you some refreshment?" he asked politely, looming over her as she sank gratefully into an armless chair.

"No, thank you. I believe my next partner is looking for me."

"Well, he can wait a moment. This is not the place, but I want to have a talk with you," he announced gravely.

"Do you have news of Delia?" Gwyneth asked, suddenly worried.

"She is fine, sends her love. She seems to be coping well with her husband's absence," he reassured her.

Relieved, Gwyneth looked more kindly on him. "Well, I suppose you can call tomorrow if your duties permit. I cannot imagine what we need to discuss."

"I regret the way we parted and want to make amends," Giles said almost ruefully.

Surprised at his diffidence in referring to their last unhappy encounter, Gwyneth wondered if he meant to apologize for trying to seduce her. This was so out of character she could not imagine what his motive would be, but she acquitted him of trying to renew his assault on her senses.

Before she could question him, her next partner, a fellow officer, appeared, nodded to Giles, and bore her away.

Later that evening after returning from the party, Gwyneth could not avoid Nancy's probing about Giles as her father listened.

"I suppose you know that your fascinating major is a viscount, the heir of the Earl of Selkirk," Nancy informed her with some pride. She had wrested the information from Lady Prevost.

"No, I did not know, but it does not surprise me. He's arrogant enough to be a duke," Gwyneth snapped, trying to hide her dismay.

"Really, Gwyneth, I don't understand you. Here is

this wonderful opportunity for you to cultivate a man of substance and breeding, and you behave as if he had a contagious disease.''

Gwyneth wondered what Nancy would say if she told her of Giles's attempt to seduce her.

''I don't like his airs and graces, ''she replied.'' He acts as if he is doing a favor even to talk to us. I wish he would return to his milieu in London.''

''You met this man in Detroit, I take it, Gwyneth,'' her father intervened.

''Yes, he was helpful to Delia and me when we were living under the occupation. It was not easy for Delia, you know, since she was the wife of an enemy.'' Gwyneth hoped that her father would see the reasonableness of this explanation and not take the matter further.

''Well, we must thank him for that,'' Walter said, and the matter was dropped, much to Nancy's disappointment. She wanted to learn more from Gwyneth but was wise enough not to challenge the girl before her husband.

Later, alone in her bedroom Gwyneth wondered what Giles's sudden arrival in Montreal meant to her. Her feelings about the man were so chaotic. He infuriated, fascinated, and frightened her all at the same time. Would he renew his efforts to get her into bed? Did she want a more honorable proposal from him? Was she so impressed with his title, address, and charm that she had forgotten that he could and did behave with the utmost disregard for not only her virtue but her feelings? She admitted to herself that she had found it difficult to banish all memories of their time together. She recalled their understanding on the ride up the river when he had told her about

Isaac Brock's death and what it meant to him. But that was just one moment in a score of less pleasant encounters. She had escaped the danger once. Was she to fall again under his spell, ignoring all the evidence that he was a womanizer who had little respect for her? When he called, how would she receive him? Well, she would have to wait upon events, and with this sensible decision she went to sleep at last, but her dreams were troubled.

As it happened, she did not have to face him the following day. When he called, she was absent, shopping for some much-needed replacements to her wardrobe. But she heard a glowing account of the viscount's manner, appearance, and conversation from Nancy. Like Delia she found him both polite and charming. Her stepmother implied that Giles had not been too disappointed to find Gwyneth unavailable and had found Nancy a more than acceptable substitute. Gwyneth could not help but wonder if Giles had set up a flirtation with her stepmother. She had to concede that Nancy was a very attractive woman and probably was thrilled at the attentions of such a man, one who in normal times would rarely cross her path. Chiding herself, Gwyneth wondered why she objected to Nancy's enthusiasm. Surely it could not affect her one way or the other.

"He stayed for some time, taking tea with me. I found him very agreeable," Nancy preened, hoping to rouse some reaction in Gwyneth Then as she saw that the girl would not respond, she went further. "No doubt he enjoyed the association with a mature, sophisticated woman."

"No doubt he did, Nancy. Lord Fitzalen-Hill has his faults, but he is quite polished. Delia liked him immensely," Gwyneth conceded.

"And I gather you don't," Nancy replied sharply, trying to discover more about Gwyneth's real relationship with the fascinating lord.

But Gwyneth would not be drawn, and she left her stepmother unappeased. Nancy decided that Gwyneth was jealous that Lord Fitzalen-Hill had enjoyed his visit with her. Just like the girl. She didn't care for him herself but resented his interest in a more understanding woman. She smiled with satisfaction, believing that a little light flirtation with a lord would brighten her winter immeasurably, and irritate her stepdaughter, too.

But Nancy would have to tread carefully. That evening at dinner, her husband quizzed her about Lord Fitzalen-Hill's call.

"I suppose he came to see Gwyneth," he said, frowning. He was not sure he liked the idea of his daughter attracting one of England's noblemen. He had rather strict standards about Gwyneth's behavior, and he was astute enough to think that the man had no honest intentions toward her.

"Well, yes, but he was quite content to stay and take tea with me," Nancy replied, unable to repress her satisfaction, although she might have been wiser to keep her own counsel.

"There will be a number of these high-toned officers in Montreal with the war heating up in the spring. But, Gwyneth, just how friendly are you with this lord?" Walter asked, ignoring Nancy's innuendo.

"Not very. He is probably bored and is looking for some distraction." She thought that was an accurate assessment.

"I don't want you talked about. Montreal is a hot-bed of gossip, so behave circumspectly," Walter Win-wood warned her. He was not unaware of Gwyneth's tendency toward rebellion, and she and Nancy were at daggers drawn, not a comfortable situation. The girl might easily be lured into a scandal. Walter loved his daughter, but he did not understand her, and her reputation was his chief concern. What he felt about his wife's endorsement of this lord he was not prepared to examine. His friends had implied he was a fool to marry a woman so much younger, and his pride would not allow him to consider that his wife might find him inadequate in any way. No, Gwyneth was the problem. He wished she would marry, but although she always had beaux, she never seemed to carry any of the relationships further. He could hardly send her back to Detroit, but it looked as if he might have to take some action if he were to insure peace in his home. He had been too occupied with business lately. With this devilish war and the threat to Montreal, he had spared little time for his family. But damn it, a man should not have to worry about his daughter's virtue and his wife's boredom. He deserved better than that.

So it was a somewhat silent dinner, the trio absorbed with their own concerns, which would have shocked each of them had they been revealed. Gwyneth thought to herself that it might be a long and difficult winter.

# Chapter Seven

Montreal society, under the threat of attack, entered into a feverish round of gaiety to distract itself from what could be a desperate conflict. Older citizens remembered the American occupation in 1775 when Sir Guy Carleton had surrendered the city without a shot being fired. They had every assurance that Sir George intended to make a fight of it, and they feared the outcome. The best distraction was a spurt of hectic routs, theatricals, even balls to keep their minds from dwelling on the spring when the battle for the city loomed.

As an aide to Sir George and a personable escort, Giles was in great demand. However, despite the many lures which were held out to him, he seemed to prefer the company of Gwyneth Winwood. Some harpies implied that Gwyneth herself was not the attraction, but that her stepmother had established a cozy rapport with the viscount which was more to his taste.

Certainly Giles spent a great deal of his free time at the Winwoods.

The promised talk with Gwyneth had not gone entirely the way he wished. The day after his tea with Nancy, he had sent a note to Gwyneth asking her to ride out with him while he inspected the fortification. Since she knew she could not forever postpone a meeting, she agreed. But unlike the drive down the river in Detroit, this jaunt did not have as happy an outcome.

It began badly when Gwyneth arrived in the drawing room to find Giles exchanging pleasantries with Nancy. Her stepmother, looking smug and satisfied, was obviously enjoying Giles's stock of flattering remarks. She tossed her head in irritation when Gwyneth appeared but did not allow Giles to see her annoyance.

"I do wish you had told me you had an engagement with Lord Fitzalen-Hill, Gwyneth," she complained, but in dulcet tones. She believed gentlemen disliked women quarreling.

"Why?" Gwyneth queried bluntly.

"Well, after all, Gwyneth, I do serve in some respects as your chaperone and I am not sure you should be riding out without one. It might lead to supposition," she simpered, turning to Giles as if to receive his endorsement of society's rule.

"Possibly you would be correct in London, Mrs. Winwood, but surely matters are more relaxed here in Canada," he said, smiling. He had no intention of inviting Mrs. Winwood to accompany them, but he was too skilled to antagonize her.

"Yes, that's true, but Montreal is not Detroit. I fear Gwyneth has fallen into careless ways during her stay in the frontier.'' Nancy did not like Giles paying attention to her stepdaughter, but she realized she would have to go carefully. He was not a man to be challenged.

''That's nonsense and you know it, Nancy. I have been riding out with men for some time without you finding it in the least bit scandalous.''

Retreating swiftly, Nancy agreed. ''Of course, my dear, you will do as you please. I was only trying to protect your reputation.''

''Giles, what have you done to appear as a threat to my virtue?'' Gwyneth mocked, angering both Giles and Nancy, the former because that was just what he was, and he didn't like her reminding him of it, and Nancy because she was thwarted in her attempt to spend more time with Giles.

''If you are quite finished with your strictures, Nancy, shall we be off?'' Gwyneth said sharply.

''Of course,'' Giles agreed and politely helped her into the warm green pelisse trimmed in beaver she was holding. Without more ado Gwyneth walked to the door, leaving Nancy to make what she would of her defiance. Gwyneth suspected Nancy had designs on Giles and she wished her luck, but she was not about to encourage her foibles.

The weather matched her mood, gray and gloomy, with snow threatening. As Giles poled up the horses, a splendid pair of matched grays, she said tartly, ''We haven't chosen a good day for this expedition.''

''No, but I wanted to get you alone, and this seemed the best opportunity,'' Giles admitted. He cursed Mrs. Winwood silently for putting Gwyneth in a foul mood and did his best to soothe her.

''I don't see why. We have said everything we have

to say to each other, I believe," Gwyneth insisted obstinately.

"Really, Gwyneth, you are so harsh in your judgments. Granted I tried to have my way with you that night in Detroit. But I realize that is not to be and want you to accept my apology," he said, not entirely truthfully.

"I'm not sure I want to do that. It might encourage you to try again," she said sulkily.

"Well, let us forget Detroit and pretend we have just met," he said appeasingly.

"To what end?"

"Why, friendship, of course. I suspect you are feeling aggrieved because I was flattering your stepmother. I was only trying to make things easier for you. Obviously you do not have a pleasant relationship with her. Are you jealous?" he asked with a slight lift to one eyebrow.

"Of course not. But Nancy would not have been my choice for a stepmother, if I had to have one. There were several more agreeable widows my father could have selected. She is a snob and a toady, and tries to cause trouble between Father and me."

"Well, I am sure you can handle her. You never seem to be daunted by these challenges." Giles felt his own temper rising at her obdurate attitude. Why did he bother with the girl?

"I am not meek by nature, but you know that," Gwyneth agreed, laughing a bit, for she saw the justice of his remarks. "But enough of Nancy. Tell me about Detroit," she invited.

"Proctor is digging in for a siege, but I think he will have to come out and fight if he hopes to hold on to the outpost. And it's vital if Canada is not to be invaded, even conquered."

"Surely the English regulars are a match for any American force of settlers."

"Those Kentucky men are fierce fighters. I am not sure. After all, they beat us once," he admitted ruefully.

"But your best generals refused to serve in the Colonies, and I feel your hearts were not in it."

"Do you want Canada to become part of the new United States?" he asked, surprised at her defense.

"No, I don't. And I despise this war."

"Well, on that, at least, we agree. Can't we also agree on becoming friends?"

"Quite frankly, Giles, you are not the type of man that women look upon as a friend."

"You have me there. I admit my relationships with your sex are not notable for friendship." He refused to be baited.

"So why choose me for your experiment?" Gwyneth asked, but her bad temper was abating. And for the rest of the ride around the deplorable fortifications, they sparred in an amiable fashion. Giles confessed he feared Prevost would have a difficult time defending the city if the Americans attacked and he himself would recommend immediately repairing matters. As they rode along at a spanking pace, the weather worsened and snow began to fall. Gwyneth shivered and buried her hands in her beaver muff. She was accustomed to Montreal's harsh winters, but somehow she found today especially trying. As they turned to ride back to the city, one of the horses stumbled and Giles pulled up, exclaiming, "What the devil." He reined in the horses, handed the leads to Gwyneth, and stepped down to survey the damage.

They were still some miles from the center of the city, and the snow had increased in volume, accompanied by a stiff, dampening wind. Gwyneth prayed the horse was not seriously damaged because she knew it could delay their journey, and darkness was closing in on this short January day.

"I'm afraid the horse is lamed and I will have to walk him back," Giles announced after running his hands over the strained tendon and returning to the curricle.

"Poor animal. Well, it can't be helped. Shall I get down and walk, too?" asked Gwyneth agreeably.

"Thank you for being so accommodating, Gwyneth. Some females would wail and blame me. You are a real Trojan," Giles approved.

"I can hardly accuse you of causing the horse's problem. Let's get on with it," she said stoutly. "I will walk. Fortunately I have on fur-lined boots. It will not be too bad, only about five miles. I am sure to an old campaigner like you, it's a short hike."

"Thank you," he said and helped her down. They began to trudge forward, Giles leading the horse and Gwyneth speaking soothing words to the animal, a high-spirited beast who did not take kindly to his predicament.

It was almost dark when they finally reached Sherbrooke Street and the Winwood house. Gwyneth had marched along sturdily, apparently unfazed by the snow and cold, although she must have been uncomfortable. Giles was impressed by her lack of complaint and her stoic acceptance of their dilemma. He thought what a relief it was that Mrs. Winwood had not prevailed upon him to allow her to go on the ride. She would never have accepted a five-mile walk through the miserable weather with such aplomb. Gwyneth was an unusual girl and would make a fine mate for a serving soldier, he thought idly. But not this soldier, he concluded. However attractive the girl was and however valiant, he was not about to be trapped into an unlikely alliance with a Colonial. Nancy and Giles had one trait in common. They were both snobs.

Whatever opinions of Giles Gwyneth might be harboring, she did not review them now, her energies completely engaged in slogging through the miserable day. By the time they reached her home, she was thoroughly wet, tired, and disgusted. However, she could not blame Giles for her predicament, and she had to admit he remained amazingly imperious to the weather and the misfortune of the lamed horse.

Still, she was not in the best of humors when they finally limped into the hall of her home. The maid who admitted them could hardly restrain her curiosity, but before Gwyneth could offer any explanations, her father emerged from his library.

"Well, Gwyneth, where have you been? This is a very late hour to return from an afternoon ride," he said, glowering at the picture of his daughter looking disheveled. He cast an equally disapproving eye over Giles.

"I believe you have met Major Lord Fitzalen-Hill, Father," Gwyneth offered, annoyed at her father's admonition and even more at his lack of courtesy. She had hoped to escape to her room and a hot bath without recriminations.

"Good evening, Major," Walter Winwood said sternly. "I suppose you have some explanation for keeping my daughter out all day and returning at this very late hour."

Giles, not liking Walter Winwood's tone and unaccustomed to having his actions criticized, was astute enough to realize that taking umbrage would not ease matters.

"Yes, sir. My horse pulled up lame and we had to walk the last few miles through the most appalling weather," he explained cheerfully as if there was nothing exceptional in such a mishap. "Gwyneth must be very tired and uncomfortable, but I have to admire her stoic behavior."

"That may be, but I am sure you realize that her reputation could suffer if this escapade becomes known. I understand Mrs. Winwood offered to accompany you and you refused," Walter complained starchily. If he felt any compassion for Gwyneth's plight, he was not prepared to show it or abandon his grievance.

Giles, now becoming annoyed, had enough good sense to believe that Walter Winwood had been worried and was just releasing his concern with an irritable burst of temper, but he did not like his attitude.

"Just as well she did not come. I doubt if she would have enjoyed the tramp back," he said suavely. Before Walter could reply, Nancy came from the drawing room, uttering cries of dismay.

"Just look at you, Gwyneth, dripping all over the rug," she protested sharply, then reverting to her usual coy manner with Giles, "And Lord Fitzalen-Hill, you look as if you have had a vexing adventure. Do come in and have a drink." Turning to Gwyneth, she said, "Of course you will want to have a bath and change. Dinner will be ready shortly. I have had Cook hold it back. Perhaps you will join us, sir," she invited, turning with a smile to Giles.

"How kind, Mrs. Winwood, but I must return to headquarters. I regret that Gwyneth has had such an uncomfortable time of it, but I am sure she will recover after a good meal and a rest. She behaved splendidly." And bidding them a curt goodbye, he made a rapid retreat.

Gwyneth, more amused than angry at the turn of events, ignored both Nancy and her father, and trudged upstairs.

Walter said angrily to Nancy, "She has not heard the last of this, traipsing around the countryside with that officer and exposing herself to gossip. The girl has no sense of decorum. You should never have let her go, Nancy."

"And how could I have stopped her, Walter? You know she will take no heed of my effort to control her," Nancy wailed. "I cannot blame Lord Fitzalen-Hill for an accident, but I agree Gwyneth should not go racketing around alone with him. It may give rise to all kinds of talk." Thus, she managed to slide out of her own responsibilities, excuse Giles, and put the blame on Gwyneth, a typical maneuver on her part.

After a rather chilly dinner that evening, Walter ordered Gwyneth into his study, where he spoke sternly to her about her conduct, insisting she mend her heedless ways.

Gwyneth, tired and annoyed that her father should blame her for an unavoidable situation, bit her tongue and then explained calmly, "What else could we do, Father? We were some miles from town when the horse floundered. There was no one about to come to our aid. We just had to make the best of it. I think you are refining too much on the accident."

"You are not on the frontier now, Gwyneth, and you must behave with some circumspection. Riding out alone with officers for hours is not proper. I must

say you seem on very intimate terms with this Lord
Fitzalen-Hill. Is he courting you?"

"No, he is not, and if he were, he would not be
acceptable. He is just an acquaintance I met in Detroit
under unusual circumstance. I might remind you that
he saved me from an attack by two Indians," she
reproved sharply, wondering why he was making so
much of this and wishing for a little compassion.
Really, her father appeared to care more for appear-
ances than her safety.

"Don't take that tone with me, girl. You behave
like a hoyden and then expect sympathy. Just because
there is a war on, you cannot abandon all the proprieties. I can see your stay in Detroit did nothing to
improve your judgment. If you continue this way, you
will become a scandal."

The injustice of her father's attitude irritated Gwyneth, but she refused to offer any apologies for what
was beyond her control. "I am sorry you feel that
way, Father, and I might say I think you are making
much over a regrettable, but not sinful situation. If
you have quite finished reproving me, I would like
to go to bed. I am very tired." And without waiting
for his permission or any more criticism, she abruptly
left the room. Walter, realizing he had handled the
affair badly and feeling a trifle ashamed, for he really
loved his daughter and had perhaps been unfair,
brooded about what he might do to alter matters.
He was neither a foolish nor stupid man, and he
acknowledged that the abrasive relationship between
Nancy and Gwyneth was spoiling the tranquillity he
wanted in his home. What could he do to retrieve
matters?

The unhappy incident with the horse did not mean

the end of Giles's visits to the Winwood household nor his attentions to Gwyneth. Nancy found him intriguing and encouraged him, believing in her vapid fashion it was really her company he enjoyed. But Walter was not deceived. The major's attentions to his daughter worried him. He was not convinced she did not have a *tendre* for the haughty lord and thought little but trouble could ensue from their continued friendship, if that was what it was. Her other beaux, including the feckless Johnny Tremayne, were intimidated by Giles and had left the field, and Giles and Gwyneth were becoming the talk of Montreal society. Walter was reluctant to quiz Giles on his intentions, but the situation bothered him. It was unfortunate she and Nancy did not get on. A mature woman might offer advice, but Gwyneth would heed no counsel from Nancy.

He dithered as February deepened into March. He could see nothing but eventual unhappiness for his daughter if she continued to see Giles, and she showed no signs of abandoning the man. But when his partner in the Northwest Company mentioned the affair archly during a business lunch, he decided he would have to take a stand.

Arriving home after the luncheon, he challenged Nancy as to Gwyneth's whereabouts.

"She has gone to a party at the Maitlands," Nancy told him.

"With that major, I assume."

"Yes, Giles escorted her," Nancy agreed. "Don't you approve of Giles?" she asked her husband slyly, having a very good idea of the tenor of his thoughts.

"I don't believe he has honorable intentions toward her, and she is becoming talked about," Walter grumbled. He knew Nancy admired Giles, and although he had too much self-esteem to be jealous, he did not like his wife favoring the man.

"Well, she has always been difficult. But surely you don't believe she could be lured into an indiscretion," Nancy purred, as if shocked.

"Indiscretion, bah. She is in danger of losing her virtue if she's not careful."

"Oh, no, Walter. I believe Giles is an upright gentleman. He would not risk a scandal by trying to persuade Gwyneth to behave badly."

"Seduce her, you mean. Don't be mealy-mouthed. He certainly would if she encouraged him, or even if she doesn't," he stormed.

"Well, what can you do?" Nancy asked.

"I can send her away, and that is what I am going to do." He spoke resolutely, having finally made up his mind.

"She can't go back to Detroit. It's too dangerous," Nancy protested, not minding the idea of banishing Gwyneth but unwilling to show Walter her true feelings.

"She can go to England to my cousins, the Endicotts. Ships will be getting through any day. The river is breaking up early this year." He had been mulling over the idea for some time, but today's luncheon discussion had forced him to come to some conclusion.

"You will not ask Giles his intentions, then?" Nancy asked, sensing a confrontation.

"Well, I suppose I might be traducing him. I will sound him out, invite him to dinner, and I will put it to him. A damn awkward situation, and not a word to Gwyneth about this, mind," he warned. Having settled the affair to his satisfaction, he dismissed Nancy's flutterings and felt he had handled matters expeditiously. That Gwyneth would be angry and embarrassed he discounted. She was his responsibility, and he owed it to his own standing in the community to manage his daughter properly. He would not admit he felt guilty. Any decent father would act as he had. He sat down immediately and wrote to the Endicotts. He had earlier hinted at the possibility that Gwyneth might visit them and had received an enthusiastic reply. Now he would confirm the fact that she would be coming to England. He would suffer no disobedience from Gwyneth.

If her father had become alarmed by Giles's attentions to his daughter, Gwyneth herself was wondering what that arrogant lord had in mind. She acquitted him of trying to get her into his bed. He had his career to think of, and Sir George Prevost would never entertain with complaisance his aide seducing a daughter of a prominent member of Montreal society and a pillar of the business community. Giles might be haughty and conceited but he was not stupid. No, she was beginning to think he really cared for her, and her own feelings were confused but far warmer than they had been a few months ago in Detroit. Since arriving in Montreal in January, he had behaved like a man who was attempting to attach her interest. At every rout, dance, and dinner he had been her partner, monopolizing her so that any other young man would think he had a prior claim. Now that she thought of it, her father's fixation that Lord Fitzalen-Hill was making her a spectacle did not seem so strange.

But why was Giles doing it? She wanted to believe he genuinely admired her, even had come to care for her, but a niggling doubt remained. He could just as easily be amusing himself, indifferent to her own feelings. She sighed, wishing that she had never met him. By comparison the company of the young men she had known in Montreal for years appeared drab and boring. They had none of his address, his air of command, nor did they have his assurance bred from years of privilege. His conversation, his manners, his appearance quite put them in the shade. Was she as gullible as Nancy, impressed by a title and a sophistication alien to this society?

In all these months she had never really come to know the man behind the facade of the dashing officer. Wary of her own feelings, suspicious of his, Gwyneth sometimes wished that Giles would suddenly be recalled to England, leaving her to the life she had hitherto accepted. If she was coming to love him, she did not trust him, hardly a basis for marriage, if that was what he wanted. Surely she could not genuinely care for a man whose motives she suspected? She was determined to be sensible, to examine her situation with intelligence not emotion. What she did not account for were circumstances that could sweep all rational thought aside, for the passion that could overcome the most stringent scruples.

# *Chapter Eight*

Gwyneth's good resolutions were put to the test two evenings later. They had attended a dinner at Sir George and Lady Prevost's, where it was apparent Giles stood in high favor. Gwyneth felt a bit shy at the august company, not a normal reaction for her, and one she despised. She had little use for Nancy's maneuvers in society, her obsequious manner toward the governor's lady, and would not try to emulate it. Certainly neither Lady Prevost nor her husband had the haughty manner Gwyneth had come to associate with the English ruling class. The governor, who had a Swiss father, spoke fluent French and had been able to conciliate that portion of Montreal who heretofore had regarded themselves as a conquered people with little interest in aiding their masters in repelling the Americans.

An experienced diplomat, Sir George knew he did not have the resources to go on the offensive. His whole thrust was to fight a defensive war, if he was forced to fight at all. In this he was far different from Isaac Brock and at times his caution annoyed Giles, who vastly preferred the bellicose methods of his former chief. But on the whole the major managed to get along well with the governor, who viewed him as a clever and coming young man.

The governor's approval of Giles was evident to Gwyneth during the dinner, given in honor of Colonel de Salaberry, who would command the Canadian forces in the event of a battle. Gwyneth, whose understanding of French was rudimentary, was impressed with Giles's easy fluency in the language and realized not for the first time that her cavalier was accustomed to moving in circles she had never encountered. However, the dinner went off smoothly, and her hosts treated her with kindness. Later, on the drive home, Giles insisted she had made a very favorable impression on the Prevosts and the other guests. He appeared to take a possessive and proprietary attitude toward her, which raised a few eyebrows, but she accepted it casually, while wondering again what his real feelings were.

"The governor seems to believe that the Americans will not attack Montreal," she said as they clopped through the empty streets on the way to her home.

"I think he's wrong, but I hope he is right because Montreal's defenses are weak, and I am not sure the Canadian militia will fight with any conviction," Giles informed her.

"Whatever happens, many young men will be killed," Gwyneth insisted, "and for what? A war that neither side really wants. What a waste."

"Yes, especially since our real concern is Napoleon."

"You want to return and fight in Europe, don't you?"

"Of course. While I dally here in this backwater, the real contest is heating up and Wellington will prevail. But he is not having an easy time of it."

Ignoring Giles's reference to her town as a backwater, Gwyneth pressed him. "Will you be going back soon, do you think?"

"Who knows? I want to, but I have blotted my copybook with Wellington, a stupid affair of a duel with a fellow officer, and he banished me."

"A duel!" Gwyneth was shocked. She had heard rumors of the affair, but now it appeared they were true. "Over a woman, I suppose."

"Really, Gwyneth, you are much too sharp and suspect me of all kinds of licentious behavior, but, yes, it was over a woman, and one not worth it," he confirmed with a laugh. "I have forgotten her name."

Gwyneth, suspecting he wished her to react angrily, would not be drawn, and the matter was dropped. At last they reached Sherbrooke Street, and Giles jumped from the carriage and assisted her down after tethering his horses to the post. He walked her to the door, and before she could pound the knocker for admittance, he suddenly swooped her into his arms and began to kiss her with a hungry ferocity. He held her hands behind her back, expecting a struggle, but she gave none, surprising herself and him with the depth of her response.

Finally he released her, smiling at her rosy confusion.

"You go to my head, Gwyneth," he admitted.

"You should not have done that, Giles," she murmured, bemused. Was this just a casual embrace? It had not seemed to be, but he made no protestations of love, only looked at her with a hot glance that brought more blushes to her cheek. Sensing that if she stayed there a moment longer, she would make an admission she would later regret, she pounded frantically on the knocker. Almost immediately her father opened the door and glared at the couple balefully.

"There you are, Gwyneth. Don't linger on the step. It's a chilly evening. Thank you for bringing her home, Major," he said repressively, making no move to invite Giles inside.

"Good evening, Gwyneth. I will see you soon. You were a great success this evening. *Au revoir,* sir," he said dismissively to Walter Winwood, and ran down the steps to his horses.

Gwyneth slipped inside, refusing to meet her father's eyes, and scurried across the hall to the stairway. For a moment it appeared her father would recall her, but shrugging his shoulders, he went into the library. Giving a sigh of relief, Gwyneth continued to her room. What had her father suspected? She was afraid she looked a guilty party, blushing from that fervent embrace and barely out of Giles's arms. He, of course, never turned a hair, his aplomb remarkable as always. Damn the man. How dare he use her so. She preferred not to remember that she had done nothing to repel him and had, indeed, enthusiastically returned his kisses. Oh, why had this disturbing man ever entered her life?

Later before falling asleep she went over every moment of that impassioned scene and decided regretfully that it probably meant little to Giles. He was an accomplished rake and thought the kisses nothing more than a suitable finale to an enjoyable evening. He probably thought her a brazen hussy, and she had not disabused him. On the one hand she wanted him to leave Montreal, and on the other she wanted him to stay and commit himself, but she felt that was most unlikely. Giles would never offer for her, and she must resign herself to that and get on with her life in which he could have no part. On that sensible resolution she went to sleep, with the unhappy suspicion that she would not abide by her decision.

Later that week she was to recall those fruitless musings. Nancy had duly invite Giles to dinner, and he accepted with some reservations. He found Mrs. Winwood's flirtatious flutterings tiresome, and he sensed that Walter Winwsood neither approved of his interest in his daughter nor trusted him. Not that the Winwood's opinion bothered him, but he disliked accepting hospitality from a pair who each, in his or her own way, were irritating. However, he did not want to offend Gwyneth, who was an innocent party in this situation. As long as he must remain in Montreal, she offered the only relief from his formal duties.

The evening of the dinner, he found to his dismay that he was the sole guest. Gwyneth looked especially fetching in a heavy aquamarine silk gown, well-cut and trimmed only with a small band of ruching at the neck and skirt. Nancy, on the other hand, had chosen a heavily embroidered pink gauze overskirt atop a cream shift, a costume much too elaborate for a simple family dinner. The meal passed off with vapid pleasantries. Walter's attempts to quiz his guest about the war met with little success that did little to improve his temper. Finally, the ladies adjourned, leaving the men to their port.

"How much longer do you think you will be in Montreal, Major?" Walter asked, sipping austerely at his glass.

"I have no idea, sir. I am hoping to return to England before long and eventually rejoin Wellington's staff in the Peninsula."

"You people believe your first priority is defeating Napoleon. We are certainly not receiving the support we need to fight the Americans," Walter said truculently.

Understanding that any Canadian would feel that way, Giles did not take offense, although he thought Walter Winwood was overly curt. "That may be true, but England has only so many ships and men to allocate to this war. Most of our emphasis has to be in Europe."

"The Liverpool government looks upon us as wretched Colonials, undeserving of help, I warrant. You should have learned your lesson with the American War. I am a Loyalist, but Liverpool strains my patience."

"I can see that, sir, and would feel the same in your position," Giles agreed affably, refusing to be drawn into a defense of Liverpool, whom he, in truth, found much too cautious in pursuing both wars.

"Your real interests and concerns are with England, then?" Walter nodded as if Giles's remarks agreed with his assessment.

"Well, naturally, I would never neglect my duties here to Sir George," Giles said, wondering at the direction of the conversation.

"Since this is only a temporary post and you are

eager to return to England, any relationship which you form here would only be a temporary one, I fancy," Walter continued a bit ponderously.

Giles, sensing that whatever answer he made would be the wrong one, wisely kept silent.

"I will be quite frank with you, Major. Your attentions to my daughter have caused a great deal of speculation, even ribald talk. I think I am within my rights to ask you what you feel for her."

Keeping his temper with difficulty, Giles played for time. He did not appreciate being reproved by this Colonial cit who had delusions of power.

"I am very fond of Gwyneth, for she is an unusual girl," he said in a noncommittal fashion, hoping that Winwood would go no further.

"That's not good enough. Do you intend to offer for her?" Walter asked bluntly.

"I am not in a position to offer for anyone, sir. Soon I hope I will be returning to the battle in Europe. My military duties preclude my making any personal decisions," Giles said suavely, thinking that should be enough for Winwood.

"Well, I suppose that means you have just been dallying with her to pass the time here. If you do not wish to marry her, I must insist that you forgo her company. In short, you are no longer acceptable as an escort for her and will not be received in this house," Walter said boldly, a bit flushed in the face but determined to make his point.

"I regret that you feel that way, sir, but I must abide by your decision. I hope you will let me make my adieu and my apologies to Gwyneth if I have in any way damaged her reputation," Giles said smoothly, although inwardly he was cursing this Montreal bumpkin who had took him to task. He rose and walked to the door without waiting for Walter's permission, and strode angrily to the drawing room, where Gwyneth and Nancy were waiting.

Nancy looked up with a wavering smile as she glimpsed his furious expression, and then dropped her eyes. She had urged Walter to confront Giles and now she was regretting it.

"I must make my farewells, madam. Your husband has made it clear I am no longer welcome here, but before I leave I want to see Gwyneth alone."

"Really, my lord . . ." Nancy sputtered, and then thought it wiser not to continue. Gwyneth rose and followed Giles to the door without a word. She had some idea of what her father must have said, and she could not decide who disgusted her more, Giles or her father.

She crossed the hall, indicating Giles should follow, and walked into the small morning room at the back of the house. It was a pleasant, restful room, furnished in flowered chintzes, overlooking the back garden, but neither Gwyneth nor Giles were in a position to appreciate its amenities.

"I suppose you put your father up to playing the heavy guardian, Gwyneth. But let me tell you I am not to be caught by that ploy," he said, facing her with fury in every lineament.

"You can suppose what you like, Giles," Gwyneth answered calmly, not intimidated.

"A few kisses and one accidental mishap on a drive do not constitute a reason for marriage. I refuse to be badgered into a declaration," Giles said sullenly.

"I quite agree, and your effrontery in thinking that I would accept you if you did offer is beyond all reason. From the beginning I have been aware that you consider me fair game for an affair but hardly

worthy of your exalted rank and conceited opinion
of your attractions. You would make a vile husband,
and I find your insinuations that I cooperated in
whatever my father demanded both insulting and
reprehensible. You are a cad, Giles," she said, refusing to give into humiliation.

"You are entitled to your opinion. I am sorry you
feel that way, and I certainly had no designs on your
virtue or meant to damage your reputation," he said
unblushingly. For he had certainly hoped to get her
into bed, and she knew it.

"There is nothing more to say. I think you had best
leave before we descend to name-calling. Goodbye,
Giles." And before he could protest, she had whirled
through the door, determined he would not see her
tears. As she crossed the hall, she met her father
coming from the dining room. He looked a bit fearfully at her and tried to stop her, but she jerked away
from him.

"I will never forgive you for this, Father," she cried
and ran up the stairs Walter would have followed her,
but just then Giles came out of the morning room,
nodded brusquely to Walter, retrieved his hat and
coat from the maid, who had watched the fascinating
drama wide-eyed. He closed the door quietly behind
him, disdaining to slam it, whatever he felt.

Walter, a bit embarrassed, went into the drawing
room not prepared to discuss the imbroglio with
Nancy at length. He did not feel triumphant about
his handling of either Giles or Gwyneth, and he was
not about to expose himself to any criticism from his
wife.

In her room Gwyneth gave into the tears of humiliation and anger she had repressed in front of Giles.

Whatever hopes or tender feelings she might have entertained toward him were now banished in a welter of disappointment and fury. Then, taking several breathes to calm herself, and drying her tears, she sat down to consider how she had fallen into this mess.

She should have ruthlessly refused Giles's attention when he arrived in Montreal. No doubt he would have found some complaisant girl who would have satisfied his desires. Whatever his faults, and they were legion, she was not blameless, gulling herself with the notion he might come to really care for her. Well, she knew better now, and if the realization was wounding, she would recover. Whatever talk had sprung up around their relationship, Montreal society must just enjoy it. Soon grave matters would replace her tarnished romance in their minds. But she would not easily forget her father's role in placing her in this unenviable position, nor her own foolishness in being lured by the blandishments of an accomplished rake. She wished she were back in Detroit in the satisfying and undemanding company of James Brush, who had always treated her in the most gentlemanly way. Giles lacked all the qualities she had found so pleasing in James, and she was a fool to have even considered for a moment that he cared for her in any but the most insulting manner. No good repining, she must make the best of it, and remember in the future not to be cozened by a lordly manner and a sophisticated address. Somehow this did not comfort her, and she retired to bed after locking her door. She was in no mood for either Nancy or her father's company. She finally fell asleep, hoping morning would bring some relief from her unhappy state.

* * *

What morning did bring was an inevitable interview with her father. Gwyneth came down to breakfast, stubbornness and hostility evident in every line of her body. Nancy, for once at a loss on how to behave, had cravenly pleaded a headache and remained in bed. A wise decision, for Gwyneth would not have accepted a word of criticism from her stepmother, nor allowed her to make any snide references to the previous day.

Ensconced behind his desk in the library, Walter looked at his daughter with some compunction. If she had shed any tears, she did not show it, looking neat and stylish in a warm woolen maroon frock, her hair tidily arranged. In truth she was a sight to lure any man into indiscretion. But if she could not depend on her father to protect her, where was she to look?

"I am sorry, Gwyneth, that last night's situation gave you reason to rake me, but I felt steps must be taken. That man had no honorable intentions toward you and was causing your name to be bandied about in a most insulting manner. I could not just ignore the insinuations I was hearing, even in my club," he justified himself.

"You are probably right, Father, but I wish you had handled it in some other way. I did not enjoy facing Giles after you had tried to blackmail him into offering for me."

"I did what any father would do. But now we must put it behind us. I am sure that you will soon forget him. And I have a plan to help you do just that," Walter said kindly, not at all sure that she would accept his suggestion.

"I don't see what you can do," Gwyneth answered, feeling a bit comforted by her father's concern. However foolishly he had behaved, she knew he really cared for her happiness. She should not take out her own misery on him.

"I can send you to England, away from all this gossip and the possibility of that man accosting you again," he replied firmly.

"England! How can I go there and what would I do when I arrived?" Gwyneth asked, intrigued and alarmed at the same time.

"You can visit my cousins Sir Fergus and Lady Endicott. They could never have children, which they both always regretted, and thus they would love to have a young relative to cosset. They are quite well placed in London society and could give you an enjoyable time. As they are eager for a visit, you can leave almost immediately, as soon as the St. Lawrence makes a passage possible."

"You have already arranged this, haven't you, expecting that Major Fitzalen-Hill might cause a problem?" Gwyneth said shrewdly, but not angrily.

Feeling the first hurdle had been jumped, Walter agreed. "I don't want to force marriage upon you, Gwyneth, but you must know girls in your position have very few alternatives. In England you might find a suitable husband, a man you can respect and care for," he urged.

"Right now the last thing I want is a husband, but I would like to see London and enjoy all the sights," she admitted thoughtfully, thinking that it was an acceptable alternative to the slights and snubs she would endure if she remained in Montreal.

"Montreal will not be a pleasant place in the next

few months. You will be out of danger, both romantic and physical. We will be attacked, I fear," he confided with a worried frown.

"And I will be deserting my country. Still, I think you have chosen well. Thank you, Father. I am sorry to be such a trouble to you. Perhaps some of the fault was mine for this mess." Gwyneth's natural honesty forced her to accept her own culpability.

"We will say no more about it. I know living with Nancy has not been easy, and although she suits me, she has not made a good stepmother. You will be better apart, although I will miss you, as I do Delia."

"And I will miss you. I have always known that you love me, Father, and I agree it would be best to forget this recent disagreement." Gwyneth realized that her father's solution had eased her mind, if not her heart. She would do her best to make her stay with the Endicotts memorable and easy, and cause no trouble to either her hosts or her father.

"Can you tell me more about Sir Fergus and Lady Endicott? I have barely heard of them."

"Of course. He has an important position in the Foreign Office and she is a reigning hostess, but for all that they are very kind and unpretentious people," Walter informed her and went on to describe his cousin enthusiastically. He was grateful to Gwyneth for accepting this offer and behaving with so much tolerance toward his own behavior. All would work out for the best, he thought.

# Chapter Nine

*At sea, April 1813*

Gwyneth stood aboard the *H.M.S. Rodney* and watched as the ship sailed past the heights of Quebec, the famous Plains of Abraham with the Laurentian Mountains in the distance. She marveled at the sight of the ramparts and wondered how General Wolfe had ever climbed the sheer cliffs to conquer the town some fifty years ago. She had never been to Quebec, for many years the center of French Canada, and wished she could have some time to explore, but the *Rodney* sailed on, impervious to the ice blocks that floated desultorily in the St. Lawrence.

The last month had been chaotic as she prepared for the trip to England, leaving her little time to think about her relationship with Giles. Since her father had so summarily dismissed him, she had seen him at a few gatherings, but they avoided each other by tacit consent. She suspected his *amour-propre* was

wounded by the confrontation with Walter Winwood.

Now she could put the whole disagreeable situation
behind her. She was sailing toward a new life, and if
she thought about the danger of crossing the Atlantic,
she discounted it. Her father, concerned with her
respectability, had put her in the charge of Mrs. Sylves-
ter Taylor, a Montreal merchant's wife who was going
to England on a long visit to see her ailing parents.

The *Rodney* was full of well-to-do Canadians
returning to the sanctuary of England with war threatening Montreal, as well as several English officers
on leave who hoped for reassignment in Europe. It
promised to be an exciting voyage. Fortunately Mrs.
Taylor was an easygoing and cheerful woman who
would not take her chaperone duties very seriously.
And even more fortunate, Gwyneth had a small cabin
to herself, a gesture inspired by compunction on her
father's part. He had paid the extra passage to insure
some privacy for Gwyneth, which she greatly appreciated.

As the *Rodney* plunged bravely up the St. Lawrence,
she clutched her warm, fur-lined cloak more tightly
and wondered what lay ahead for her in England.
She was leaving behind friends, family, and the familiar life she had always known, but she was young
enough to hail it as a thrilling adventure. No doubt
she would be homesick at times, but the experience
was bound to be enlightening. At the last moment
her father had wavered, wondering if he was con-
signing his daughter to peril and if he would ever
see her again, but Gwyneth reassured him. She had
determined to take whatever England offered and
enjoy it, and most of all, she would forget Giles Fitza-

len-Hill and be wary of any aristocratic gentleman
she encountered abroad.

That evening as she entered the dining salon with
Mrs. Taylor, her best resolutions were put to the test.
No sooner had they been seated at a table for six
than she was approached by the very man she had
never expected to see again.

"Well, Miss Winwood, we meet again," Giles said
somewhat ironically.

"Good evening, Lord Fitzalen-Hill. May I introduce
Mrs. Taylor," Gwyneth said with an aplomb she did
not feel. How furious her father would be, after all
his trouble. If he had known that Giles would be
sailing aboard the *Rodney*, he would have cancelled
her passage.

"How do you do, ma'am?" Giles bowed, impressing
Mrs. Taylor with his address.

"Delighted, my lord," Mrs. Taylor responded, falling beneath his spell. She had not been apprised of
Giles's role in Gwyneth's life, and if she had heard
the Montreal gossip, she discounted it under the spell
of his charm.

Her round flushed face looked happily on the pair,
who did not share her delight. Gwyneth looked warily
at Giles, and he returned her gaze blandly.

"I have been recalled by Wellington at last and am
eager to join him again," Giles explained, his manner
easy and relaxed.

Gwyneth, tense, nodded. That explained it. He
must have booked his passage at the last moment.

"We will meet later, Gwyneth," Giles promised,
then bowed again and made his way across the salon.

"He is dining at the captain's table," Mrs. Taylor
said, obviously impressed.

"His father is the Earl of Selkirk," Gwyneth offered dryly. Mrs. Taylor, like most of Montreal's matrons, loved a title.

But further explanations were halted by the arrival of their fellow diners, two young officers and an elderly couple, acquaintances of Mrs. Taylor. The officers brightened at the sight of Gwyneth, and after introductions were made, they managed to seat themselves on either side of her and engage her in spirited conversation. The young men were both lieutenants, regular army, returning home after two years' service in Canada and happy to put the besieged colony behind them. Charles Randall, the elder of the two, was an engaging raconteur with blond hair and bold brown eyes. His companion, Robert White, a stocky redhead, was much shyer and unable to compete, so he contented himself with gazing admiringly at Gwyneth. She responded to them both, thinking they would make a fine defense against Giles. However, she should have realized that two callow officers would be no match for the sophisticated viscount.

The meal passed pleasantly, the young men fascinated by Gwyneth's tales of frontier life. Both of them had been with General Brock at Queenstown, but refused to give details of the battle that cost the hero his life.

"A bloody mess, if you will excuse me, Miss Winwood, and not fit for your ears," Charles insisted. "Let us talk of what awaits you in London instead. You will set the town on its heels, I vow," he flattered.

"I don't think so, Lieutenant. Provincial Colonials are no treat for that society, I believe. But I hope to enjoy myself in a quiet way."

"Somehow I don't think your arrival on the scene will go unnoticed. Your cousins, the Endicotts, travel in very *ton*nish circles," he informed her with an attempt at a blasé air. "Not that I am accustomed to such rarefied heights myself, but perhaps you will let me show you some of the town," Charles urged.

"Unfair, Charley," Robert broke in, blushing at his temerity. "I make a claim to some of Miss Winwood's company when we reach home."

Gwyneth quizzed them eagerly as to what she should see in London and how she should go on. Altogether the dinner cheered her spirits, and she resolutely postponed any thoughts of what Giles's presence on this voyage might mean to her. Stealing a quick glance at the captain's table, she saw him engaged in a serious discussion with that austere gentleman, probably discussing the war, she surmised. Then, reproving herself for even noticing him, she turned back to her fellow guests.

Mrs. Taylor, engaged by the elderly couple for a game of whist, politely invited Gwyneth to join them after the meal, but pleading that she had not finished unpacking, Gwyneth declined.

Charley and Robert, now flushed with Gwyneth's presence and a good deal of wine, insisted on escorting her to her cabin, and after prettily obtaining Mrs. Taylor's permission, Gwyneth consented. As they left the room, she was conscious of two hard dark eyes boring into her back. Well, let Giles think what he might. He had no claim on her time.

Fending off attempts by the officers to walk about the deck, Gwyneth shut the door of her cabin firmly in their protesting faces, promising to see them tomorrow. At last alone, she dropped her air of careless camaraderie and sank down heavily on the narrow bunk. Giles's appearance, so unexpected, had shaken her. Could she still have some feeling for this man who had treated her in such a cavalier fashion? If so, she must root it out and not allow herself to fall under his spell again. They would be at sea for at least a month, a long period in which to remain aloof. Would she never escape his insidious influence? He had shown quite clearly that for him she was not suitable for any role except as a casual mistress. Was she so besotted with the man that she would let him renew his efforts to seduce her? Of course not. She had too much self-respect to play the doxy. Well, she had a say in the matter, and the two officers she had met would serve very well to parry any advances Giles might make.

The following day dawned bright and clear with a crisp wind that scudded white fleecy clouds across the sky and drove the *Rodney* on its course into the Gulf of St. Lawrence. Leaning over the side in the company of Robert and Charley, Gwyneth caught a fleeting glimpse of Newfoundland in the distance. When the ship passed that landmark, they would be out in the open sea with no landfall until the shores of Ireland. It was a sobering thought, for in the weeks that followed they would be at the mercy of the sea.

Charley flirted with her and Robert continued shyly to show his admiration, but Gwyneth refused to take the young officers seriously. They were pleasant companions, however, lightening the tedium of the voyage, and would serve as a safeguard against Giles. So far on this first day out he had not approached her, but as the trio walked about the deck that afternoon, they passed him strolling with a very attractive blonde, and he raised a wry eyebrow at her after they exchanged brief greetings. This did nothing to relieve her feeling that eventually he would confront her.

Once into the Atlantic the days developed a routine of their own—walks along the deck, card games with Charley and Robert, and a courteous attention to Mrs. Taylor, who smiled benignly on Gwyneth's two escorts. But Gwyneth was edgy and restless, expecting Giles to pounce. Yet when he finally approached her some three days into the Atlantic, she was not prepared. She had just finished breakfast alone, since Mrs. Taylor was beginning to find the pitch and toss of the ship as they sailed into deeper waters disturbing. Gwyneth, who was determined not to be seasick, discovered that sailing exhilarated her, and she had found her sea legs. Giles caught up with her just as she was leaving the salon.

"Good morning, Gwyneth. How are you enjoying the voyage?" he asked as he held the door for her to walk onto the deck.

"Very much. It's exciting, although I suppose the novelty will wear off and I might become bored. But now a bit intimidating to see nothing but billowing waves, no land at all," she confided cheerfully.

"So far it has been calm," he agreed as they strolled along the deck toward the stern. "But I fear we will encounter some storms before we reach port, and that is never pleasant."

Gwyneth wondered if they would go on chatting about the weather and the ship or if Giles had something else on his mind. If so, she did not want to hear it.

"I should see how Mrs. Taylor is getting on. She was not feeling quite the thing this morning and could not face a meal," she said firmly, turning as if this random meeting was over.

"She does not seem to take her chaperone duties very seriously," Giles offered, placing a restraining hand on her arm, causing Gwyneth to flinch. Even a casual touch from this man sent a frisson through her body, and she hoped he had not noticed.

But he had. "Come, Gwyneth. I am not about to attack you with the ship's crew looking on. You didn't always seem so averse to my touch," he mocked.

Gwyneth, deciding that she would not dignify that taunt with an argument, felt a blush of discomfort stain her cheeks and hoped he would attribute it to the wind blowing steadily from the north. She knew he was referring to those passionate kisses on the stoop of her house in Montreal.

"With your father hundreds of miles safely behind us, surely you can spare me some of your company," Giles continued, not releasing her.

Convinced he was taunting her, Gwyneth rose angrily to the bait, despite her best efforts to remain cool.

"I cannot think you desire my company. You seem to have established a comfortable relationship with Miss Ellington," she accused. Then she felt a fool for letting him know she had noticed him with the lovely blonde.

"Are you jealous?" he asked, assessing her with a nasty smile.

"Don't be ridiculous. Giles, there seems no point to this conversation. I realize you must have found the interview with my father uncomfortable. But you must be used to indignant fathers quizzing you about your intentions. Just because he is not on hand to protect me doesn't mean I will fall under your spell again."

"Then you do admit there is some unfinished business between us."

"Not at all, "she replied hotly." You have made your position quite clear. I am useful for a diversion but a permanent relationship is not possible. Do you think I would chance my reputation just for a little attention from you? You have been insultingly obvious about how you regard me."

"I think you are mistaken, Gwyneth. I only thought since we are fellow passengers on this tedious voyage you might like a little amusement. Or do those young officers provide enough?" he sneered.

"Yes, they do. The lieutenants are very fine fellows," she protested.

"I think you will be thoroughly tired of their inanities before the voyage is over, but good luck to you. I think the shyer one would make a better husband." With that, Giles strode off, having had the last word.

Gwyneth, humiliated, scuttled down the ramp to the cabins, realizing that Giles had lost none of his ability to raise her hackles. Whatever she said or did, he managed to get the better of her, and she hated that. But why did he bother? Why couldn't he leave her alone. Was it because she represented a challenge to him? Well, she would not give him the satisfaction of riling her again. Composing herself, she knocked on Mrs. Taylor's cabin door and, hearing a weak voice allowing admittance, hurried in to do her duty.

Later that evening, escorted by her cavaliers, Gwyneth entered the dining salon, which had a somewhat forlorn air. Many of the passengers had been laid low with seasickness, for the wind had freshened during the day and the ship was rolling hard.

"I am happy to see you have not succumbed to

vertigo and nausea, Miss Winwood," Charley said, seating her.

"Not so far, but I am promising nothing," Gwyneth replied pleasantly. She noticed that the elegant Miss Ellington was absent. She could not restrain a grin of glee at the thought of the blonde charmer giving in to the current malady. Of course Giles was at his usual place, but she tried to ignore him.

"If all we suffer is seasickness, we will be fortunate," Robert said diffidently.

"What do you mean?" Gwyneth asked, dipping into her soup with a hearty appetite.

"He means we have not sighted an enemy sail yet," Charley explained.

"You must not frighten Miss Winwood. This is a fast ship, probably could outsail any war vessel," Robert consoled.

The words sobered Gwyneth, for her apprehensions about Giles had banished any thought of the war. It had seemed miles away and no threat in the isolation of the *Rodney*. But of course, French enemy ships would be on the lookout for any victim.

"The captain is not in his seat this evening. I wonder if that has any significance," Robert said.

"It means that the winds are rising and we might be in for some rough seas," Charley insisted, giving his friend an admonitory glance.

Robert did not reply, but attacked his beef, brooding.

"You have had quite enough of the war, I expect, Gwyneth," Charley said, hoping to distract her by reminding her of her brush with the Indians, a tale she wished now she had kept to herself as the officers appeared to regard her as some sort of heroine.

"I hope my sister is safe in Detroit," she said, thinking of Delia, and chagrined she had not considered her sister's plight in days.

"We still hold Detroit, the last I heard. But isn't her husband an American?" Charley asked, intrigued by this division of loyalties.

"Yes, and a soldier. But he is safe in Ohio. I suppose now that spring has arrived he will go into battle and try to regain Detroit."

"Our supply lines are stretched too thin," muttered Robert, who appeared to take a gloomy view of the war's progress.

"Well, we can do nothing about it. Our job is to defeat Napoleon," Charley said blithely.

Gwyneth, who had heard enough of the Corsican and of the threat he represented, shook her head. "I don't want to talk about the war."

"Quite right. Not a suitable topic. Let's talk about what you will do in London instead," said Charley cheerfully.

Although the rest of the meal passed with a spirited discussion about what Gwyneth would enjoy in London, the war was not so easily put aside. Later as the trio struggled onto the deck, Gwyneth realized the significance of the guns she had barely noticed earlier. The *Rodney* was an armed merchantman, its speed promising to outrun most frigates, but prepared to stand and fight if necessary. She knew that if the *Rodney* made landfall in England without incident she would be most fortunate. Of graver concern for the moment was the worsening weather that the *Rodney* might not be able to outrun. To avoid French warships, the captain had chosen a northerly route where the enemy was not apt to lurk, for they preferred the warmer waters about Chesapeake Bay.

During the night the winds rose to gale force, and

the next morning Gwyneth awoke suddenly, aroused
by the clattering of her boxes as they tumbled from
the shelf where she had stowed them. She heard the
lash of water against the hull and staggered to her
feet. Washing and dressing in the sway of the ship
was an ordeal, and she wondered how she would
manage to reach the dining salon for breakfast. She
struggled to Mrs. Taylor's cabin, next to hers, to find
that poor lady moaning and miserable, convinced she
would never reach land. Gwyneth tried to comfort
her and tended to her needs as best she could. The
steward assigned to them made a brief appearance,
then rushed off to care for other ailing passengers.
Gwyneth could only be grateful she had not succumbed to the malady. Finally she was free to seek
some food, surprised to find she was hungry, the
rough weather having little effect on her appetite.

The dining salon was almost deserted. Even Charley
and Robert did not make an appearance, but she was
not surprised to see Giles, who came over to her table
and dropped into an empty seat.

"I am relieved to see you in such hearty spirits,
Gwyneth. Most of the passengers have taken to their
beds," he said cheerfully.

"Yes, I am feeling fine," she agreed. Giles's dark
eyes glowed with excitement, as if he found the sea's
challenge exhilarating.

"Not frightened?" he asked as if he really cared.

"If I am, I'm not going to give into such fears,"
Gwyneth insisted with a certain bravado.

"Good girl," he nodded. Then, hesitantly, he suggested, "Would you like a turn around the deck?"

"I should get back to poor Mrs. Taylor, but why
not?" she agreed, disregarding all sensible ideas that
it might not be the best plan to expose herself to

Giles's blandishments again. But she could not resist the challenge of braving the storm.

Outside the salon they were met with a hearty gust of wind, but both were dressed in sou' westers, so it did little harm. Beyond the rail Gwyneth could see the water curling into a white spray, and the deck shifted beneath her feet. She heard the creak of canvas and saw the top gallants straining against the wind. Giles held her in a firm grip, and she felt safe, yet invigorated. Their voices could not be heard above the howling of the wind, but they marched along companionably, each enjoying the contest against the angry water and the force of the wind.

# Chapter Ten

Most of the day Gwyneth spent dutifully calming Mrs. Taylor, who was not only sick but frightened, sure she would breathe her last aboard the wretched ship. The majority of the passengers kept to their cabins, unwilling to chance a journey on the slippery decks. The *Rodney* plowed on, straining every timber, attempting to outrun the gales, but the storm kept pace with her.

By dusk Gwyneth was thoroughly tired of being cooped up indoors. Mrs. Taylor finally dropped off to sleep, and she tiptoed from the cabin, intent on finding some food. But meeting the steward in the hallway, she learned that the dining salon would not be serving that evening because of the storm. He promised to bring her a bite in her cabin, and she had no recourse except to retire back there.

After a sparse meal of bread, cheese, and cold meat, she tried to read, but the oil lamp swayed so dangerously she gave it up. Peeking through the porthole, she saw water lashing against the glass and began to wonder if the ship would survive. As darkness fell, her fears deepened, and she shivered as much from fright as the cold damp air which seeped through the small cabin. She craved company in her ordeal but did not want to disturb Mrs. Taylor, who was, in any case, in no condition to offer any. Not even in those fearsome days when Detroit was poised on the edge of a dreadful battle, not even when the two Indians had broken into Delia's house, had she felt so desolate. Then she had been supported by the fort's inhabitants, by the need to comfort and protect Delia, and when the Indians had attempted to ransack the house, she had been angry, stirred to action. But now there was no action she could take. She was at the mercy of the sea.

Somehow she must get a grip on her nerves. She was not worse off than the other passengers, better even because she was not ill. But that did not comfort her; it only made her feel more isolated. Suddenly she began to cry, a stream of tears trickling down her cheeks, and she made no attempt to wipe them away. As the ship lurched, she cried out, certain she was destined to be pulled beneath those terrifying waves. Just when her hysteria reached an unbearable peak, there was a hard knock on the door.

"Come in," she cried in a wavering voice, eager for any human face.

Giles stepped across the threshold, dressed in his sou'wester and slicker. Taking one look at her pale face in the dim light he tossed aside his streaming coat and hat.

"What a woebegone girl. Where is all that stalwart courage in the face of danger? Come, Gwyneth, don't be frightened," he said gently and took her in his arms. She nestled against his damp shirt.

"I'm frightened," she moaned. "I fear we are all going to be drowned."

"Perhaps, but I doubt it. I have been in worse storms at sea."

"I feel so alone," she whispered, still hiding her tear-stained face in his chest, comforted by the steady beat of his heart beneath her cheek.

"Well, you are not alone now." He raised her head with his hand and looked into her eyes, his own steady and clear.

Gradually Gwyneth's shaking eased, and she felt a warm glow spread through her shivering body. Here was comfort and reassurance.

Hardly aware of what she was doing, she lifted her face imploringly to his. He bent his head and kissed her with a sudden passion. Comforted by the contact, Gwyneth made no effort to repulse him. On the contrary she found the kiss driving all fear from her, and she responded, scarcely aware of his warm hands roaming her body. Her blood coursed heavily, and a languor stole over her.

"You want this as much as I do. And this time you cannot stop me," he muttered, almost as carried away as she was. Mindless under a barrage of emotion, Gwyneth made no protest as he guided her to her cot. The sound of the wind and the thud of the sea was forgotten, and Gwyneth submitted to the clamoring of her senses.

Hours later she woke from a deep sleep to find herself alone and naked beneath the quilt which had been tucked around her. Beyond the porthole she

was conscious that the wind had dropped and the
waves seemed to have diminished. The *Rodney* had
outrun the storm. Staggering to her feet, she looked
through the porthole. The terrors of the night
receded before the sight that met her eyes. Although
the wind was blowing briskly, filling the sails and
speeding the ship forward, it had lost its former
strength, and the water no longer raged against the
hull as it had.

Realizing she was not going to drown memories of
the night before brought her to gasping acceptance
at what had happened. She had allowed Giles to
seduce her, had given into him in her terror. What
a credulous fool she was. Despite her best intentions
she had surrendered to his pressing demands under
the impetus of loneliness and fear. She would never
forgive herself nor him. In time-honored fashion he
had taken advantage of her. How could she face him
now?

Wrapping a warm dressing gown around her, she
huddled on the edge of her cot. She had no illusions
that he would behave honorably and offer for her.
For him the conquest was just one in a long line.
From the very start, from the day he had appeared
in Delia's house, he had meant to have her and now
he had. No good chastising herself. To repine and
rail against her reckless behavior was useless. She
must dress and face whatever the day brought. But
she had learned a valuable lesson. She had never
dreamt she could be such a wanton, and the desperate
situation she had faced during the night was a poor
excuse. She knew now that she was not the fearless,
strong, and independent spirit she had always
thought. She was as gullible and vulnerable as any
housemaid, and he had treated her as one. She

blushed as she remembered in some confusion her eagerness and cooperation. His lovemaking had drugged her into acquiescence, but no longer. She had finished her contest with Giles, and he had been the victor, but that was the end of their relationship. If some inner voice hoped for a different outcome, she pushed the traitorous idea from her and dressed.

After calling on Mrs. Taylor and finding that ailing lady much recovered, Gwyneth walked slowly toward the dining salon. To her surprise she realized she was hungry and craved her breakfast. On reaching her table she found Charley there before her, looking a bit green and sheepish, but determined to put a bold face on his former weakness.

"Good morning, Gwyneth. How did you survive the night? For a moment there I was sure we would founder and disappear beneath the surging sea," he quipped a bit feebly.

"Oh, I survived, but it was a terrible storm," she replied, hoping her discomfort did not show. Then, to change the direction of the conversation, "And where is Robert?"

"I left him snoring away. He was sick most of the night, and the rest will do him good," Charley informed her masterfully.

"The dining room is still quite empty. I suppose most of the passengers are resting after the fright they had."

"Yes, but I see that some of the ship's officers are at table, so the danger must be truly past."

Gwyneth looked about a bit warily, but she saw no sign of Giles, thank goodness. Repressing all thoughts of him with some difficulty, she made an effort to respond to Charley's innocuous gossip. His buoyant manner was rapidly returning, and he distracted her with stories of another voyage he had endured, making an amusing tale of it. After breakfast the two ventured on deck, laughing as they were buffeted by the still-strong winds.

In the days that followed the storm, the sea returned to its former benign state, and the *Rodney* sped through the waters, apparently unscathed by the fury of the storm she had weathered.

Mrs. Taylor regained her sea legs, apologized to Gwyneth for neglecting her, and took a sterner view of her chaperone duties. It was pose that Gwyneth encouraged. And her two cavaliers remained steadfast, fending off any other admirers. Gwyneth caught a glimpse of Giles at meals, but he made no attempt to approach her, hardening her belief that he no longer wanted her and had never seen her as anything but an easy conquest.

In that she was wrong. The morning following the storm, after leaving her alone, he regretted his actions. He knew she would never have surrendered to him in the normal course of events. At first he wanted to go to her and make some explanation, but she was always surrounded either by Mrs. Taylor or those two cubs who had adopted the role of protectors. And his anger was roused when one afternoon as he passed her on the deck where she was escorted by Robert and Charley, she averted her eyes and did not acknowledge him. For some reason this momentarily shook his poise. In the past, the aftermath of his romantic escapades had never induced any emotion but boredom, yet somehow he could not easily shrug off his seduction of Gwyneth. She had challenged his self-esteem and he had taken his revenge, but it brought him little satisfaction. Probably she was right to ignore him, but it left a bitter taste. Knowing he could not leave the affair unresolved, he decided he would have to corner her and judge her reaction.

After a week, tired of being studiously ignored, he strolled over to her table as she and Mrs. Taylor were finishing their meal.

"Good evening, Mrs. Taylor. I wonder if you could spare me Gwyneth's company for a moment. I will not keep her long, and I suspect you are anxious to join your whist partners," he said suavely, bringing an approving smile to Mrs. Taylor's face.

"Run along, my dear. Lord Fitzalen-Hill can deliver you to the cardroom when you have had your chat," she agreed. If her curiosity was aroused by the rebellious look on Gwyneth's face and her obvious reluctance, Giles's winning manner dispelled it.

Seeing there was no help from that quarter, Gwyneth marched out of the room, hostility in every line of her body. Giles could have nothing to say that she wanted to hear, she promised herself.

Taking her arm and resisting her efforts to pull away, he guided her up on the deck, where he stopped and turned her to face him as he leaned negligently against the rail.

"This won't take long, Gwyneth. I apologize for taking advantage of Mrs. Taylor's eagerness to oblige a lord, but you are deuced hard to get alone."

"I don't want to be alone with you," Gwyneth said stubbornly.

"No, I suppose not. Such a practiced seducer represents a horrid threat, I agree. I cannot say honestly I regret what happened between us on the night of the storm, but I realize you do."

Gwyneth drew her lips together and refused to respond. He was at it again, trying to charm her and excuse his callous behavior.

Giles sighed wearily. "I know I took advantage of your fright, but admit it, Gwyneth, you did nothing to fight me off."

She still refused to answer. What answer could she give him, for he only spoke the truth.

"You think I should do the honorable thing and marry you," he blurted out, surprised by his irritation at her stubborn refusal to talk to him. He had no intention of offering for her, but her attitude aggravated him. Getting no response but a lifted eyebrow and an ironic scoff, he continued. "If that is what you want, I will marry you."

"I wouldn't marry you if by refusing it meant I remained a spinster to my grave," she cried furiously, for she knew he regretted his impulsive words almost as he said them.

Amused, he mocked, "There's little likelihood of that, I warrant. I would not make a good husband, I agree, but since you have adopted this pose of the outraged virgin, I feel it's my duty to make the offer. Think about it. I may not repeat it," he said arrogantly.

"You conceited oaf. You think I should fall gratefully into your arms, thrilled at becoming the wife of the great Lord Fitzalen-Hill. Well, you are wrong. I would rather marry Charley or Robert or any decent dustman than you." As the words tumbled out of her mouth, she was aghast.

"You are no doubt absolutely right. But I have given you your chance," he insisted.

Gwyneth felt both ashamed and wounded at his casual dismissal at what she deemed an outrage. If he had made any attempt to take her in his arms, express regret, tell her he cared for her, she might have weakened. But his air of weary acceptance of a tiresome responsibility infuriated her. Before she could rail at him like a fishwife from both disappointment and anger, she whirled away and disappeared down the ramp to the lower deck. He did not attempt to follow her.

"Damn, I handled that badly. But what did the chit want, an expression of undying love? Any such protestation would have lacked sincerity, and she knew it. We would deal very badly together," he tried to convince himself. He admired her tempestuous rejection of him, knowing that many a woman in her position would have snapped at his offer. She genuinely disliked him, and he would have to accept that, although it damaged his *amour-propre*. Well, there were plenty of other available females who would be thrilled by his attentions, he decided. Then, laughing at himself, he realized Gwyneth was right. He had a very good opinion of himself, and in her case, it was not warranted.

Giles leaned over the rail, watching the water scud before the thrust of the hull. What a shrew the girl was, with no idea of proper behavior. She would cause a tempest in London if the Endicotts tried to introduce her to the *ton*. Would probably insult the Prince Regent if she thought he was too forward in his attentions.

She had caused him some uncomfortable soul-searching, but during that memorable night she responded with all the ardor of the most brazen Cyprian. What would happen to her? Would she accept the hand of that nodcock Randall in a fit of pique? An unaccountable girl. He was well rid of her. Once off this ship their paths would rarely cross and he could forget her.

Having taken what he considered a sensible deci-

sion, he continued to stare out to sea, feeling that
he had missed an opportunity for a rare relationship.
That was nonsense. His malaise sprang from this isolation at sea, the knowledge that in Spain, in England,
great events were taking place and he was not part
of them. This was natural reaction of a soldier who
disliked missing a battle, that was why he had succumbed to this strange depression, so foreign to his
usual sanguinity. Once on dry land with a promising
new posting awaiting him, he would regain his spirits.
Still, he remained at the railing, staring out to sea,
impervious to both wind and chill.

Gwyneth was having no second thoughts, anger
having swamped all other emotions. Pausing for a
moment before joining Mrs. Taylor in the cardroom,
she hoped her cheeks had cooled and her heavy
breathing calmed. If this last encounter with Giles
had done nothing else, it had convinced her the
man had no decent scruples; his own self-interest was
paramount in every relationship he undertook. His
grudging offer of marriage had been an insult. Some
girls might have leapt at the proposal, but Gwyneth
had too much pride to adopt the role of a grateful
victim. The man was a monster and never again would
she fall under his dominion. Life held a great deal
more for her than Giles Fitzalen-Hill, and she would
dismiss him without a qualm. Shaking off the burden
of these troublesome thoughts, she walked into the
cardroom, greeted Mrs. Taylor, and settled into a
riotous game with Robert and Charley. Mrs. Taylor
beamed fondly at her charge, never dreaming that
behind Gwyneth's merry facade lay a resolute girl
who refused to succumb to despair.

For the next fortnight Gwyneth entered into the
amusements offered on the voyage, fetched and car-

ried for Mrs. Taylor, and allowed Robert and Charley
to entertain her. She was becoming quite attached
to them both, for they formed an eager bodyguard
that protected her from any of Giles's attempts to
talk to her. Not that he tried. He seemed equally
occupied with Miss Ellington, who was apt to smile
condescendingly at Gwyneth when they passed on
deck, as if to say, "My dear young woman, you had
no chance of attracting a man of Lord Fitzalen-Hill's
stamp. You only offered a little variety, but now he
has sought out his proper mileu." Gwyneth, if she
had read her correctly, could only agree.

As the *Rodney* entered the final stages of the voyage,
sailors kept a sharp eye out for enemy sails. Charley
had informed Gwyneth, with an expert air, not at all
justified, that the French lurked outside the Channel
and near Ireland, hoping to seize unguarded prizes
such as merchant ships entering home waters. But
the *Rodney*, if indeed she was a target, escaped any
threats, sailing into the Bristol Channel without
encountering any ships except those of the Royal
Navy. The *Rodney* docked in Bristol, a safer port than
Plymouth in these days of conflict, a little more than
a month after leaving Montreal, pleasing both passengers and crew.

As Gwyneth waited with Mrs. Taylor to disembark,
rather thrilled by the bustle of landing and happy
to put the sea behind her, Giles approached them.
Ignoring her averted head, he spoke pleasantly to
Mrs. Taylor and then turned to Gwyneth.

"This is farewell, then, Gwyneth. It has been an
interesting voyage with some memorable moments.
Perhaps we will meet again in London," he said
smoothly, conscious of Mrs. Taylor's avid ears.

"I doubt it, Lord Fitzalen-Hill. Goodbye," Gwyneth turned away, determined not to offer her hand.

Giles raised a rueful eyebrow at Mrs. Taylor and said softly, "I seem to have offended Miss Winwood. Have a pleasant journey to London," he concluded, bowing and then sauntering away.

"My dear, you were quite abrupt with his lordship, such a charming manner he has, too," Mrs. Taylor twittered, a question in her voice. But before she could speak her questions aloud, she discovered that she had mislaid one of her cases.

"I thought all five were here, but I only see four. What could have happened to it?" she wailed.

"I will run down and check the cabin, Mrs. Taylor," Gwyneth said agreeably, and departed on her errand. She would have been most surprised to discover that Giles, standing by Miss Ellington, watched her departure with hard angry eyes.

# *Chapter Eleven*

*London, May 1813*

Gwyneth craned her neck out of the window of the hired coach, unable to suppress her excitement. She had never seen such sights: a bewildering, noisy medley of vendors crying their wares, cursing draymen, smart phaetons driven recklessly, scurrying clerks, and harried shoppers, all jostling each other as they went about their business. Walking the streets of London must be a dangerous if exciting chore. But before long the carriage wound its way into a more fashionable, quieter section of London, where the tall, stately gray-stone houses spoke of wealth and position. When they finally came to a halt on Charles Street just off Berkeley Square, Gwyneth was completely bemused by what she had seen. Mrs. Taylor was hardly less overcome but tried to hide her naiveté.

"What a charming house," she said, impressed by

the imposing home of the Endicotts, its marble steps
and tall windows evidence of the owners' status.

"My cousin, Sir Fergus Endicott, holds an
important post in the Foreign Office," Gwyneth
informed her dryly. She had a very good idea of Mrs.
Taylor's impressions but did not fault her for them.
"You will come in for a moment and meet them,
won't you?" she invited, knowing Mrs. Taylor could
not resist.

"Thank you, my dear. It has been a tiring ride and
I could do with some refreshment before I journey
on to my parents in Richmond."

Gwyneth barely had time to mount the steps, trailed
by Mrs. Taylor, when the door opened and a butler,
in formal livery, welcomed her.

"Good day, Miss Winwood. I hope you had a pleasant
journey. Sir Fergus and her ladyship are awaiting you
and your companion," he greeted, looking down his
nose a bit at Mrs. Taylor, apparently not finding her
up to his rigid standards. Taking their cloaks and hats,
he ushered them across a vast marble hall, which had,
to Gwyneth's delight, a knighted figure in full armor.

"Mrs. Taylor and Miss Winwood," the butler
announced, throwing open the double mahogany
doors.

Gwyneth's first view of her cousins instantly dispelled her reservations. Sir Fergus, who hurried
across the room with his hand outstretched, was a
portly, cherubic man, of no great stature, but with a
pair of twinkling brown eyes and a high complexion.
Gwyneth dropped a curtsy, but before she could utter
a word, she was clasped in a fond embrace by Lady
Endicott, who was taller than her husband but equally
rounded, with bright blue eyes and blond hair wound
about her head in unfashionable braids.

"My dear, we are so thrilled to have you," she said, releasing Gwyneth and turning to Mrs. Taylor cheerfully.

"And you must be Mrs. Taylor who kindly chaperoned Gwyneth on what I am sure was a long and tiring voyage. Now both of you sit down and I will ring for some tea. You must be exhausted."

Mrs. Taylor was guided to a comfortable chair by the fireplace, in which some logs glowed despite the warmish May afternoon. Gwyneth was led to a settee across from her, and Lady Endicott seated herself beside her.

The room with its high decorated ceiling, furnished in polished Chippendale pieces and rose chintz, had a stately aura which was completely lacking in its owners. The Endicotts plied Gwyneth with questions and over tea and cakes put Mrs. Taylor at her ease.

After a suitable interval, Mrs. Taylor, delighted by her warm reception, reluctantly took her leave. She had found the Endicotts a surprisingly informal pair, not at all her idea of the *haut monde*. She would have much to tell her parents.

Sir Fergus escorted Mrs. Taylor to her coach and sped her on her way, inviting her to call whenever she was in the neighborhood. He then returned to the drawing room where his wife was telling Gwyneth all the exciting plans she had for her.

When she could get a word in, Gwyneth opened her reticule and handed Sir Fergus the letter her father had entrusted to her for his cousin.

"My, my, your father has been most generous. He has enclosed a large letter of credit for your wardrobe and expenses. Not at all necessary as we were quite prepared to frank you."

Lady Endicott joined in. "You see, my dear, we

have no children and are hoping that you will be here for a long stay. And I must take you straightaway to my modiste to fit you out for the season. We have invited several friends to meet you at a small ball in a fortnight," she rattled on, describing all the festivities she intended to offer Gwyneth.

Surprised by her relatives and cheered by their welcome, she could not help but contrast the atmosphere in their home, grand as it was, with Nancy Winwood's tepid reception of her when she returned from Detroit. Cosseting and comfort were very agreeable after her tempestuous voyage.

At last Lady Endicott took her to her room, a large pleasant chamber, obviously recently done up for Gwyneth's arrival in soft shades of green and overlooking a garden in which spring flowers bloomed.

"I hope you will be happy with us, Gwyneth. It's such a treat to have a young relative in the house. We are apt to sink into the doldrums. I dare say you will find us old fogies, but you will soon settle down, I am sure," Lady Endicott said with a chuckle.

This merry lady was hardly an old fogy, Gwyneth thought and confided, "It's lovely to be here and to be made so welcome. I am sure we will deal very well together."

"Thank you, my dear. And after you have had a nice rest and a bath, which I am sure you are craving, we will have a coze. No guests for dinner tonight, thank goodness," she informed Gwyneth, who suspected, despite the disclaimers, that the Endicotts had a great many friends and led an active social life.

In the days that followed, her first impressions of her cousins were confirmed. They were popular with all sorts of people; politicians, aristocrats of high rank, and even Cits, whom many members of the *ton*

scorned to entertain. Lady Endicott pressed Gwyneth
to invite any friends she might have met on the voyage
to their home, and when Robert and Charley called,
they were received with great enthusiasm. Gwyneth's
days were crowded with shopping, sight-seeing, and
introductions. She rather dreaded the small ball
which Lady Endicott had mentioned, but she was
determined to behave with suitable gratitude. Lady
Endicott had insisted on providing her with a gown
for the occasion, a fashionable silver gauze over cream
lace, not at all in the *jeune fille* mode, and sent her
own maid, Fletcher, to dress Gwyneth's hair which
was styled à la Sappho for the occasion.

Looking at herself in the long cheval mirror when
the maid, as cheerful and as round as her mistress,
had completed her task, Gwyneth thought she would
not embarrass her relatives.

"You do look a treat, miss," Mary, her own abigail
announced, while Fletcher signaled equal approval.
Rather overwhelmed by all the attention, Gwyneth
could not help comparing her present circumstances
to her rugged pioneer life in Detroit. Lady Endicott
had been both horrified and thrilled with Gwyneth's
account of Delia's frontier household in Detroit and
thought she was a heroine to have handled the whole
experience with such courage and skill. But now she
would need different, and in some ways more
demanding, skills to cope with the sophisticated company in which she found herself. She suspected that
meeting London society would prove more challenging than fending off bellicose Indians. However, she
knew she would have the guidance and support of
her cousins.

Descending the stairway a bit later, she found Sir

Fergus, his body threatening to burst the seams of his formal evening clothes, waiting for her with an admiring look.

"You will do us proud this evening, Gwyneth. How fortunate we are to have such a delightful cousin. Will you spare the first dance for this old codger? I am putting my claim in now, for I know you will be besieged. Such a fresh and lovely face will excite all the jaded beaux who sometimes find our simpering misses a trial." Then feeling he may have been unkind, a sentiment Sir Fergus rarely entertained, he added, "Of course, there are some charming debutantes this season, but you offer a great deal more than just beauty."

Gwyneth, touched by his old-fashioned courtesy and compliment, reached up and kissed his cheek. "You have been so kind to me, giving me this ball and most of all your affection. I am so grateful, Sir Fergus," she said, bringing a gratified smile to his face. "Of course I want to have the first dance with you."

Beaming, he offered her his arm and escorted her to the drawing room, where Lady Endicott was waiting. "We are having a few friends to dinner first. Nothing too frightening, although you may find Castlereagh a bit off-putting. Brilliant man, but a bit stiff," he confided as they crossed the hall.

Looking a sight in a mauve satin gown, but distinguished for all that, Lady Endicott expressed unqualified approval of Gwyneth. Although her figure did not flatter the current styles, Lady Endicott had enough fashion sense not to ape the more outrageous plumes and turbans some of her contemporaries favored. She really looked quite elegant, Gwyneth decided.

After inspecting Gwyneth with a critical eye, Lady Endicott turned to her husband and said, "I hope you have reassured Gwyneth about this evening."

"Of course, of course. We were just discussing Castlereagh."

"He sounds frightening," Gwyneth admitted, thinking of the Foreign Secretary.

"Just shy, poor man, and his wife is rather outrageous. Why, at the Devonshire Ball she wore his Knight of the Garter insignia in her hair. But all the Herberts, that is her family, are a bit strange. There will be plenty of exciting young men to entertain you, so you won't be forced to put up with the Castlereaghs and such. We had to invite them, for he is Fergus's chief at the Foreign Office." And so Lady Endicott dismissed one of the most eminent men in England.

As it turned out, the Foreign Secretary was neither as austere nor as forbidding as Gwyneth had feared. He quizzed her about her experience in Detroit and confided that the war in the Colonies could not compel England's full resources as long as Napoleon was threatening. Lady Castlereagh was indeed a caution, dressed in a flamboyant purple satin gown and dropping outrageous remarks to all, but her husband treated her with the grave courtesy that had become his hallmark, which Gwyneth found most endearing.

They sat down twelve to dinner, most of the guests friends and associates of the Endicotts and not at all intimidating.

Lady Endicott had invited a handsome guardsman to serve as Gwyneth's escort and to provide some younger companionship. A captain in the Blues, a fashionable regiment, Roger Eastbrook was charmed by the new arrival and impressed with her experiences in Canada. Not until later did Gwyneth learn that he was a marquis, for he had none of the airs and graces she had expected in a peer. The dinner was a simple one, consisting of only five courses, including a saddle of mutton and garden peas, and ending with a syllabub, following which the ladies retired to the drawing room. Lady Endicott cautioned her husband not to delay the gentlemen too long over their port as their other guests would be arriving within the hour.

Gwyneth discovered that the ladies were all enthralled by Lady Endicott's description of Gwyneth's experiences, and they questioned her avidly, especially interested in her confrontation with the Indians. Gwyneth, by now heartily tired of recounting that episode, changed the subject by asking them about General Brock. They all praised him lavishly, hailing him as the savior of Canada, and mourned his loss. Unfortunately these encomiums reminded Gwyneth of Giles, but she resolutely put the thought from her. She would not allow her memories of him to mar her introduction to London society. Finding herself the center of attention a strain, kindly although her interlocutors were, she was relieved when the gentlemen joined them and Roger Eastbrook hurried to her side.

"I want to claim the supper dance," he asked. "I know you will be surrounded by a host of rubbishy fellows once we enter the ballroom, and I must take advantage of our prior acquaintance."

Telling him she would be delighted to dance with him, Gwyneth then asked him what she could expect from the evening.

"You will be the toast of the town. London society is rather jaded, and any new arrival, especially one so lovely and sponsored by the Endicotts, will have a huge success," he informed her with engaging candor. "You see, you are so different from the usual crop of debutantes, nice girls many of them, but on the whole rather boring, having just come from the schoolroom."

Intrigued by his analysis of her contemporaries, Gwyneth reminded him that in Montreal the same situation prevailed. "The only reason I did not follow that path was that I went to Detroit to be with my sister and was caught there by the war."

"Yes, none of us expected it would come to a conflict, but the Americans are feeling their oats, quick to take offense. In some ways I hoped to be posted there to see for myself what the wilderness is like, but the real action is in Spain now. I have been serving as an attaché at the Foreign Office, a nodcock's post. I will be leaving within a few weeks for the final fight against Napoleon," he confided proudly.

"You men are all so anxious to fight," Gwyneth answered somewhat shortly.

"That's what we trained for," Roger said simply. "But I shouldn't be talking about war to such a lovely girl."

"Nonsense. I am not some delicate female unaware of the dangers you face. But do tell me more of London society," she insisted.

Roger obliged with some amusing and scandalous tales, including a scathing description of Almack's, the Marriage Mart, where young women were introduced to eligible men. Receiving a voucher to the sacred portals on King Street was "the crowning achievement of the young ladies' season," he informed her with a wry expression. "A dreary place on the whole, but being denied acceptance is a cruel blow. You will see its dusty charms for yourself and then you can tell me what you think."

"Oh, I doubt I will be invited. A merchant's daughter and a Colonial is simply not up to snuff," Gwyneth laughingly demurred.

"Nonsense. Lady Endicott is hand in glove with the patronesses, and she will see you have a voucher."

That lady herself now crossed to them and interrupted this fascinating discussion about the rules of London society that Gwyneth found confusing and, if truth be known, rather ridiculous. She was grateful for Roger's information but wondered how she would find her way among such hidebound people.

"I am delighted to see that you and Roger are enjoying yourselves, Gwyneth, but we must really be taking our places in the reception line. A tiresome duty but etiquette demands it, I'm afraid," she said.

"Yes, of course, Lady Endicott," Gwyneth agreed, bidding Roger a reluctant farewell. She thought him a very agreeable young man and was pleased he had asked her for the supper dance.

The Endicotts and Gwyneth repaired to a large reception room behind the drawing room, leaving the dinner guests to follow, and formed a line just inside the door.

"You'll never remember all these people, dear," Lady Endicott whispered. "Just nod and smile. That's all they expect."

The butler Bradley appeared, very imposing in tails and white gloves, to announce the guests. What Lady Endicott had promised to be a small ball turned out to be a crush of three hundred people, including the Prime Minister, Lord Liverpool. Remembering her father's angry words about this powerful statesman, Gwyneth was surprised that he appeared so kindly and diffident. Lady Liverpool was as haughty as any duchess, but her husband had all the tact of the diplomat that he had been for many years. The cares of state did not appear to rest heavily on his shoulders although Sir Fergus had told Gwyneth that Liverpool had a difficult time managing his Tories and the irreconcilable Whigs. As the men and women streamed by, Gwyneth recognized a few names as eminent, but aside from Lord Liverpool most of them were a blur, a collection of glittering jewels, lavish gowns, and the black and white de rigueur formal dress of the men.

Toward the end of a long line, Gwyneth was pleased to greet Charley and Robert, kindly invited by her cousins to provide friendly support during her great evening. Charley had adopted an air of sophistication, but Robert was obviously ill at ease, overcome by the honor of mingling with such august personages.

At last Gwyneth was freed from her duties and took the floor with Sir Fergus in the opening dance of the ball. For the first few bars they danced alone but then were joined by other couples. As soon as the set ended, Gwyneth was mobbed by a cluster of young men, eager to claim her hands and investigate this interesting new addition to society. Her card was filling rapidly, and she hardly took in the names of the gallants who besieged her. Fending off the extravagant flattery of several beaux, she looked up as the group around her parted only to see Giles before her.

"Good evening, Gwyneth. I see you are having a resounding success, which does not surprise me," he greeted her suavely, lifting an eyebrow at her expression of stupification.

"How did you get here?" she gasped, ignoring the interested eyes watching them.

"I was invited, of course," he informed her blandly, not at all discomposed by the listening eyes and ears. "I hope you can spare a dance for me." Ignoring her hostile glare, he took her card from her unresisting hand and scrawled his initials on a space toward the end of the evening. Before she could voice her displeasure, he bowed and strolled away. Fortunately Charley appeared at her side to claim his dance, the next one, and as the orchestra had begun to play, she had to join him on the floor.

Persuaded that Giles had used his considerable influence to gain entrance to the Endicotts, she was more than annoyed but had to hide her anger, for this was not an occasion when she could rail at him. Lady Endicott had not shown her the guest list beyond requesting if she had any friends she wished to invite. Charley and Robert had been included, and she knew no other young men in London. What did not occur to her was that Giles had entrée into most *ton* houses, including the Endicotts. That he would seek her out puzzled her. What could he want? Well, she would discover that soon enough. Now she owed it to the Endicotts to enjoy herself, and she was determined not to let Giles think his appearance mattered to her one bit. So she devoted herself to her partners with enthusiasm.

Roger Eastbrook found her a rewarding and fascinating supper partner, marveling at her frank enjoyment and flattering interest in his tales of the Army and society.

"Tell me, Lord Eastbrook, do you know Lord Fitzalen-Hill?" she asked during a pause between bites of lobster patty.

"Of course. Everyone knows Giles. He's Lord Selkirk's son and heir and a fine officer," he replied, wondering at Gwyneth's interest in Giles and not liking it much.

"I met him in Canada. He was an aide to General Brock," she explained.

*Damn*, Roger thought. *If Giles is in the running, I have little chance with this intriguing Colonial.*

"Do you like him?" he blurted out, abandoning all caution.

"Not particularly," Gwyneth answered briefly.

"He has a fearsome reputation with women," Roger warned. Then because he was a fair man and did not want to appear critical, he added, "Not that it is all his fault. He's handsome, rich, and gallant, all attributes attractive to women. Girls have been after him since he came on the town some years ago."

"I suppose so. But he's also arrogant, conceited, and fond of his own way," Gwyneth replied.

"You sound as if you know him well," Roger said, a bit taken aback by her fierceness.

Gwyneth shrugged as if throwing off a burden. "Too well, but let's forget him. You haven't revealed anything I didn't already suspect."

Perceptive enough to realize that Gwyneth did not want to say more, Roger turned to the topic of the Prince Regent's latest extravagance, hoping to distract her. But he wondered just what the relationship was between Fitzalen-Hill and Miss Winwood. It did not bode well for his own interest.

# *Chapter Twelve*

By the time Giles came to claim his dance, toward the end of the evening, Gwyneth had regained her poise and decided upon her attitude. She would treat him with cool indifference, the only protection she had in this trying situation. And he could not quiz her during the dance, which was to be a spirited reel.

But once again Giles foiled her best resolve. When he approached her as she was thanking her previous partner, he suggested they sit the dance out in one of the niches off the ballroom.

"You must be exhausted with your success tonight and could do with a little respite," he said masterfully, guiding her to a chair before she could demur.

"Not at all," she protested. "I am enjoying myself. So many interesting partners have introduced themselves," she said, endeavoring to let him know other men found her acceptable.

Watching her set face, Giles realized she had not forgiven him. Whether it was his seduction or his proposal she found offensive, he could not tell . Probably both. But he was not deterred. .

"I had hoped you had forgiven me. Is there any reason you should treat me like a leper?" he asked whimsically.

"I would rather not treat you at all. Whatever happened between us is in the past and best forgotten. The intimacy of the voyage and our peculiar introduction in Detroit forced us together. Now there is no longer any reason for us to meet," she said coolly.

"Oh, Gwyneth, I think you will find I am not so easily dismissed," he argued, repressing a surge of disappointment.

Gwyneth, deciding that this fencing was serving no purpose, turned to him and said bluntly, "Giles, there is no point in us continuing this fruitless discussion. I thought once we could be friends, but that is no longer possible. I don't know why you are bothering to pursue a hopeless relationship. We do not have anything in common. You are only interested in me because I am different from your usual conquests and my hostility represents a challenge. I am sure there are hundreds of girls who would welcome your attentions. Forget me and concentrate on them."

"You know, Gwyneth, your frankness is most appealing. Of course, I must honor your request. I thought you might welcome a friendly face among all these strangers, but I notice you seem to deal very well without me," he said plaintively.

For a moment Gwyneth wondered if he was really wounded by her rejection, then she dismissed such a foolish notion. Giles only wanted to assuage his own conceit by luring her into a liaison. Stubbornly she set her lips and refused to offer any more explanations. They sat quietly for a moment, neither one willing to make the first move, ignoring the covert glances of many of the guests. Gwyneth was relieved when Robert White came to partner her in the final set. Whatever Giles's motives in seeking her out, they would not profit her, and she must remember that. Nodding briefly to him, she went away on Robert's arm, chatting gaily. She only hoped it deceived him.

If Giles had suffered a rebuff, he was too skilled in the social niceties to show it. Standing up, he noticed Roger Eastbrook, having delivered his partner to the chaperone's corner, making off toward a passing footman for a drink He joined him, hailing him casually.

"Deuced hot in here, Eastbrook. How about a stroll in the garden?" he suggested.

If Roger thought Giles's approach odd, he accepted it without demur, and the two men made their way out of the ballroom. Gwyneth watched them go and wondered what ploy Giles had in mind. Well, if he was warning Roger off, she did not care. Despite her success at the ball, she was not in the market for an English husband. A sudden longing for home assailed her. The picture of James Brush came to her mind. She wondered where he was and if he were safe.

James was a great deal nearer and in greater peril than Gwyneth could have dreamt. During the fall of York to the American forces in late April, James had been captured and sent with a boatload of prisoners to England. Two days before the Endicott ball he had landed and managed to escape en route to prison in Devon. A resourceful young man who had survived several bloody engagements, he had not lost his taste for fighting. He was determined to make his way home and rejoin the army, although he had no idea how he would accomplish this daunting task. During the long dreary months of the past winter while soldiering on the Ohio, his thoughts had often turned to Gwyneth, wondering how she was managing in Detroit. Isaac Sibley, who had several letters from Delia smuggled through the lines, told him that she had left for Montreal, causing James some anxiety. James had hoped to be in the contingent bent on relieving Detroit and rescuing her. Instead, he joined the militia intent on taking York, and then determined to go on to Montreal, which the American general Henry Dearborn insisted the Americans could easily invade, a task Thomas Jefferson was also convinced could be managed. Once in the city, James meant to find Gwyneth and renew his courtship. He was a young man both stubborn and determined, and he wanted Gwyneth for his wife. In Detroit he had come close to achieving his objective. His capture and the trip to England in the reeking hold of the ship had not dampened his ardor. He must get home, and to that end he made his way toward London.


Of course Gwyneth had no knowledge of James's adventures, but he was often in her thoughts, as an antidote to Giles, perhaps. The morning after the ball, she rose and dressed quite a bit later than usual, still tired from the festivities of the night before. After clearing away her breakfast tray, an indulgence Lady Endicott had insisted upon, Mary told her that the mistress required her presence. Gwyneth, knowing that lady would want to discuss the ball, agreed and knocked on Lady Endicott's chamber door.

"Come in, come in," Lady Endicott called with eagerness.

Gwyneth found her propped up in bed, wearing a pink embroidered jacket and matching cap. On her breakfast tray were a host of envelopes.

"We are popular today," Lady Endicott said, indicating the missives. "Flowers are arriving every moment, and we have received a great many invitations for the season's events. All due to your great success at the ball, my dear," she insisted, patting her bed, suggesting that Gwyneth should sit down and hear about all these bids which signified her popularity.

"That's very kind of you, Lady Endicott, but I am sure you are such a skilled hostess that my debut would be hailed even if I were squint-eyed and gauche. And I am the latter, I fear," Gwyneth insisted, taking her place gingerly on the vast canopied bed.

"Not at all, my dear. You will become the rage. Roger Eastbrook was definitely *épris*, and loads of other eligibles found you enticing." She hesitated a moment and then rushed into speech, unable to restrain her curiosity. "I saw you sitting out with Lord Fitzalen-Hill." Her tone held a questioning note.

"I met him in Canada. I was somewhat surprised to see him here," Gwyneth explained reluctantly. She did not want Lady Endicott to exercise her fertile imagination about her relationship with Giles.

"His father, Lord Selkirk, is an old friend, and we have known Giles for ages. Of course, he received an invitation, but his singling you out was an honor. Although I must warn you, if you have not already noticed, that he is an accomplished rake, the naughty boy."

"I am quite aware of Giles's womanizing tendencies," Gwyneth said, hoping that would end the quizzing.

"Of course, he has to marry before long. If only this war would end, these young men would give up ideas of martial glory and attend to their marital duties," Lady Endicott quipped, but not entirely in jest.

"Please don't have any ideas that Giles is interested in me that way, despite our friendship," Gwyneth pleaded, alarmed at her patroness's matchmaking plans.

"Don't you like him? Most women find him irresistable."

"I don't. I thought Lord Eastbrook much more inviting," Gwyneth offered, hoping to distract Lady Endicott.

"He's a marquis, you know, and equally eligible," Lady Endicott replied with a complacent smile. She was enjoying this talk of beaux and marriage, and would not be put off.

"I am in no hurry to be married, especially since you are providing all these treats," Gwyneth said.

"Of course, of course. You must enjoy the season. That is why you are here. And incidentally, here is a letter from your father. He must be missing you."

Grateful for the diversion, Gwyneth accepted the letter and prepared to take her leave, thanking Lady Endicott again for the ball.

"Tonight we are going to the theater to see Edmund Kean. He's quite the rage, although I find him a bit *farouche,* but you must see him." Lady Endicott was basking in her role as chaperone to the Colonial who had captured the attention of the *ton.* "And tomorrow is Almack's. Your vouchers just arrived from Sally Jersey."

Realizing that Lady Endicott considered this a real coup, Gwyneth made no objection, although from what she had heard Almack's might be a dead bore. Longing to escape but not wanting to offend Lady Endicott, she suggested she would be available for any errands if her hostess required her services.

"I really feel the need of some exercise. Can I go to the shops for you?" she offered.

"Oh no, dear, that's all taken care of. But if you want to go out, you might walk over to Hatchard's and pick up some books I have ordered. Jane Austen's new novel, for one."

"I will gladly oblige. A walk is just what I need."

"It's just a step to Piccadilly, but be sure that Mary accompanies you. I know you might find it strange, but young women are not supposed to walk about London unescorted. Silly rule, but you must not sully your reputation," Lady Endicott warned, wondering if Gwyneth would object. But she need not have feared a rebuff, for Gwyneth was so eager to escape the luxurious confines of the Charles Street mansion for a time she would have agreed to a phalanx of abigails. She was finding the protocol of London society a trifle depressing, for during the past few weeks she had rarely been alone.

"I will just read Father's letter and be on my way." She bade Lady Endicott an affectionate goodbye and hastened to her room. Her father's letter was full of fears for the safety of Montreal, as the Americans appeared ready to attack, but he also mentioned he had heard from Delia, who was standing up to the occupation of her town bravely and had heard from her husband. He hoped she was enjoying herself and not being a trouble to her hosts, to whom he sent his best regards. Only toward the end of the letter did his real message appear. He had learned that Giles Fitzalen-Hill had left to return to England. He sincerely hoped she would not encounter him, and if that should happen that she would depress any attempts on his part to renew their friendship. Evidently he did not know that Giles had traveled on the *Rodney*. If he had, his warning would have been more stringent, Gwyneth suspected. Well, he need not worry. She had had enough of Giles to last her a lifetime. Putting aside her letter, she donned her shawl and bonnet and rang for Mary, anxious to get beyond all advice from her relatives both in London and abroad.

For the next few weeks Gwyneth was besieged with invitations, all thoroughly vetted by Lady Endicott. They attended Almacks', Drury Lane, routs, receptions, luncheons and dinners, and even the Manchester ball, a grand affair at which Gwyneth was undoubtedly the belle, not endearing her to the season's debutantes. Gwyneth rather regretted their jealousy and hostility, for she greatly craved a friend with whom she could exchange confidences. Giles was often at these affairs but only once did he approach her and that was to introduce his father, the Earl of Selkirk, a tall gray-haired man who wore his years lightly and had none of the wry cynicism of his heir. The Countess of Selkirk had been dead for some years, Gwyneth understood. She liked the earl and only wished his son had inherited more of his father's character. The earl, who always appreciated an attractive young woman, was equally pleased with Gwyneth.

"I knew you would approve of Father, even if you find me lacking," Giles said to Gwyneth sarcastically as they parted.

The Manchester ball had been a triumph for Gwyneth. The "Colonial beauty" had indeed become the rage, as Lady Endicott promised. The house on

Charles Street was thronged with young gallants requesting Gwyneth's presence on rides, picnics, and expeditions of all sorts. Her bedroom began to look like a flower shop. Gwyneth naturally enjoyed her popularity but was sometimes frustrated that the war, both in Europe and in Canada, did not appear to concern London society. Neither her beaux nor the contemporaries of the Endicotts discussed the progress of the Army beyond decrying its effect on the season, as it robbed their circle of proper escorts for the females. Gwyneth wished she could find another opportunity to talk with Lord Castlereagh, but the Foreign Secretary had his own agenda at social evenings and did not bother with unfledged girls, for which she could hardly blame him.

On the morning after the Manchester ball, some four weeks after she had arrived in England, she awoke feeling logy, headachy, and nauseous. At the first bite of her breakfast egg, she rushed to the basin and was wretchedly sick. Finally, the bout passed and she took a restorative gulp of her tea, wondering what was the matter with her. It must have been the lobster patties which she enjoyed. The weather had been quite warm and possibly they had been tainted.

Relieved that she was feeling a bit more the thing, she rang for her abigail and dressed for the day. Roger Eastbrook was taking her with a party to Richmond, and she was looking forward to it. Roger would be leaving at the end of the week for the Continent and had pleaded with her to spare him as much time as possible. However, much as she enjoyed his company, she should not be sorry to see him go, for she feared he was coming to care for her, and she could not return his affections. She often wondered what was wrong with her that she could not fall in love and make a commitment. Certainly Roger was all that a girl could desire in a man; considerate, handsome, and well-born. He never overstepped the bounds of propriety and obviously respected and liked her. If Giles's reactions toward her were different, she did not want to think of him. But he had made her wary of men's attentions. She could be deceived by Roger as she had been with Giles.

The trip to Richmond proved a huge success, and Gwyneth equally enjoyed the theater party that evening. But the next morning she was sick again, and she wondered what was wrong with her. Mary, her abigail, had a suspicion when the bouts of sickness continued, and at last she summoned the courage to speak to Gwyneth.

"Miss, you shouldn't be having this morning sickness. Could you be pregnant?" she blurted out after five mornings of clearing up after Gwyneth. A country girl, Mary was neither shocked nor disapproving, only curious as to whom had seduced Gwyneth.

Appalled, Gwyneth paled and looked at her abigail fearfully. That one night with Giles on shipboard! Surely she was not paying for her loss of virtue. It had only been the once. But she then remembered that her monthly courses had not come. She had thought it was due to the travel and the excitement of coming to London. However, Gwyneth was not a complete innocent as her sister had described her own stages of pregnancy in some detail. It could be true. What was she to do? Lady Endicott would be furious and disgusted, might even turn her from the house. In these cases it was always the woman who paid for a lapse of conduct and paid the price in suffering and disgrace. Girls of her sort did not surrender no matter how compelling their emotions.

And she did not even have the excuse of an over-whelming love. She had been frightened of the storm and turned to Giles for comfort, a situation he had turned to his advantage. It was not as if she had not had plenty of warning. He had tried to seduce her in Detroit and only the arrival of Judge Woodward that evening had saved her. Why had she been so foolish, so weak-willed? But it did no good to repine. She would have to face the situation and she would have to tell Lady Endicott, a poor repayment for that lady's wonderful kindness to her.

Gwyneth was no coward. But the idea of confiding in Lady Endicott was not a pleasant one. Whatever that comforting and tolerant woman said to her could not be worse than the castigation she deserved. Still, she must face her, and she must insure that Mary did not spread the tale in the servants' hall.

"If what you suggest is true, Mary, you must keep it to yourself. If I find you have been the source of rumors belowstairs, I will have the Endicotts send you home to Devon in disgrace," Gwyneth told her abigail sternly.

"Oh, miss, I won't breathe a word," the abigail wailed. She thought Gwyneth a kind and easy mistress, and shuddered at the thought of returning home to the crowded laborer's cottage and her angry mother, who was ambitious for her country-bred daughter and welcomed the money the girl sent to the distressed household.

Gwyneth doubted the girl would be able to hold her tongue, but at least she was intelligent enough to realize that her continuing service depended on her silence. Gwyneth dismissed her with another reminder that her own future lay in keeping her tongue quiet.

After Mary left, Gwyneth sat down to regard her own bleak future. The prospect of having a baby without a husband was overwhelming. She would have to leave London, and what excuse could she give? There would be no mercy from the fashionable society that had hailed her success. Not that the *ton* had moral scruples, but she would have committed the gravest insult to the *haut monde*. Certainly adultery and sexual license abounded in that world, but the unforgivable sin was in being unmasked.

Well, she had managed to live happily most of her life without the approval of the *ton*, and she would survive this shameful situation somehow. What was most dispiriting was the knowledge that her father had been right in his suspicions of Giles. And so had she.

Not one to delay an unpleasant confrontation, Gwyneth walked down the hall and knocked on Lady Endicott's door. The sooner that lady heard her appalling news, the better. No use to hope this could be a false alarm. Gwyneth accepted that she was pregnant, for she remembered Delia's tales, and knew she could not be mistaken.

"Come in," Lady Endicott called, and Gwyneth marched into her hostess's bedchamber, finding Lady Endicott as usual ensconced in bed, her breakfast tray on her knees, with Fletcher in attendance.

Stifling the impulse to delay any confidence, Gwyneth said, "Could I speak to you alone, Lady Endicott?"

"Of course, my dear. That will be all, Fletcher. I will ring when I am ready to dress," Lady Endicott said, giving Gwyneth a welcoming smile, unsuspecting of what would all too soon be revealed. Fletcher sniffed and made her departure, closing the door behind her softly but for all that signifying her displeasure.

"Pay no attention to Fletcher, Gwyneth. She takes offense easily," Lady Endicott said, dismissing her disapproving maid casually. "Now what can I do for you?"

Gwyneth ignored Lady Endicott's indication that she should sit down and stood squarely at the end of the bed, wondering how soon her kind hostess would revile her.

"I am in deep trouble, Lady Endicott, and there is little you can do for me, I fear."

"Oh, my dear, I hope not. Fergus and I have become so fond of you, so proud of you, that we will do all in our power to help you. Now what is this trouble?"

"I greatly fear that I am pregnant," Gwyneth blurted out, determined not to cry but having a sudden desire to throw herself on Lady Endicott's bosom and wail like an erring tweeny.

But Lady Endicott surprised her. "Well, these things happen. Who is the man. Not Roger?" she asked mildly.

"Of course not. He's much too honorable," Gwyneth said, taken aback, not only by Lady Endicott's suggestion but by her calm acceptance of this ghastly mess.

"Do you want to tell me the whole story? I think you must so we can decide what to do," Lady Endicott asked. Then feeling that perhaps a bromide would help, she added, "There is a remedy for every trouble, you know."

Overcome by Lady Endicott's charity, Gwyneth

could barely restrain her tears. The relief of sharing her predicament with a comforter was almost too much for her.

"You were quite right about Giles Fitzalen-Hill. And I cannot claim to have been deceived by him. I suspected he was a rake from the moment I met him, but he caught me with my guard down. Not that I have any real excuse for behaving like a doxy," she accused herself. And then she recounted the whole sorry tale of the night aboard the *Rodney*.

Lady Endicott listened sympathetically, making no comment until Gwyneth had finished.

"He will marry you, and the sooner the better," she said decisively.

"He won't, you know. After that night he offered, but I refused him and told him I would rather wed a dustman," Gwyneth informed her a bit shakily.

"Well, I don't know of any dustman who will oblige. But Giles will. Selkirk will insist. Fergus will speak to him," Lady Endicott replied firmly.

"Sir Fergus will be disgusted. I don't see why you are not," Gwyneth told her champion.

"You are not the first gently bred girl to be seduced by a cad," Lady Endicott comforted. "But believe me, Fergus has the power and so does Selkirk to compel Giles. He will make an unenviable husband, but that can't be helped. If he refuses to do the honorable thing, Fergus can see to it that his military career is ruined, and believe me, that matters to Giles," Lady Endicott said shrewdly.

"I am so sorry to bring this disgrace upon you, Lady Endicott," Gwyneth apologized.

"Nonsense, my dear. There will be no disgrace. Giles is about to leave for the Peninsula. You will be married quietly before he goes, and no one will wonder at the suddenness of it all. Leave it to me. We will manage beautifully. Now you must stop abusing yourself and try to regain some calm. It is not good for the baby," Lady Endicott insisted. "Ring for Fletcher, my dear. I must get dressed. There is quite a lot to do. Just run along and try to get some rest. This has all been most distressing for you."

Gwyneth leaned over and gave Lady Endicott a hug, completely overcome by her kindness and her acceptance. She seemed almost to be enjoying her role in this domestic tragedy, for that was what Gwyneth felt it to be. That she would escape scorn and scandal seemed impossible, but Lady Endicott was going to make it her task to see that all would be managed with decorum even if the result would not insure Gwyneth's happiness. After all, most of her friends made marriages of convenience, and that was what this union would be.

# Chapter Thirteen

If Sir Fergus's reaction to Lady Endicott's news of Gwyneth's pregnancy was one of disgust, he gave no evidence of it. That evening, after Lady Endicott had been closeted with him in the library when he returned from the Foreign Office, he met Gwyneth with a comforting hug and warm reassurances. Dinner that evening was necessarily a rather sober affair, although Lady Endicott did her best to keep the conversation on cheerful topics. Bradley's stoic face gave no sign that he knew of her predicament, but Gwyneth felt sure the servants' hall was abuzz with her disgrace. No matter how Sir Fergus and Lady Endicott behaved, and their manners were impeccable, Gwyneth was certain they viewed her in a different, less acceptable light.

She shuddered to think what her father would think. After all, he had prophesied just such an outcome from her relationship with Giles and had done his best to avert a scandal. That it could be nothing else, Gwyneth was convinced. There were bound to be sniggers and ostracism even if Sir Fergus prevailed on Giles to marry her. Despite Lady Endicott's almost casual reception of her news, Gwyneth knew that the resolution of her dilemma would not be as simple as her cousin had explained. She wished she had the courage to leave London for a small hamlet, have the baby in secrecy, and endure whatever came after the birth.

Sir Fergus had the means to compel Giles, Lady Endicott insisted, but that did not assuage Gwyneth's disgust at herself. And she accepted that Giles would be furious and frustrated, even if he honored his obligation. The earl, that kindly but proud man, would not be pleased either. He may have wanted Giles to marry, but certainly not in this degrading fashion.

Whatever coercion Sir Fergus applied to Giles, her next meeting with him was bound to be humiliating and uncomfortable. Sir Fergus did not confide in her as to his methods, only saying that all would be well.

Gwyneth could not believe that the Endicotts would not eventually alter their affectionate regard for her, but she was wrong. Later that evening, after Gwyneth had retired early, Catherine Endicott discussed the situation with her husband. "I don't blame Gwyneth. Giles Fitzalen-Hill is a fascinating man and he took advantage of her. He has gone through life supremely confident that he would never have to pay for his transgressions. Now his sins have caught up with him," she told her husband.

"Yes, and he will have to behave honorably. His father will insist, even if I do not. But I think he will make the poor girl a bad husband," Sir Fergus replied. "I will see Selkirk tomorrow. Fortunately he is in town for several weeks, and I will not have to go down to their place in Sussex."

"I wonder how the earl will react."

"Selkirk is a man of great sophistication and probity, a difficult combination, but he will see that only one solution is possible. And he will compel Giles to marry Gwyneth."

"I hope you are right," Lady Endicott said with a grimace.

The residents of the Endicott mansion in Charles Street all passed a somewhat sleepless night. Gwyneth's mind churned with the dread of the coming interview with Giles, Lady Endicott grieved for her cousin, and Sir Fergus tossed and turned as he marshaled his arguments in anticipation of his meeting with the earl.

Whatever Sir Fergus said, it must have been effective, for two days later Giles arrived at Charles Street and asked to see Gwyneth alone.

Lady Endicott was tempted to refuse, feeling that she should be present at the interview in order to protect Gwyneth from Giles, but on second thought she believed it would be better for the young people to come to some understanding without her interference. Her manner toward Giles was neither judgmental nor angry, but he was aware that she held him responsible for the situation, which irritated him. He disliked being in the wrong, so that when Gwyneth finally appeared, looking wan and apprehensive, he scowled at her ferociously.

For some reason his obvious fury steadied Gwyneth, and she faced him bravely.

"Well, Gwyneth, you have caught yourself an eligible husband," Giles said nastily.

If his words were wounding, Gwyneth showed no sign of it. "I wasn't in the market for a husband. I regret this whole affair as much as you do, and I doubt very much if we will make an amiable couple," she retorted, color rising in her cheeks.

Giles smiled sarcastically as if he did not believe her protests. "We will have to be married quickly. I have received my orders and must be off to the Peninsula next week," he informed her. "If you are fortunate, you might be a widow before the baby is born."

"Much as I dislike you, Giles, I don't want you killed," Gwyneth replied, refusing to lose her temper. She might have known Giles would adopt a cynical attitude, but she could not entirely blame him. She had not been an unwilling participant in their shipboard affair, brief as it was.

"That's charitable of you." He turned away and walked toward the window, staring unseeing at the street. He was slightly ashamed of his stance. After all he had seduced the girl, but his father's harsh criticism had made a wounding impression. Whatever his sins in the past, his father and he had remained friends. But the earl took this latest transgression badly. Unfairly, Giles thought, he laid the blame entirely on Giles's shoulders.

"Sir Fergus and Lady Endicott will make all the arrangements, I understand," he muttered, still not facing Gwyneth. Her candid eyes and calm demeanor increased his guilt, and he disliked being regarded as a blackguard.

"I suppose so, and since we can have little more to say to each other that will not be full of recrimina-

tions, I see no purpose in prolonging this meeting,"
Gwyneth said sharply. She had hoped for some indication of affection, even if it was spurious, but she should
have known better.

"As you wish," he said in a surly fashion. "But
before you turf me out, not to meet again until the
ceremony, I suspect, I must give you this betrothal
ring. My father insists. All Selkirk brides have worn
it." He crossed over to her, not meeting her gaze,
and proffered a large sapphire ring. He made no
effort to put it on her finger.

Gwyneth repressed an urge to throw it in his face
and turn him from the house, and took it meekly.
He did not seem at all interested in the coming heir,
when it would be born, or any arrangements that
might be made. Well, she could manage beautifully
without his cooperation. Obviously he felt little but
annoyance and disgust at this embroglio and wanted
to put it behind him as soon as possible.

"Goodbye, Giles," she said firmly and walked from
the room, her shoulders straight, and closed the door
softly behind her. Whatever she felt she would not
give Giles the satisfaction of seeing her unhappiness
and dismay.

Left alone, Giles frowned. The chit had courage.
Why had he ever embarked on that seduction? She
deserved better than a rake and a cad whose life had
little purchase. Well, if he should meet his just desserts
in the Peninsula, she would be well-served and, no
doubt, as a wealthy, attractive widow, have little trouble in catching a more amenable and likeable husband. Somehow this gloomy picture did not give him
any satisfaction. After all, he should not be so down-
hearted. He had to marry eventually. His father had
made that quite clear to him, and the earl approved

of Gwyneth, if he did not welcome the situation that ensured he won a daughter-in-law.

In different circumstances Giles might even have enjoyed the thought of claiming Gwyneth as a bride. But he disliked being forced, and he realized she would have preferred another man, maybe even Roger Eastbrook, whose credentials were as sound as his own and who would never have acted so shamefully. She was a damned attractive girl, with a deep well of passion and a staunch character. Why couldn't he just accept this marriage and try to make the best of it? Giles sighed, not liking what he saw in his own character, and then shrugged. He would marry the girl and return immediately to his proper milieu, the battlefield, where such musings could be ignored, if not forgotten.

Gwyneth made a lovely bride, dressed in a cream silk gown and matching bonnet. It was a quiet ceremony in St. Margaret's Church, the traditional wedding choice of London's best families. Only the earl, the Endicotts, and a fellow officer of Giles's attended. The vows were spoken quickly, but after signing the register the earl insisted they all return to his Grosvenor mansion for a wedding luncheon, a surprisingly cheerful affair, due in part to Ned Waterford, Giles's best man. Like Giles he was a career soldier, who had served under Sir John Moore and been wounded in the retreat at Corunna. A stocky, rather ugly man whose charm lay in his disposition and happy facility for always looking on the bright side of life, he appeared to find nothing untoward in this hurried wedding and congratulated Giles sincerely on winning such a lovely bride. The earl and the Endicotts, all skilled in handling ticklish situations, smoothed over any awkwardness, and the luncheon was quite pleasant. Only the newlyweds seemed a bit distrait, but at a warning glance from his father, Giles finally bestirred himself to behave with some modicum of interest in his bride.

Giles and Gwyneth were to spend their wedding night in the Berkeley home, the earl returning immediately to Sussex, where Gwyneth would join him eventually for the birth of the baby. In the meantime once Giles had departed, she would be living with the Endicotts.

At last the guests departed, and Giles and Gwyneth were alone. The earl had embraced Gwyneth heartily before he left in his carriage, telling her how much he looked forward to introducing her to Selkirk Hall. If Gwyneth had a fleeting wish that Giles had inherited some of his father's manners and character, she abandoned it. His father had a lot to answer for in allowing his son to go his heedless way without restraint. For the Endicotts she felt nothing but admiration and real affection, and wished she could go home with them now instead of spending the coming hours with an irate and sullen husband. But Giles surprised her. When the door closed on the retreating guests, he turned to her and said easily, "Well, Lady Fitzalen-Hill, that all went off in a spanking fashion, don't you think?"

Somewhat surprised at his insouciance, Gwyneth responded in kind, "Yes, the Endicotts are wonderful organizers."

"And now you are alone with the ogre," he mocked, offering her his arm and leading her into the library.

"I don't think you are an ogre, Giles, only a spoiled, self-assured rake who never expected to pay the penalty for his ways," Gwyneth reproved. Then feeling that perhaps she had sounded like a prissy scold, added, "But, of course, I am not blameless in this business."

Giles raised his eyebrows and went to the drinks tray laid out on a side table. "Can I offer you some wine?"

"No, thank you." Gwyneth felt tongue-tied and ashamed of her hard words. He was trying to make the best of a difficult situation and she was not helping. Recriminations and criticism were of no use now. She looked at her new husband, who stood awaiting her pleasure.

"We must somehow pass the next few days until I sail. I suppose we cannot show our faces in the likely places of amusement, such as the opera or the theater. We are supposed to be panting for intimacy," he teased.

Realizing that Giles was trying to put the best face possible on their situation, Gwyneth did her best to cooperate, but she was ill at ease, and he noticed it, of course.

"Come, Gwyneth, you know I enjoy taking you to bed, and now that we have sanctified our passion by the bonds of matrimony, we should take what the gods offer." He crossed to her and looked down at her with an unmistakable glint in his eye.

An unexpected shiver of excitement shook her. She wanted to deny him, but her instincts were swamped by other more passionate emotions. He bent and kissed her gently at first, then with rising warmth as she responded.

Without further words they left the room and hurried up the stairs. However much she resented the reason for this marriage, she could not deny him. On reaching the bedroom she scarcely noticed the rich appointments as her eyes were filled with the sight of the huge fourposter bed. Morley, Giles's batman, was bustling about and chatting with Gwyneth's abigail flirtatiously. Gwyneth thought fleetingly that she must speak to Mary about Morley. Like master like man, and she thought he might have designs on her attractive young maid. But Giles had no patience with either of them and dismissed them curtly. Gwyneth caught the sly smiles between them as they left the room, having a good idea of what they were thinking, but Giles, in his usual arrogant fashion, gave them no heed. Within moments of their departure he had unbuttoned the dress uniform jacket that he had worn for the ceremony and turned to Gwyneth.

"Are you going to be missish about a perfectly natural desire, Gwyneth? After all we are married," he mocked.

Not wanting him to know how much she dreaded a soulless coupling, she shrugged and turned her back. "Since you have dismissed Mary, you will have to help me out of my dress. I am sure you have had lots of experience in maiding young women," she snapped.

He smiled and obliged, and within moments they were together in bed.


The next morning Gwyneth awoke, stretched, and immediately felt the usual pangs of nausea. She barely reached the basin in time. Giles woke, heard her retching, and groaned. At last she finished and, wrapping herself in a pale peach peignoir, sat down in a chair before her dressing table. Giles stumbled out of bed, donned his own dressing gown, and taking one look at her pale face beaded with perspiration, attempted to console her.

"I do hope my lovemaking has not made you sick," he joked, not entirely certain how to approach his wan, miserable wife.

"It's the baby. Delia was ill every morning for three months, and then it passed and she was in fine fig," Gwyneth informed him. "Most women have morning sickness."

"How unfair. What can I do for you?"

"Nothing. I am all right now. But I would like a cup of tea," Gwyneth said weakly, rather surprised as Giles bent over and kissed her gently on the forehead.

"You are little more than a baby yourself. It's a shame. But last night would probably have started a baby if we had not anticipated our vows," he teased.

Gwyneth, tempted to make a sharp reply, bit her lip.

"I know. It's all my fault. But I am sorry. Truly, Gwyneth," he consoled her.

"Well, we must just accept it. No doubt when the baby arrives I will have forgotten all about being ill and enjoy it."

"And I will not be here to share it with you," Giles said uncomfortably. "That is unless we manage to beat the Corsican in time."

"Don't worry. I will have Lady Endicott to support me. And I am sure your father will be a doting grandfather." Gwyneth wondered why she felt the need to cheer Giles. She had some nebulous idea that he was rushing into danger, and much as he infuriated her at times, she wished him safe.

That little encounter brought them into a more charitable state, and the next two days before Giles's departure flew by. He took her shopping to Rundell's, the royal jewelers, and bought her a delicate ruby and diamond necklace, over her protests.

"A new clasp will have to be fitted, my lord," the clerk told Giles, who obviously was a favored patron. Gwyneth wondered how many demi-reps had received gifts from this impressive establishment, tokens of his interest. But she said nothing, only promising to pick up the necklace when the work was done.

Giles, amused, had no difficulty in deciphering the tenor of her thoughts.

"A wife deserves the best, wouldn't you say, Horton?" he said to the clerk, who, remembering Giles's purchases in the past, only nodded. If he thought that at last the racketing peer had met his match, he said little, only offering his congratulations to the pair. Nothing was mentioned concerning the price, which Gwyneth realized must have been steep. Somehow she had not realized that she had married a wealthy man Nor had she expected to be bowed from the shop with many "my ladies." Her new status had insured that she would be treated obsequiously, and she did not know if she liked that. Giles understood and commiserated.

"You will be a countess someday, if I don't succumb in the Peninsula. Doesn't that please you?" he quipped.

"Don't be ridiculous, Giles. I never thought of it."

"Knowing you, I don't suppose you did," he said,

remembering her independent spirit and lack of ambition. "You must just put up with it." And he flicked his whip at his chestnuts as they drove down Piccadilly.

The next forty-eight hours passed all too swiftly, and Gwyneth awoke on Giles's last morning, for once not sick, and watched him as he dressed to leave. They had decided that she would not accompany him to Portsmouth where he would board his ship. He said the journey would be bad for her and the baby. Rather touched by his care of her, Gwyneth agreed. She did not like farewells, and she suspected he would not approve of any overt display of emotion. After all, he had been yearning for this assignment all during the past year. He would be relieved to be returning to war and the fellowship of other officers, away from the distractions of women. She did not blame him for this but wondered a bit at her own reluctance to let him go.

He was off directly after breakfast, accompanied by Morley. His farewells were brief as if he were impatient to make the break, and Gwyneth understood his mood.

"Don't get into trouble and take care of yourself. I suspect I will miss you," he said casually, and then belied his coolness by giving her a passionate kiss. Finally, tearing himself from the embrace, he laughed a bit hollowly. "You could become an addiction, Gwyneth. I will write."

Then he was gone, the bedroom door shutting with a decisive snap, leaving Gwyneth prey to regret mingled with irritation. How like Giles to rush off without any soothing words. That he was as moved as she never crossed her mind. But Morley received the brunt of Giles's humor on the road to Portsmouth and wondered if his master had at last succumbed to the spell of a woman.

In the days that followed Giles's departure, Gwyneth removed herself, her abigail, and her belongings to Charles Street, where the Endicotts welcomed her enthusiastically. The announcement of the marriage had appeared in the *Gazette*, and if there was speculation about the haste and secrecy, most of the gossips accepted that Giles's hurried assignment to the battlefield was the reason. The Endicotts depressed any overt hints of scandal and escorted Gwyneth on a round of entertainment. As yet her pregnancy was not evident, and in fact, she had never looked more attractive. There was a great deal of moaning among her past gallants that she had been wrested from their grasp by Fitzalen-Hill, but that did not alter her popularity. The Colonial beauty was still the rage. The cynics suggested that an absent husband only added to her appeal.

Once settled at the Endicotts, her life returned to its previous round of parties, theaters, balls, and shopping, but she had lost the zest for London's attractions. She wished now she had decided to travel to Selkirk Hall as soon as Giles left. A desire to see his ancestral acres made her regret that she had accepted the Endicotts' invitation, but she could not wound her hosts, who had been so hospitable and tolerant. A fortnight after Giles had left she received a notice from Rundell's that her necklace was ready, and she decided to pick it up herself and perhaps buy Lady Endicott some trifle to show her regard. Giles had given her a healthy allowance and his man

of business had called to tell her of the disposition
of his will, a depressing occasion. Generously he had
left her everything with a separate provision for the
heir, but she refused to consider that the will might
ever be implemented.

The June morning was warm and sunny when she
set out in the carriage with Mary for Rundell's, and
it raised her spirits. She thought of Giles on the seas
and hoped he was enjoying an equally good day.
Somehow this strange marriage had calmed her usual
tempestuous spirits, and even the memory of the letter she had written to her father refused to dampen
her good humor. At Rundell's she duly admired her
necklace and bought a small sapphire and diamond
spray for Lady Endicott, hoping it would suit. As
before, the clerk was more than obliging, and Rundell
himself bowed her out to her carriage. As she looked
back to thank him, she started with shock. Surely she
knew the man just emerging from offices down the
street. It seemed impossible, but she was certain it
was James Brush, here in London, sauntering along
as if he had not a care in the world.

Her first instinct was to call out to him, but with
the coachman, footman, and Mr. Rundell, as well as
Mary watching, she could not bring herself to make
the move. She drew back into the carriage, hoping
James would not see her, for the complications of a
meeting here on the street were more than she could
bear. As the carriage moved away, she looked once
more at the well-remembered figure moving purpose-
fully but easily away. He appeared unaware of any
danger, yet he was in the very midst of enemy territory.
What was he doing here in London? She had thought
him back on the Ohio, thousands of miles away, not
only from London but from her life. Confusion and

apprehension reigned as the carriage rode serenely on, and Gwyneth tried to hide her dismay.

Once back in Charles Street, Gwyneth presented the diamond and sapphire spray to Lady Endicott, who was fulsome in her thanks, and they had a delightful coze about baby clothes and the arrangements for the birth. By the time Gwyneth had gone to her bedroom for a short afternoon rest, she had almost forgotten that strange encounter outside of Rundell's. But lying on her bed, she could not deny that she had really seen James Brush. Of course, he had no idea she was in London. But then she sat up, remembering that the announcement of her marriage had been in the *Gazette*. Could he have seen it? If so, why hadn't he sought her out? Did he feel it might be dangerous? Somehow she doubted that James would be deterred by that possibility. And if he did contact her, what would she do? How could she explain her marriage to a man for whom she once had feelings? Now she must discount them, refuse to entertain any thoughts of what might have been. She felt guilty that in the past weeks she had given no thought to him, to the situation in Canada, being completely caught up in Giles's spell and her own predicament.

If James should suspect the truth of her marriage, he would be both disappointed in her and disgusted. If Giles had not sailed eagerly away to fight Napoleon, she might not have considered James a threat, but somehow she did. She was thousands of miles from familiar friends and family. Was that why she thought longingly of James? She was married and he should have no place in her new life. She lay down and composed herself. She was behaving like a hysterical ninny, raising specters of the past and fears for the

A RAKE'S JOURNEY 167

future. James might be just a figment of her loneliness and isolation from all she had known, a ghost from the past. It was probably just some clerk who had some slight resemblance to him. Determined to forget the incident in the Ludgate, she finally fell asleep.

# *Chapter Fourteen*

If Gwyneth had decided to relegate James Brush to the past and concentrate on her new position, he was determined to seek her out. James's adventures since escaping from his captors had been many. He had tried to sign on as a seaman on a Dutch ship bound for Halifax, but the first mate had looked on him with suspicion. Recalling the reason for the war between his country and England, he had avoided the docks after that experience, afraid of being impressed, forced to serve aboard a man-of-war. But he had to find employment if he were to survive until he found a way to get home. Trained in the law, he thought his best recourse was to try to find a position in some solicitor's office as a clerk. He might claim to be a Canadian trapped in London by the war and needing employment. He was fortunate enough to discover a small firm whose youngest clerk had gone off to join the Army in a burst of patriotism. James had duly been hired without too many queries by

Snodgrass & Smith, a company with few illustrious clients, which exactly suited his needs. With his employers as a reference, he had found suitable lodgings near his office and so rarely ventured into the more fashionable haunts of London.

But one evening while having his supper in a shabby café behind St. Paul's, he picked up an old copy of the *Gazette*. Leafing through it casually, he was brought up short by the announcement that Maj. the Viscount Giles Fitzalen-Hill, son of the Earl of Selkirk, had been married quietly at St. Margaret's to Miss Gwyneth Frederica Winwood, of Montreal, a cousin of Sir Fergus and Lady Endicott. He was shocked. Surely this was not his Gwyneth. But it was an unusual name, and there could not be two Gwyneth Winwoods from Montreal. But how had she met this man? Why had she come to London? He thought her safely in her home in Canada. Of course, a year had passed since their last meeting. Evidently it was out of sight, out of mind with Gwyneth, he concluded bitterly.

Well, he was not prepared to leave it at that. If Gwyneth was really in London, married to some haughty lord, he would find her and discover what had lead her to such a pass. And if the lord objected, he could damn well put up with it. James had all the frontier American's dislike of the English aristocracy and would countenance no condescension from Gwyneth's husband. Surely this marriage must be a hoax. In Delia's letters to Isaac months ago, she had mentioned casually that the English officers occupying Detroit had been very kind and protective. Could this fellow be one of the officers Delia meant? How else would Gwyneth have met him? Perhaps it had been a whirlwind courtship in Montreal. He had never heard of these cousins, the Endicotts, but then there was a great deal about Gwyneth that appeared mysterious. He had not known her as well as he thought. He disregarded fears for his own safety in contacting her. If Gwyneth were truly married, denied to him, he might as well be in prison, James concluded sorrowfully. Despite this gloomy prognosis, his natural optimism could not be repressed for long. The whole story in the *Gazette* might be a hum, and he would not be satisfied until he had learned the truth. Just how to accomplish this was the problem, and James spent several days deciding on the best method of acquiring the information he craved.

On the following Sunday, returning with the Endicotts from church, Gwyneth was informed by Bradley in disapproving tones that she had a visitor, a Mr. Brush, who refused to state his business but insisted on waiting. Lady Endicott, noticing Gwyneth startled reception of the news, drew her own conclusions.

"Is he someone from Canada, Gwyneth? If you don't wish to receive him, I will make short work of him."

"I'm sure you could, Lady Endicott, but I think I must see him. He probably has news from home," she said warily. What tale had James spun to insure his safety? He surely had not marched in and announced himself as an enemy officer. He had probably claimed to be from Canada. That seemed the likeliest tale. She felt guilty at deceiving Lady Endicott, but she would not be responsible for turning James over to his enemies.

"If you think it best, my dear. And since you are a respectable married lady, there is no need for me to be present. I am sure you have much news to exchange. Why not invite the young man to luncheon after your talk," she invited smoothly, deciding that she must leave Gwyneth alone to see him, but would quiz him herself and find out his business over a meal.

"That's very kind of you, Lady Endicott," Gwyneth replied, having a good idea of the lady's methods. The woman had not become a skilled society hostess without learning tact and diplomacy.

Giving her bonnet and gloves to Bradley, she followed him into the drawing room, where he had installed James, not without some hesitation.

"Thank you, Bradley," Gwyneth said, almost closing the door in his face as she slipped into the room.

"James, what are you doing here? You could be in the most dreadful danger," she cried as he took her hands and bent to kiss her warmly on the cheek.

"Not at all. I have a respectable position and am posing as a loyal Canadian. But what are you posing as, Gwyneth?" he asked sharply.

Her first relief now changed to anger. "I am not posing as anyone." Then seeing that James remained obdurate, and not liking his expression, she suggested in her most polite tones, "Shall we sit down? I don't like you looming over me, glaring."

"I have a lot to glare about, I think. When I left you to go off to war, I thought you felt some affection for me and it was only time and events that prevented us from becoming engaged. Now, barely a year later, I find you in London, supposedly married to some lord, and swanning about society with your high-toned new friends."

Although Gwyneth could see some justice in his remarks, she was not about to be berated like some erring schoolgirl. She sat down composedly, folded

her hands in her lap, and was determined not to lose
her temper, and indicated that he settle on the settee
opposite. Frowning and looking not at all like the
cheerful obliging James she remembered, he did so.

"Well, I am waiting," he grumbled.

"I am not sure I owe you an explanation. You had
no real claim on me, although it is true we had a
warm friendship in Detroit. But much has happened
since then. You went to war, the English occupied
Detroit, and very unpleasant that was with their Indian
allies threatening and the commander a dreadful
man. If it had not been for Major Lord Fitzalen-Hill,
my position could have been very uncomfortable."

"And I suppose this gallant major rescued you from
death and so earned your love," James sneered.

Excusing his sarcasm because she realized his disappointment, Gwyneth still felt irritated. All very well
for him to accuse her of wayward and inconstant
behavior when he had no idea of what really had
occurred.

"Actually he did rescue me from some marauding
Indians who broke into Delia's house. When I faced
them, one of them tried to tomahawk me," she
explained simply.

"Oh, my God. Isaac said some civilians had been
attacked, robbed and killed when the English
marched into the fort. It was due entirely to that old
fusspot Hull, who refused to challenge them. We lost
some good men, too," he informed her, his eyes
clouding with the memories of that bitter time.

Gwyneth, somewhat assuaged by his words,
launched into an edited account of her days in Detroit
and her subsequent return home.

"And once back in Montreal I suppose this major
pursued you, persuading you to come to London

where he could offer you the earth," James concluded
without waiting to hear the rest.

"Not quite. He did come to Montreal, posted there
to Gen. Sir George Prevost, but my father thought I
might enjoy a holiday with my cousins, and so I came
to London. It was just coincidence that Giles happened to arrive here about the same time to take
up his military duties in the Peninsula," she said
carefully, omitting any suggestion of what really had
happened.

"Where he is now, I hope," James offered rather
cruelly.

"Where he is now," she agreed.

"But somehow before he left he managed to get
you to the altar and doomed all my hopes," James
said in a far gentler voice, realizing just what the
major had robbed him of.

"I'm truly sorry, James. So much has happened
since we last met, and the war changed everything,
your life as well as mine. Perhaps, if the war hadn't
come . . ." Her voice trailed off as she realized she
was not explaining her feelings very clearly. In fact she
did not understand her reaction to James's sudden
appearance after all this time.

"Well, the war did come, and if I hadn't been
such a muggins, I would not have gone off on that
expedition to York. Then I stupidly allowed myself
to be captured," James admitted, too tactful to
remind her that if he had not wanted to see her again
he would probably have stayed with Isaac on the Ohio.

But Gwyneth was not deceived. She liked James
and was concerned for his safety, but she realized
that she did not love him. He would have made a
respectable, reliable, caring husband, but now he
seemed dull and too cautious. If he had showed an

ounce of passion back in Detroit, she might have succumbed to him. What had changed her opinion of him? Was it Giles, so different, so reckless, so fascinating, so undependable? Still, she owed James some loyalty. She must help him get back to America. And the notion that her efforts would be some recompense for his disappointment was strengthened by the realization she must get him out of her life. Guilt forced her to offer her help.

"We must think of some way to get you on a ship for home," she said with more decisiveness than she felt.

"Have you any ideas?" James asked a bit gloomily. He had to accept that Gwyneth was lost to him and now his chief priority must be escaping from London.

"No, but I will think of something. We cannot stay here much longer. Lady Endicott will be wondering what we are about. She has invited you to luncheon and will quiz you unmercifully."

"I won't accept. I'll plead another engagement."

"Give me your direction, and if I can arrange some way to find you a ship, I will send you a message. Do take care, James." Gwyneth stood, signifying the meeting was over.

James had no recourse but to do the same. They parted uneasily, both aware of their changed relationship. James disliked the idea that Gwyneth thought of him as an irksome problem, someone she must help because of a past loyalty. He did not enjoy that position and decided he would be wiser to discourage any intentions of aid she had.

"Forget about me, Gwyneth. Your life lies in a different path now. I regret that but I am sure you don't.

Be happy," he said. Then he kissed her gently on the forehead and took his leave.

Guilt and remorse dogged Gwyneth after his departure, and she resolved she would find some way to help him. She parried Lady Endicott's tactful queries at luncheon and then retired quickly to her room to decide what plan she might concoct. Even more than James she was a captive, owing the Endicotts her loyalty. They would be appalled to learn they had been entertaining an enemy, although she suspected Sir Fergus did not approve of the war. So foolish this war when neither side felt any real commitment to its cause. Of course, the English should not have impressed American seamen, but the government was desperate to man its ships in the struggle against Napoleon. Liverpool had enough sense to repeal the Orders in Council, but his action had come too late and now men were dying for little reason. Not for the first time Gwyneth damned men and their pride and their thirst for glory. Giles was a good example of where such unadmirable traits could lead one. But she wished he were here. Somehow she sensed he would neither be shocked or irritated by James's appearance. He would admire his ingenuity and think of some way to send him safely home.

Gwyneth, a little annoyed at her wish for her reluctant husband, determined to handle the matter cleverly. Then she would tell him about it when he returned. If he returned. Suddenly she remembered that Giles was in danger as frightening as James was and for a far better cause. Well, she would contrive some method of ridding herself of her rejected suitor. Delia and Isaac, if no one else, would applaud her efforts.

That evening at dinner, as Sir Fergus was discussing the war, Gwyneth casually asked him about neutral ships. Were they attacked by the English on the high seas?

"No, not unless the captain believes Englishmen might be aboard, or even Americans. I am afraid that the government thinks the former Colonials are fair game, really disguised Englishmen who should serve in our navy—a regrettable stance."

"I think my friend Mr. Brush wants to go home to Canada, but dreads embarking on what can only be a perilous voyage," Gwyneth suggested tentatively, knowing she was giving Lady Endicott the opportunity to quiz her on her relationship with James.

"Is he a close friend, my dear?" that curious lady asked. She suspected James of being a previous claimant for Gwyneth's hand and wondered if her charge was regretting her hasty marriage already.

"At one time. But, of course, Giles changed all that," Gwyneth said dulcetly, feeling the veriest deceiver.

"A small convoy of merchantmen will be leaving for Halifax next week. We might get him a passage on one of those ships," Sir Fergus suggested kindly. Perceptive but much more reticent than his wife, he believed Gwyneth wanted to place herself beyond temptation, rid herself of a former suitor who might cause problems. Sir Fergus was not an unsophisticated man and had always viewed Gwyneth's hurried wedding with some misgivings. Of course, she had no choice, but perhaps she secretly preferred this other man. Best to get him away.

"That would be splendid, Sir Fergus. James has not found London quite what he expected," she confided gently.

No doubt he expected to find Gwyneth still available, Sir Fergus decided shrewdly. Yes, this Mr. Brush must be dispatched with all speed. He would make the arrangements forthwith.

A man of his word, Sir Fergus booked James's passage the next day and informed Gwyneth she should notify her friend. She realized that traveling under Sir Fergus's aegis would do a great deal to insure James's safety, if she could warn him to continue to play the patriotic Canadian eager to return home. She sent James a letter immediately, suggesting he call and learn of her plan. The footman dispatched to the rather seedy offices of Snodgrass & Smith found it rather odd that his master should be championing such a dubious Colonial, but delivered the letter, turning up his nose at his surroundings.

James had a strange reluctance to honor Gwyneth's request that he call, although he was grateful for her attempt to help him. After all, she was abetting the enemy, and if her high-toned husband and relatives discovered the ruse, she could pay dearly. She might be lost to him, but he still admired and cared for her. Should he accept her offer? Summer was passing, and he should try to get home before the fall campaigns began. James was always conscious of his duty, but the news of Gwyneth's marriage had altered many of his earlier beliefs. Suppose her aristocratic husband fell in battle. Then she would be a widow, available once again. Suppressing thoughts of what that might mean to his own chances, he wavered over whether to go or to stay. He discounted his personal peril. Well, it would do no harm to accede to her invitation, and he wanted to see her again. James did not easily abandon a cause, no matter how hopeless.

He duly presented himself the following Sunday at

the Endicott residence, disgusted at accepting the hospitality of an enemy but wise enough to behave as a trustworthy friend and patriotic Canadian. This time he remained for luncheon, and Lady Endicott delicately questioned him as to his former relationship with Gwyneth. But James was not skilled in the law for nothing. He easily parried her attempts to discover how well Gwyneth had known him, and turned the conversation to the Army's success against Napoleon and the Corsican's Russian campaign.

Gwyneth, apprehensive at James's bland deception, wanted to have a word alone with him, but that seemed difficult due to the Endicotts' hospitality. Finally, she was able to draw him away just before he took his farewell.

"Do be careful, James. If the Endicotts discover your real allegiance, you could end up back in prison, if not worse," she warned.

"It was a bit tricky when Sir Fergus suggested I call at the Foreign Office, but I think I evaded him nicely, pleading my work," he assured her. Somehow he feared exposure for Gwyneth more than any threat from the authorities. He still found her an attractive, compelling girl, whose marriage only seemed to make her more appealing.

"I will come down to see you off," Gwyneth said, determined to offer this last testimony to their friendship. "And when you arrive home, take care in the fighting."

"I lead a charmed life," he insisted, half believing it. He may have lost the girl he wanted, but he was not such a sapskull that he was willing to abandon everything for a hopeless love.

Past experience had taught James that Gwyneth could not be dissuaded from what she thought she should do, so he made no protest. He only said, "Take care yourself, Gwyneth. I will be a long while forgetting you. I wish events and this wretched war had turned out differently."

"Goodbye for now, James. I will see you at the dock."

As Gwyneth watched him walk sturdily away without a backward glance, she felt bereft. James was a touch of home, a fading memory of her girlhood, those days in Detroit, when life seemed simpler, if more rigorous. What lay ahead with Giles, or without him, suddenly seemed unreal.

# *Chapter Fifteen*

While Gwyneth was relieved to have played some part in sending James Brush on his voyage to home and safety, she could not help but think he had accepted her offer rather supinely. Certainly he had showed a certain boldness in escaping from his captors and finding a job to sustain himself in London, as well as deceiving his employers and the Endicotts as to his real identity. It was mean-spirited of her to think he lacked initiative or courage, but she felt instinctively that Giles would have managed without enlisting the aid of the girl he had at one time wanted to marry. Whatever Giles's faults, he took charge of his life, not depending on others to extricate him from whatever perils he encountered along the way.

Perhaps she was not being fair to James, a stranger in an enemy stronghold. In the past she had compared Giles unfavorably to James, who possessed all the probity, consideration, and unselfishness that Giles lacked. Still, she thought of those days in Detroit and wondered if she would have succumbed had James shown more ardor, more daring in his courtship. No doubt the very traits that would make him a steady husband inspired caution. However, if he had loved her as much as he claimed, he should have made a more passionate effort to win her. How unfair she was being, and how critical. Giles had behaved with a callous disregard for her feelings despite his more considerate efforts in the days just before he sailed. And she had changed, altered by the events that had forced her into her present situation. Could they ever reach a calm domestic plane? No, life with Giles would always be exciting, irritating, even unhappy, but it would not be dull. She wondered a bit wistfully if he was thinking of her, or were the demands of military life swamping gentler emotions. She scoffed. Giles did not have gentle emotions. Passionate, virile, demanding, he seized the moment with no thought for tomorrow. She blushed, remembering how he had inspired an equal passion in her, even while she resented his power to do so. She realized that James would never have called up those feelings, that response to his lovemaking. But that did not mean he was the lesser man, only not the man for her.

Confused by her feelings, she decided that her pregnancy must be affecting her judgment. Whatever she had felt for James it could matter little now, for she was committed to Giles and the coming child, and she had best forget what might have been.

Gwyneth would have been surprised to know how often Giles thought of her on the long voyage to Spain. At first his mind had been fully occupied with his coming assignment. He had missed Wellington's stunning victory at Vittoria in June when "Old Nosey" had defeated King Joseph Bonaparte. Now Wellington was poised to invade France. Napoleon, retreating from Russia and the terrible losses inflicted by the Czar's army, was at last on the run. At least, Giles believed that he would be in on the final battle to overthrow the Corsican. Somehow this did not fill him with the exhilaration he expected. He missed Gwyneth and wondered how she was coping without him. Probably very well, he decided, a bit aggrieved. He should have remained at home, missed the coming campaigns, been present for the birth of his son. A strange parental pride filled him with the thought of his heir, and he was convinced it would be a boy. He scoffed at his excess of emotion. He was a soldier and had his duty to perform, a duty more important than any woman. But Gwyneth was not just any woman. She was his wife, however reluctant he had been to claim her. If Gwyneth was confused by her feelings, Giles was hardly less so. He embarked at San Sebastián with less eagerness than he expected and prepared to join Wellington and face Marshal Soult, who had replaced the fleeing King Joseph as commander of the French troops.

On the day scheduled for James's departure, Gwyneth awoke with an eerie feeling of misgiving. She could not really believe he would get off without some hitch in the proceedings. How dreadful if he were unmasked, revealed as an enemy officer, and hauled off to prison. She wished Sir Fergus could accompany her, but a last-minute crisis at the Foreign Office took precedence over his private affairs, and only her maid

Mary would ride with her in the coach to the docks. The day matched her mood, gray and overcast with a threat of rain.

Lady Endicott, seeing Gwyneth's sober face, suggested she might forgo the trip. Surely she need not personally bid farewell to her Canadian friend, she said, wondering a bit at Gwyneth's obdurate decision to do so. Lady Endicott did not voice her suspicions, however, and sent Gwyneth off cheerfully. Not entirely deceived by her young charge's explanation of her previous relationship with Mr. Brush, she wondered if he knew about the pregnancy, if Gwyneth had told him the whole story of her relationship with Giles. She realized that Gwyneth was concealing something but decided she did not really want to know and turned her attention to other matters. Once he had been dispatched, she thought, Gwyneth would forget this rather mysterious stranger from her past and concentrate on the baby. Long adept at denying uncomfortable thoughts, Lady Endicott believed strongly in "out of sight, out of mind."

It was not that easy for Gwyneth. As the coach rumbled over the cobblestones, past St. Paul's and the Tower, into the dockland's sordid streets with their grubby alehouses and seamen's lodgings, she wished she had heeded Lady Endicott's advice. But she had promised.

At last the coach stopped by the river, where the masts of countless ships, England's lifeline, rose staunchly, the keels of merchantmen jostling for position. Escorted by Edgar, the Endicotts' coachman, his grizzled face expressing disapproval, she walked to the company offices where she was to meet James. He was waiting for her outside, his trunk beside him.

"This must be a happy day for you, James," Gwyneth greeted him, aware of the inanity of her words but unable to think of any sensible conversation.

"I don't like leaving you, Gwyneth," he protested, low-voiced. He looked at her searchingly, then rushed headlong into speech. "I wish you were going with me. I wish you had never come here, that neither of us had." Then, aware that the coachman was listening, he said stumblingly, "Of course, I am eager to depart."

"Is it time to board?" Gwyneth asked, suddenly wanting this painful leave-taking to be over.

"I am afraid so. I hope I will see Delia before too long. Any messages?" he asked, embarrassed, unwilling to surrender to more regrets.

"Just my love, and tell her I will be writing," she said, subdued. Impulsively she reached up and kissed James on the cheek, and then he hoisted up his trunk. They stood uncertainly for a moment, and then as Gwyneth turned away, a drunken sailor loomed up from the fog and jostled her, muttering curses. She stumbled and fell heavily, crying out, so that James, who had stepped toward the gangplank, turned back.

"Are you hurt?" he cried, swearing at the sailor who lurched off muttering.

Gwyneth made no answer, only groaned. James, abandoning his trunk, distraught, knelt beside her and was joined by the coachman, who muttered angrily, "She shouldn't be here in her condition. The master will have my hide."

James, now thoroughly alarmed, began to chafe Gwyneth's cold hands, murmuring comfort, but helpless before her waxen face and still body. What was wrong? Was she seriously injured?

"I'll get her maid, sir. You had best be off," Edgar urged.

"I can't leave her like this," James argued, appalled as he saw no sign of Gwyneth reacting to his feeble ministrations. Edgar hurried away into the fog as James continued to rub Gwyneth's hands and call fruitlessly to her. She must have fainted, but surely she should be coming around by now. However, Gwyneth seemed beyond any comfort as a sudden pain gripped her and she twisted in agony.

Distraught, James stood by, sweat beading his forehead. Thankfully he saw Gwyneth's maid and the coachman run up to them, and Mary took a vial from her reticule and waved it under Gwyneth's nose. Moaning, Gwyneth slowly regained consciousness but was obviously in pain.

Mary, worried, wailed. "The baby! She might be losing it."

James, appalled, gasped, "A baby? Is she pregnant?"

"Yes, sir," Mary answered, wondering how she could get her mistress home.

Just then came a distant shout of "All aboard," and Edgar cried, "You must go, sir, if you don't want to miss your sailing. We will attend to milady," he insisted with more confidence than he felt.

James wavered, then suddenly picked up his trunk and dashed toward his ship in a daze. The sailors yelled curses at him but allowed him to board just as the gangplank was raised. He looked to the dock, once upon the deck, but could see little in the mist that was shrouding the area, guilt and anger warring in him. Why hadn't she told him she was pregnant? Up to the last minute he had been tempted to beg her to flee with him, to return home, abandon this hateful marriage. Should he stay? If she lost the baby, there might still be a hope she would heed his pleas, but then he heard the cries of the sailors as they cast off the mooring ropes. Too late. And how could he help her now? If he stayed, lost this chance to return home, he might lose everything; Gwyneth; his freedom; his chance to return to the only life he knew, away from these hateful haughty English whom he despised.

As the ship slowly sailed downriver, he realized that he might show no cowardice in the face of enemy fire, but in a critical moment he had behaved with craven indifference to all but his own safety. He had deserted Gwyneth when she was in trouble, but what could he have done if he had stayed? James would not easily forget his selfishness in the long days to come.

Back at the dock Edgar and Mary, with the help of some passing sailors, carried Gwyneth to the coach and sped her home as quickly as possible. The jolting of the carriage was agony to her, and she tossed and moaned, frightening Mary into near hysteria. Once they all arrived at Charles Street, Lady Endicott took charge with her usual practical good sense. She sent for the doctor, had Gwyneth carried to her bed, and sat beside her, wiping her clammy forehead and murmuring words of comfort. But there was no comfort to be had. Later that day, despite the doctor's best efforts, she lost the baby.

Gwyneth did not recover quickly from the miscarriage. A strange lassitude and indifference gripped her as she lay on a divan in the Endicotts' garden watching the shadowy dance of the leaves in the silver birch trees, uncaring of events around her. Lady Endicott, despairing, having tried briskness, comfort, and every other effort to rouse her to some interest, finally took her concern to her husband.

"It isn't as if she were madly love with Giles or that she desperately wanted this baby," she complained. "I wonder if her malaise has anything to do with that Mr. Brush."

"The child has had a chaotic year. It's no wonder she has fallen into despondency," Sir Fergus explained. In truth he was as worried about Gwyneth as his wife and as helpless to cheer her.

"Perhaps this letter from Giles might raise her spirits It came yesterday but I hesitated to give it to her. What do you think?"

"I think she must have it. I suppose she has not written to tell him of their loss," Sir Fergus said, reflecting.

"She might believe he will not be too upset. He is not a man cut out for domestic bliss, I fear. Now he might blame her even more than she blames herself."

"It was a grievous accident," Sir Fergus insisted.

"I knew she should not have gone to the docks to see Mr. Brush off," Lady Endicott mourned.

"I don't see how you could have prevented her. She's very strong-willed. But she must write to Giles eventually. The invasion of France has begun and he will be in the midst of the fighting. This news cannot be welcome. Men going into battle are prone to think of their immortality, their heirs, and his chance has disappeared, at least for the present." Sir Fergus could not help but feel some sympathy for Giles, although he agreed Gwyneth was their first responsibility. He frowned and then made a decision.

"Selkirk wrote today and offered to come to London, but he also suggested Gwyneth might convalesce more happily in the country. And she should visit Selkirk Hall.''

Lady Endicott brightened at that idea. "That's the very thing. How clever of you to think of it."

"I don't like you worried, my dear, and this affair has taxed you beyond measure. Why not give Gwyneth Giles's letter, and if that does not rouse her suggest she go to Sussex where Selkirk is anxious to receive her.''

"I will attend to it right now." Lady Endicott was relieved, not that she wanted to surrender her responsibility for Gwyneth, but she was genuinely concerned about the girl and felt her own efforts had been woefully inadequate. "Thank you, Fergus. You are such a comfort," she said, rising and bestowing a hearty kiss on his cheek.

Sir Fergus, who had taken the morning off from his usual duties in order to write a strong paper about the German ineptitude in aiding Wellington, returned to his work but finally threw down his pen in disgust. He shared his wife's concern for Gwyneth, but being of a less romantic turn of mind, he wondered how this regrettable loss of the Selkirk heir would affect Giles. Would he want to dissolve the marriage and endure all the subsequent scandal? Peers must seek divorce in the House of Lords, and that conservative body did not look kindly on the dissolution of any marriage except in unusual circumstances. Well, he must allow the Fitzalen-Hills to sort out their own problems. For the first time he wished Gwyneth had never come to London.

\* \* \*

Lady Endicott bustled into the garden, determined to lose no time in suggesting to Gwyneth that she accept the earl's invitation to come to Sussex. She found her charge with her hands clasped listlessly in her lap, her eyes staring unseeing at the lush display of roses lining the wall.

"Well, my dear, here is a letter from your husband. Affairs are marching well in the war and he might be back home before too long," Lady Endicott said with an optimism she did not really feel. She placed the letter on Gwyneth's lap, but the girl made no effort to open it.

"And Sir Fergus has suggested you might benefit from a stay at Selkirk Hall. Lord Selkirk is eager to have you, and after all, it will be your home someday," Lady Endicott insisted with more confidence than she felt.

"What does it matter?" Gwyneth responded tepidly.

"It matters that you are not recovering as quickly as you should. I know it is a bitter disappointment, but you are young and can have other children."

"Not with Giles," Gwyneth said, a wry twist to her lips.

"Of course with Giles. He is your husband. Now, I will leave you to read your letter, and if you want to write a reply, Sir Fergus will frank it for you." And she hurried away, afraid to say more.

Gwyneth watched her depart, feeling a pang of regret that she was causing the dear woman such anxiety. Really, she must try to show some appreciation to the Endicotts for their care of her. But it seemed too much of an effort. She dreaded Giles's letter. He would mention the baby, and she did not want to think about that disaster nor what lay ahead. Reluctantly she opened the missive. The first few paragraphs were all about the war and the chances Wellington had to defeat the French general Soult and push on to Paris. Naturally that would occupy him before all else. But toward the end of the letter he wrote of their marriage and the coming baby with a thoughtfulness that surprised her.

> *I think of you so often, Gwyneth, and regret that our marriage was based on such despicable behavior on my part. But we cannot go back and must try to make this union meaningful. You must know how much I admire your courage and independence, your ability to face up to whatever life offers. I could have married a shrew or a ninny, and you are neither. We share feelings that go beyond passion and must build on those feelings. I will try my best, when and if I return to you and our child, to make an acceptable husband. I don't promise to succeed, but I owe you my loyalty and affection and I find, surprisingly, that does not appear an onerous burden. Coming from me, I suppose you find that amusing, but believe me, what I feel for you is no light fancy. Think of me with some kindness and take care of yourself.*
>
> > *Your obedient servant,*
> > *Giles*

For the first time since the loss of her baby, Gwyneth realized that Giles, too, would be deeply affected by the tragedy. Evidently he had spent a great deal of time thinking about their situation, regretting his actions, and wanting her to think more kindly of him. She did not know whether she could do so, but she refused to go on sitting in the Endicotts' garden behaving like a spineless widgeon. She would go to Selkirk Hall. Perhaps visiting Giles's home would prove a tonic or at least force her to make some hard decisions.

# *Chapter Sixteen*

*Selkirk Hall, Sussex, November 1813*

Gwyneth galloped into the stable yard, exhilarated from her brisk ride on her gray mare, Sukie, and jumped to the ground before the groom could assist her. Her daily ride across the Selkirk acreage was one of the many innovations the earl had instituted since her arrival in late August. Now the ground was hard, and today had a dusting of snow. A brisk wind blowing in from the Channel had freshened the air, promising a hard winter to come, but Gwyneth found it stimulating.

Striding up the massive marble stairs to the Queen Anne facade of the mansion that had been in Selkirk hands since Tudor days, she scarcely noticed the vast stretch of the house. But when she had first arrived, a virtual invalid, the ancestral pile of the Selkirks had seemed intimidating. The earl had soon disabused her of any such ideas. He had welcomed her with such warmth, such true understanding, that before long she recovered under his bracing yet sympathetic manner, and was now in what she considered almost rude health. With a modest pride he had introduced her to her new home, driven her about to meet the tenants, and given her riding lessons himself. If he worried about his son, struggling across the Pyrenees and into France with Wellington's hard-bitten army, he kept his concerns to himself and shared with his daughter-in-law his zest for the countryside he much preferred to London. Gwyneth found she preferred it, too.

Often she thought that if only Giles had inherited his father's character, their relationship might have been far different. Smiling as she crossed the imposing hall with its suits of armor and huge portraits of bygone Selkirks, she admitted that if he had been younger she would have fallen in love with the earl. She admired his tolerance, sensibility, and pride in his family, and she found him a comfortable and rewarding companion.

Just as she was about to mount the stairs toward her room, the butler Hoskins approached her.

"His Lordship would like to see you in the library, milady," he informed her in his stately manner. At first Gwyneth had been a bit awed by Hoskins, but she soon learned he possessed many of the qualities that made his master so likeable.

"Right away, Hoskins, before I change?"

"I think so, milady. He received several letters this morning. I believe there is one for you from Master Giles," he said, waiting stolidly for her to precede him.

"Oh, good. It's been some time since we heard from him," Gwyneth replied, and slapping her crop against her boots, she hurried into the library.

On her entrance the earl rose from behind a massive desk which was strewn with papers. "Good morning, my dear. You look in good spirits. I am sure your ride was partially responsible," he chuckled, remembering her first reluctant efforts at horsemanship.

"Yes, it's rather brisk, but you are right; it makes me feel quite wonderful." Gwyneth crossed to him and gave him a kiss on his cheek. "Hoskins was quite insistent I come. Not bad news, I hope." For months she had expected to hear daily that Giles had been wounded, even killed, but lately, with the war news so promising, she had relinquished these craven thoughts. The earl always displayed optimism and, although he disliked the war, saw its necessity and tried to persuade her that Giles was only doing his duty. Though he wished his bellicose son would resign from the Army and come home to assist him in running the estate, he never discussed it, but he worried that his heir was in such danger.

"No, on the contrary. It looks as if we have Napoleon on the run this time. He returned from that disastrous campaign in Russia to find his empire crumbling, and he will now take the field himself and try to redeem affairs, but I doubt if he will be successful. The French are as weary as we are of war, and Wellington will be in Paris before spring, I am certain."

"I hope so," Gwyneth agreed, throwing her crop and hat on a nearby table and settling into a chair opposite the earl's desk. Only then did he resume his seat. His old-fashioned manners delighted her, for he was most punctilious in treating her as the countess she would one day be.

"But the news is from America. Detroit has been

relieved, and I am sure your sister is even now welcoming her husband home safely."

"What a relief. I know I should want the English to prevail in Canada, but I have been worried about Delia."

"And rightly so. Also you will be relieved to hear that Montreal was stoutly defended by that French colonel, so your father, too, is safe for the moment. It means that the Americans have prevailed on the Lakes but their various invasions of Canada have not succeeded. I never thought they would, but the American War has been a muddle, with neither side gaining much." Like his son, the earl did not approve of the war against England's former colonies, but he did not like the idea of Canada being annexed either, a view Gwyneth also shared.

"And here is a letter from Giles. I heard from him, too, and it seems that Wellington is settled over the Pyrenees, beneath Bayonne, and is hoping to occupy Bordeaux." He handed Gwyneth the letter. "Of course, he knows about the baby. I am sure he is as disappointed as we all were, but when he sees how fighting fit you are, he will be pleased."

"I give you a great deal of credit for that, sir. I was a miserable, complaining, weak female when I arrived on your doorstep."

"Nonsense. You had every reason to feel poorly, but now you are in fine spirits and health. Which leads me to my plan. Giles seems to have suffered what he calls a trifling wound in his shoulder during the fight against Soult's forces for Nivelle. Our army has gone into winter quarters, and I thought it might be safe for us to travel to France. Many wives of English officers are joining their husbands now that the end is in sight. Of course, I would escort you. Like to see the boy myself," he added a bit wistfully.

Startled, Gwyneth did not know quite how to respond. Would Giles welcome her appearing on the scene? His letters had been increasingly affectionate, but a meeting now after all these months?

"I'm not sure that would be a good idea. I have heard him say that women have no place near the battlefield. He sneered at those officers whose wives accompanied them to the Peninsula."

"Ridiculous. That was before he was married himself to such an intrepid girl. If we leave in the next week or so, we might be there for Christmas," he urged.

Gwyneth could see he was most anxious to go and she had not the heart to disillusion him. Giles could be enjoying this respite from his tenuous marriage, involved in military affairs, and have no time for a troublesome wife, no matter how he might welcome his father. She knew the two had exchanged some angry words about the need for Giles to marry, and she sensed that in this situation the earl's loyalties would be strongly tested. He liked her and, although disappointed about the loss of the baby, thought there was every need for the young couple to embark on a family as soon as possible. Although she understood his craving for an heir, she was not convinced that she and Giles were ready for what that entailed.

"But you read your letter, my dear. Perhaps Giles has suggested you come. I suspect he is missing you dreadfully," the earl suggested, determined to put the best face possible on this forced union.

"Yes, sir, I will do that, and we will discuss it at luncheon," Gwyneth agreed, not willing to commit herself. She smiled a bit tremulously at the earl and left the room.

The earl sank back into his seat and restrained an impulse to wipe his brow. That had been sticky. He had no illusions about the relationship between his son and Gwyneth. Despite her situation she had been a most reluctant bride. Giles, wounded, even if not seriously, would be querulous and angry, not in the best mood to renew his marriage. But little could be accomplished in mending their affairs while Gwyneth was in England and Giles in France. The longer they were separated the more difficult it would be. The earl believed somewhat ingenuously the young people could use a little experienced interference in sorting out their problems. After all they were both attractive, vital, and, he suspected, passionate. That is how they had arrived at the necessity for the marriage to begin with. Gwyneth was a sensible girl. She would see that this marriage must be settled. About Giles he was not so sure. His son disliked being pushed or persuaded against his own desires. He had always been willful and reckless. Would he be rash enough to demand a divorce with all the scandal and disgrace that would bring? No, the earl was determined he would not allow that to happen, even if he had to barricade them in a bedroom and tell them to get on with it.

Laughing a bit at his coarseness, he dismissed his wish to knock their heads together and reminded himself he was behaving atrociously. He excused himself by his fervent desire to be a grandfather and insure the continuance of the estate. Not an ignoble cause, he thought, having much pride in the Selkirk name and honor. Well, it would all sort itself out, and if he had to give affairs a little nudge, he could not be faulted for his actions, he reassured himself. Gwyneth would see it his way with a little convincing. He had come to both admire and love his daughter-in-law and would be appalled to think he might be causing her unhappiness.

Gwyneth delayed opening Giles's letter until she had a bath and changed into a yellow sarcenet morning gown, suitable for luncheon. The house suddenly seemed unusually cold, and she was glad of the fire and the warm Norwich shawl she wrapped about her shoulders. She rather dreaded learning what Giles had to say. He had been very sympathetic and comforting about the loss of the baby with no cynical remarks about the futility of their marriage. She knew he was disappointed, a feeling she shared, for even though she had recovered physically from the miscarriage, her emotions were still in turmoil when she thought about the accident. She had not mentioned James Brush to Giles. He would not look kindly on her efforts to dispatch her former beau to safety. After all he was an enemy officer and no matter how much Giles disapproved of the war in Canada, he would be abetting treason if he viewed her action with any acquiescence. She had kept James Brush a secret, not revealing the matter to the earl. He believed she had been jostled and fallen on the cobblestones while shopping, and the Endicotts had not disabused him. She lived with the guilt of deceiving Giles's father even more than deluding her husband.

Giles's letter was quite cheerful, and he only casually mentioned his wound. He was more concerned with the culmination of the battle against Napoleon and the progress of the war abroad. Wellington had refused to serve in America now that the European struggle appeared to be ending, and Giles supported his commander. Most of the letter concerned political and military gossip, and he mentioned that several officers had brought out their wives to comfort them in winter quarters. Was that a hint that she would be welcome, too? His true feelings remained a mystery to her.

However, she had the earl to consider. He wanted to go, and she owed him a great deal, beside having a true affection for her father-in-law. If she went, that would be a tacit admission she wanted the marriage to continue. Giles was her husband, and whatever the reason for their marriage, she doubted it could be ended easily. The Endicotts and the earl accepted it as a *fait accompli*, taken for granted whatever the participants felt. It had been almost five months since Giles had left. War seemed to have softened his anger and his cynicism, but when she faced him he might revert to his former sarcastic, wounding manner. Then what would she do? Resign herself to becoming a complaisant wife, enduring his infidelities, his indifference, his casual use of her body? She could not bear that.

Gwyneth sighed, thinking of those faraway days in Detroit, and her first impressions of Giles. He had a poor opinion of women then, whatever the reason, and marriage had not softened his views, she was convinced. She wanted to stay safely at Selkirk Hall, where war and men's delinquencies did not intrude, but that was a cowardly solution. Her marriage was a fact, and she must face it without timorous shrinkings and foolish vanities. Her girlhood was over, and there was no going back to those carefree days in Detroit and Montreal, although they, too, were not without their problems. Gwyneth was never one to shrink from hard choices, and she must not retreat now.

Should she confide her misgivings to the earl? He knew the reason for this forced marriage, even if he was inclined to discount it, hoping for a happy resolution. For the first time in many weeks she thought of James Brush and wondered if she would have been any better off with him. No, she did not love him. His arrival in London had proved that to her. But neither did she love Giles. She felt a certain awe of him, not a good basis for harmonious relations between husband and wife, and she neither approved of, nor understood him, which were barriers to any real intimacy. But she knew Giles would never countenance a scandal, and the earl would be deeply disturbed by any suggestion that the marriage should be dissolved.

Lady Endicott, that wise and compassionate woman, had suggested that most *ton* marriages were not based on love but on property, the need for an heir, and societal stability. But hers was not a *ton* marriage. She had little to offer—no position, no wealth, and no status. Gwyneth discounted her assets: beauty, spirit, and a certain rare courage.

Her father had been unaccountably pleased that she was now a lady, which rather disgusted her, but she should not fault him for craving acceptance and revealing a certain snobbery. His own reputation was most important to him, and Gwyneth had enhanced it by marrying the son of an earl. Really, life held so many anomalies.

The clock on the mantelpiece struck noon, startling Gwyneth out of her musings. Though she had made no decision, she rose and readied herself for lun-

cheon. She would put her doubts to the earl and
allow him to decide, a cowardly retreat, she thought,
but necessary.

"Well, my dear, did Giles have any vital news about
the war?" he greeted her when she came into the
dining room. Looking at the wide mahogany table
gleaming with polish, the Georgian silver, and the
impassive face of Hoskins ready to serve, she remembered how this room had first impressed her. She
had come to accept the grandeur of Selkirk Hall
because its master was such a modest man, not arrogant in his possessions or privilege, but genuinely
concerned for his responsibilities, of which she felt
she had become the paramount one.

"No, sir. He seems to feel Wellington has Napoleon
on the run, gives his chief all the credit, and writes
scathingly of the Germans and Blücher," she
reported.

"Of course that would be his attitude, but Blücher
has done a good job. I doubt if we could have routed
Napoleon without him in Leipzig," the earl insisted
with his usual objectivity and fairness. "Does he mention his wound or his wish for you to come out?" the
earl continued, determined to have affairs settled.

"No," Gwyneth said baldly. "I'm sure he feels
women have no place on the battlefield."

"Nonsense. You would not be in a battlefield but
snug in a Bordeaux billet," the earl said, dismissing
her objections.

Toying with her mutton chop, Gwyneth decided
she could equivocate no longer. "To be honest, sir,
you know that Giles only married me because I was

pregnant and because you and Sir Fergus pressured him. I am sure he would have preferred another wife. I doubt if his feelings have changed."

The earl paid her the respect her objections deserved. "Quite true. Giles has never liked being coerced, but he is honest enough to realize that he had a responsibility for the baby. You did not get pregnant by yourself," he suggested with a wicked little chuckle.

"Men in his position rarely marry their mistresses."

"You were not his mistress. He must have felt deeply attracted to have pursued you in London after that one encounter aboard ship. He could have dismissed the whole business."

"That's very frank talk, sir, but I don't think it really answers, and I admit that my own actions do not hold up under scrutiny. I behaved wantonly and had to pay the price."

"You are much too hard on yourself, Gwyneth, and I know my son. His reputation with women is not an admirable one and he took advantage of you. But all that is past. You must deal with events as they exist, and that means you must accept this marriage and make the best of it. I am not saying it will be easy or even enjoyable, but many couples begin with little affection and end up coming to care for one another."

While Gwyneth could not deny the earl's argument, she wondered if Giles would be so accommodating.

"You mean a great deal to me, sir. Your acceptance and care of me have gone well beyond anything I expected or deserved. I am very fond of you and would do almost anything to please you," Gwyneth replied gently.

The earl took out a wide linen handkerchief and

blew his nose, embarrassed and touched by Gwyneth's words.

"Thank you, my dear. I am fortunate in my daughter," he said gruffly. "So you will heed my pleas to go to France?"

Gwyneth laughed. "That's emotional blackmail, but I cannot refuse."

So despite her misgivings the preparations were made. The earl was an efficient organizer, and within the week they had traveled to London, the first leg of their journey.

They were already at sea when Giles received the earl's letter telling of their decision. His first reaction was one of anger. He had been enjoying the fighting until one of Soult's cavalryman had put a ball through his shoulder. His convalescence was impeded by the cold and damp, his rather dim quarters, and the knowledge that he would be out of action in the coming weeks. He was in a filthy temper, and the arrival of an irate father and an unwanted wife did not improve his humor.

Bored and disgusted by his wound, which was troubling him more than he wanted to admit, he had begun a heavy flirtation with an obliging Frenchwoman whose husband was serving in the army conveniently posted near Paris. So far the association had not advanced to a liaison, but Giles had had every intention of sealing affairs with the lady. Now he realized that he must postpone the dalliance. Despite his libertine ways and unwillingness to follow his father's strictures, he had a healthy respect for the earl, who did not look kindly on Giles's romantic escapades.

While Gwyneth was miles away, he had written affectionate letters, but now he was regretting his effusions.

If his father frowned on his amorous inclinations
outside the bonds of matrimony, Gwyneth would be
even more obdurate. She would not play the role of
a complaisant wife. Then, too, he must bestir himself
to find some suitable rooms for them all. He could
hardly go on living apart from them, although it
would be dashed inconvenient to be at their beck
and call. Five months' absence from Gwyneth had
not induced any change in his habits. He truly was
disappointed that she had lost the baby, but he had
returned to his bachelor ways, soothing his never-
active conscience with the knowledge that she would
never know about his pursuit of other women. Somehow he felt a bit ashamed of his nonchalant attitude
but was too arrogant and too lazy to change. The
Selkirks could expect a rather tepid welcome from
Giles when they finally arrived.

# *Chapter Seventeen*

*Bordeaux, December 1813*

Much of Gwyneth's first view of Bordeaux was masked by fog and rain. Wellington and his officers had been complaining for a month about the weather and the sodden, muddy ground which made winter campaigning impossible. From the ship's rail Gwyneth could see little, but the earl, who had visited the wine producing city as a young man, recognized certain landmarks, particularly the spire of the Cathedral of St. Andre and the long stretch of quays bounded by warehouses, where French ships had carried wine around the world before the hostilities. Gwyneth was in no hurry to embark, despite her eagerness to reach land. The crossing had been rough but somehow she preferred the ship to what awaited her in Bordeaux. However, the earl did not share her reluctance and bustled about seeing that his servant and Gwyneth's maid, both uneasy travelers, carried out his orders.

At last they walked down the gangplank to the dock. A crowd of officers and men thronged the quay, anticipating travelers and message from home, so that at first Gwyneth did not see Giles, so thick was the press of uniforms.

He appeared by their side suddenly, hailing his father with that casual air she had come to know, as if he were greeting them in some London drawing room.

"Good trip, Father?" he asked, then turning to Gwyneth, "I must say you look as if the voyage agreed with you, but perhaps you were spared the storms we encountered crossing the Atlantic together."

Gwyneth decided to ignore his sardonic reference to the past and only nodded, saying, "Yes, I found the trip most bracing. I seem to have recovered from those foolish fears. You look quite well yourself, Giles, despite your wound."

In fact she thought he appeared drawn, weather-beaten, and thinner, but it would never do to say so. He made no move to embrace her. Gwyneth, relieved, understood it was not the thing to display any emotion publicly, even if he felt any, and she suspected his chief mood was one of annoyance.

The earl, hoping to bridge any slight embarrassment, said heartily, "Surprised to see us. You did receive my letter?" he queried, a bit doubtfully. "But, of course, otherwise you would not be here to meet us. Have you been able to find us a place to stay?"

"Of course, the practical French are always willing to entertain an English milord with all his guineas," Giles replied carelessly.

"Your father was anxious to assure himself of your

well-being, but I knew you would have survived in
fine fashion," she said, as if excusing their arrival.
"And I thought it might make a great adventure."

"Yes, I remember, you are a great girl for adventure," Giles agreed in a tone Gwyneth was not sure
she liked. But before they could begin one of their
brangles, the carriage had drawn up, their cases were
loaded up, and Giles assisted her into the vehicle,
climbing in after his father.

"Bordeaux is a rather staid town, and of course,
the defeated French citizens are slow to recover from
years at war," he said in answer to a question by his
father.

Gwyneth was silent, watching the carriage negotiate
the crowded lanes leading from the docks into the
narrow streets beyond, and wondering what had happened to the entertaining and rather affectionate
man of the days after their wedding. Obviously their
arrival did not please him, and she wondered if he
had embarked on some affair. Frenchwomen com-
bined an inordinate interest in amour with a practical
eye for the main chance. And with Napoleon on his
last legs, it behooved the madames and mademoi-
selles to look after themselves.

Her certainty of Giles situation vis-à-vis these charm-
ers was enhanced when she heard him tell his father
that the French gave no trouble, as they were relieved
the war was drawing to a close and grateful to Wellington for disciplining his troops. Their gratitude could
easily take more tangible form, Gwyneth thought, like
casting a possessive eye on a well-born wealthy English
officer. But determined to show no concern over
Giles's lukewarm reception of them, she chatted
brightly, quizzing him about Wellington, whom she
admitted she admired extravagantly.

"Fortunate Wellington," was his only riposte. "Did you know he has finally been awarded a field marshal's baton? Long past time."

The earl launched into questions about the skirmish in which Giles had received his wound and the awkward moment passed as Gwyneth kept silent. Giles had booked them into a hotel on the Place de la Comédie, where several other English officers had established their families. In the confusion of checking into the hotel and inspecting their rooms, a rather lavish suite, Gwyneth said little beyond enquiring about arrangements. She was now even more convinced that this trip was a mistake, but would do nothing to exacerbate matters, leaving the explanations to the earl. She was not especially surprised at Giles's reaction, although she had hoped for a different reception. But now that they had arrived she must make the best of it although she had a difficult time restraining her own irritation.

However, over a glass of wine Giles seemed to realize he was behaving badly and made some effort to improve.

"The next battle will be for Toulouse. The French have lost their enthusiasm for the war and Napoleon's crack troops were decimated in Russia. We will beat him yet," he informed them confidently.

"I would like to see Paris," Gwyneth offered tentatively.

"It's far more entertaining than Bordeaux." Giles suddenly changed his tactics and smiled at her.

He left them soon after, promising to return for dinner. The earl, sensing Gwyneth's discomfort, hastened to reassure her.

"He really is glad to see us. Don't be put off by his

manner, my dear. It will all work out for the best," he promised with more certainty than he felt.

Gwyneth, who had suffered in the past from Giles's arrogance and his determination to go his own way, was not completely convinced. Her own feelings of annoyance and confusion, she discounted. If this marriage was to last, Giles would have to change drastically, and so would she. At this moment she was not inclined to suffer from his indifference and sarcasm. He had an exalted idea of his own importance and would brook no interference in his life. His reception of her had proved that. Well, perhaps intimacy would improve the situation, but she had no intention of renewing their marital relations unless he showed some sign of affection. It was too humiliating.

That evening Giles appeared for dinner with Ned Waterford, who served as a cheerful buffer against any friction. Gwyneth had liked Ned when she had met him briefly at the wedding and was grateful for his tactful efforts to smooth over any difficulties.

"How nice it is to see you again, Lady Fitzalen-Hill," he greeted her, his open face evidence of his sincerity. She had no idea what Giles had told him about their marriage, but she acquitted him of any but the best intentions.

"Please call me Gwyneth. I will never become accustomed to such formality."

"Thank you," he responded and launched into an amusing description of his conversational struggle with his landlady.

"Ned's French is horrible, but he charms all the ladies," Giles insisted.

"I'm afraid my own French, learned in Canada,

leaves much to be desired," Gwyneth admitted, turning to Ned and giving him an encouraging smile.

"I am sure it is perfect, Gwyneth. The French always appreciate a lovely lady," Ned countered.

"Stop flirting with my wife, Ned," Giles said, only partly in jest.

"Don't be selfish, Giles. You must get used to your fellow officers admiring your wife," Ned answered, not at all intimidated.

The evening passed more easily than Gwyneth had expected, due in no small part to Ned's pleasant company. But she dreaded what lay ahead. After a suitable time she left the gentlemen to their wine and retired to the bedroom, wondering what approach Giles would adopt when they were finally alone. Her maid, was brushing her hair when he finally appeared.

"That will be all tonight, Mary," Gwyneth said, dismissing her maid casually and turning to face her husband.

Giles dropped his sword on a nearby table and unbuttoned his tunic. "I let my batman have the night off. He seems to be a gay dog with several ladies on a string," he confided, slipping into his dressing gown. If he appeared unsure of his next move, he showed no signs of it.

"You're annoyed that your father insisted on this trip, aren't you?" Gwyneth asked, determined to discover his true feelings.

"What I admire about you, Gwyneth, is your honesty. No gilding the lily," Giles said ironically.

"Well, I think we must talk about this marriage. You were forced into it because of the baby, and that reason no longer exists. There is no use in pretending ours was a love match," Gwyneth replied, a little nettled.

"But we are married and you are here, so I would be a fool not to take advantage of the situation."

Gwyneth looked at the big fourposter bed and winced. "I don't want to be bedded as a convenience," she protested.

"Whatever you are, Gwyneth, you are not a convenience. And as I remember, you were not averse to the pleasures of the bed."

"Really, Giles, I had no idea you could be so crude," she said, her temper rising and a deep blush staining her cheeks.

"Look here, Gwyneth, I won't force you to resume relations if the idea is repugnant to you. We would probably start another baby and I assume that would not be to your taste."

Gwyneth, provoked by his frankness, did not quite know what to say. His off-hand acceptance of their relationship repelled her.

After a short silence, Giles said tentatively, "It's true, Gwyneth, I was not too pleased on learning that you and father were coming out here. Battlefields are no place for civilians, and don't be deceived, the struggle against Napoleon is far from finished. Bordeaux may be safe for the moment, but there are bands of French soldiers, little better than guerrillas, wandering about the outskirts of the town. And I am afraid my temper is not the best, idling around here with this trifling wound. I'm not in the mood to entertain you."

"I quite understand, Giles. I have said this trip was your father's idea." Gwyneth realized she sounded churlish and that was not her intention, for his careful explanation had made sense. If he felt her presence curtailed his activities, she could hardly blame him. But they must come to an understanding. Somehow

she must persuade him that they could not resume
their marital relationship until they felt more than
pure sexual desire.

"I realize you are my husband and have certain
rights, but under the circumstances I find it difficult
to give in to you," she said solemnly, trying to appear
adult.

For some reason Giles found her objections
endearing rather than annoying. She looked like a
little girl caught in some trifling misdemeanor. He
was prepared to make a concession.

"Come, Gwyneth, don't look so apprehensive. I
have some sensitivity, although you may doubt it from
my past actions. Let us agree to postpone what you
call so tactfully our marital relations until you are
more in charity with me, although I must admit it
will try my temper." He smiled encouragingly at her.

"Thank you, Giles," she said and without another
word climbed into the vast bed, doused her candle,
and settled herself to sleep, meaning to behave sensibly even if her heart was pounding. Giles followed
suit, and perhaps because it had been a long tiring
day, both physically and emotionally, they both went
to sleep.

The next morning when they joined the earl for
breakfast, he looked at them with some compunction.
He had wondered if he had precipitated matters best
left alone. Giles could be awkward when he thought
his father, or anyone else, was directing his life. But
surely his son was convinced that as a married man
he could not behave with the heedless abandon he
had done as a bachelor. The earl wanted this marriage
to succeed and he would do his best to see that it

did. He wanted to hold an heir in his arms before he died.

"We will not interfere with your duties, my boy. I will escort Gwyneth around town if you must report for some pressing tasks."

"I have to see the doctor about this wretched shoulder. I hope he will sign me off, and then I will ride to headquarters and see what Wellington wants of me," Giles admitted.

Evidently the doctor decided that Giles was fit enough to return to duty because for the next few days they saw little of him. He rode to headquarters and remained several days. When he returned, he seemed in a far more equanimous mood, almost light-hearted. He confessed it looked as if there would soon be a battle to take Toulouse and he would be part of it. The weather was not cooperating and little could be done until early spring, but there was little doubt that Napoleon's days were numbered.

"We will be in Paris by spring, I am convinced," he informed the earl and Gwyneth at dinner on the day of his return.

"And how have you been entertaining Gwyneth, Father?" he asked.

"We have done all the sights, including the wine cellars. I managed to buy some good vintages. Fortunately the war has prevented the merchants from sending their best bottles abroad."

"And did you like that, Gwyneth?" Giles asked, amused.

"Bordeaux is a charming town with its lovely squares and neat houses, and yes, I did enjoy our expeditions. Improved my French, too," she admitted, pleased to see Giles coming to some acceptance of her presence.

"Well, we will have to see what I can do to enliven your stay. There is quite a popular performance on now at the Grand Theatre. We will go this evening," he offered. "And you must meet some of the other wives wintering here."

Realizing that he was trying to make the best of matters, Gwyneth obliged with cheerful assent. But she was still troubled about their future and found her own feelings in turmoil. She could not deny that Giles could charm her even when she distrusted him. It was one thing for him to dally with other women when she was miles away, but she would not like to hear of his romantic adventures when she was in residence. Rather mean-spirited of her, she admitted, when she was unwilling to allow him his husbandly priviledges. But experience had taught her not to let down her guard with Giles. And he seemed to sense her doubts, for during the next few days he went out of his way to appear a devoted husband.

On Christmas morning he gave her an expensive mantilla, purchased in Spain on his arrival, showing that he had not forgotten her once removed from London. On the earl's advice she gave him a miniature of herself by Andrew Robertson, who had won a reputation by painting members of the royal family. Giles appeared genuinely touched by the gesture, and the holiday passed off in great style, culminating with a ball patronized by most of the English community at the Hôtel de Ville.

Gwyneth wore an elegant cherry silk gown and the necklace Giles had purchased from Rundell's, remembering with a renewal of guilt her encounter with James Brush. As she fastened the necklace, she wondered where James was and was surprised to realize how little he mattered now. Whatever his future, it did not concern her. How the war had changed her fortunes. If she had remained in a peaceful Detroit, she would not have met Giles, and she was still uncertain how much that added to her happiness. She only knew that life with James and what he could have offered would not have satisfied her. Did that make her an ambitious parvenu? No, it was his insidious charm that caused such heated desire. And she doubted she was the wife he would have chosen if the war had not alerted his situation. She was coming to regret her insistence on their chaste existence and feeling a certain frustration at the denial of her emotional and physical needs.

Giles, however, showed no signs of an equal frustration, which might mean he was finding satisfaction elsewhere. At the ball that Christmas night she noticed that he paid a great deal of attention to a fetching matron, Mrs. Godfrey Thorndyke, a luscious brunette who did not seem very bound by her own marriage vows. Her husband, an elderly colonel of an hussar regiment, was not in evidence. And Amelia Thorndyke did not appear to miss him.

Gwyneth, dancing with the obliging Ned Waterford, finally could not restrain her curiosity.

"Tell me, Ned, has Mrs. Thorndyke been out here long?"

"Yes, quite a while. She traveled with the army in the Peninsula. She is a good campaigner," Ned explained, a bit worried. There had been some gossip about Giles and the lovely Amelia, and Ned wondered if the rumors had reached Gwyneth. He was quite attached to Gwyneth in a brotherly way and thought Giles was a fool not to appreciate his wife.

"And where is her husband?" Gwyneth asked a bit tartly.

"At headquarters, I believe. But she prefers the more sophisticated pleasures of Bordeaux. Have you met her?"

"Briefly. She didn't seem interested in pursuing the acquaintance. I think she prefers men," Gwyneth said sharply, and then grimaced. "I do sound a veritable cat."

"You mustn't misunderstand, Gwyneth. Mrs. Thorndyke is a favorite with most of the officers. Giles is only doing the polite," he assured her anxiously.

"Poor Ned. I am a shrew to quiz you so," Gwyneth laughed, passing off the matter, but she did not forget. Was she behaving like the dog in the manger, denying Giles her comfort and complaining if he found it elsewhere? The idea of Giles wooing Mrs. Thorndyke raised her hackles. But she was hardly in a position to object.

Later that evening as they were preparing to retire, Giles, who appeared remarkably cheerful, finally noticed that Gwyneth seemed distrait.

"Did you not enjoy the ball?" he asked. "You were a great success with my fellow officers. They think I am a lucky chap."

"I think they are all so eager for a woman's company that even a Colonial like myself is a treat. But, of course, they have the fillup of Mrs. Thorndyke," Gwyneth blurted out waspishly, then felt discomforted at showing her annoyance.

"Jealous?" Giles mocked, appearing amused by her remarks.

"Of course not," Gwyneth insisted, feeling a fool. Giles always managed to put her in the wrong. He irritated her even further by sidling into bed and picking up a book, as if her presence represented no temptation.

"I wonder if I would have enjoyed campaigning. Several of the officers told me their wives thought it a wonderful experience and were a great comfort to them."

"I thought you had quite enough of war in Canada," Giles said, wondering what maggot she had in her head. If she were worried about Amelia Thorndyke's effect on him, that was a promising sign. He turned to her and put an arm around her shoulders.

"I need comforting, too, Gwyneth," he said with surprising earnestness.

"Do you, Giles? Well, perhaps I have been silly about our situation. After all, we are married," Gwyneth agreed weakly, his touch stimulating her.

"Then let us become more married," Giles suggested, pinching out his candle and turning to take her in his arms. She made no protest.

# Chapter Eighteen

The next morning Gwyneth realize that Giles felt most of their problems were solved, and he wore a smug expression which raised her hackles. If she herself felt a relaxation of tensions, she would not admit that their marriage was set on a practical course. Giles had a tendency to believe that if all went well in bed, then men and women had little to concern themselves. Her own reaction was quite different. She blamed herself for submitting so easily, but she realized she had little defense against his persuasive passion. She could only hope that this new intimacy would promote a meeting of the minds as well as of the bodies, but she had doubts. Still, Giles's temper was much improved, and he ate his breakfast with gusto.

Giles's father noticed his son's demeanor and congratulated himself on the decision to bring Gwyneth to Bordeaux. That Gwyneth was not as complacent as Giles about their renewed relationship was not immediately apparent to the earl.

"And what are your plans for the day?" he asked.

"Since I understand that Gwyneth has become an accomplished equestrian, I thought we might ride out of town. I need the exercise, and it might be entertaining," Giles suggested. He had another motive, wanting to get his wife alone.

"Would you enjoy a hard gallop, Gwyneth?" he asked.

"Just the tonic. The day promises to be fine if a bit chilly, but a ride will warm me up," she agreed.

Giles went off to see about suitable mounts, leaving the earl and Gwyneth alone. Too tactful to mention the changed relationship between the embattled pair, the earl only suggested diplomatically that Giles seemed well-recovered from his wound.

"Yes, he says he is ready for the next fight, but no move will be made until at least February," Gwyneth reported.

"Well, the waiting is tiresome, but at least the end of this wretched war is in sight," the earl agreed. Then claiming he was meeting a friend, he took his leave.

Gwyneth was left alone, prey to fears she had not considered before. Another battle meant danger to Giles, and she found she feared the outcome. He had been fortunate till now in escaping any but the most trifling wound, but his luck might be running out. She discovered that the thought of Giles's death was horrifying. Despite all that had happened between them, she found she cared a great deal about his safety and their future together. Was propinquity upsetting all her earlier ideas about her husband? Was she falling in love with him, and thus exposing herself to tragedy? Not for the first time she yearned for her home and familiar surroundings, friends who would counsel and comfort her. It seemed years since she had sat in the Maitlands' drawing room gaily recounting her Detroit adventures, warmed by their interest and concern. She even missed her father's care of her. Much as she admired and loved the earl, he could not replace Walter Winwood. Suddenly she felt bereft.

But once on the sprightly mare Giles had found for her and cantering out of Bordeaux, her spirits revived and she scolded herself for being so weak-minded. And once beyond the crumbling fortifications and into the countryside touched with a light frost, she decided her troubles were mostly imaginary. All she needed was some exercise. Giles watched approvingly as they cantered some miles without a word.

Finally, he reined in his horse, signaling Gwyneth to do likewise. They slowed to a gentle walk.

"You are a natural rider, Gwyneth. So many women slouch like a sack of potatoes in the saddle. I should have suspected you would be different in this as in so many other matters," he complimented her, bringing a pleased smile to her face.

"Your father is a good teacher."

"He has a great amount of patience, a quality I lack, I am afraid."

Gwyneth did not disagree. But she did not want to discuss Giles's faults when this ride had put her in charity with him. She spurred her mare into a fast canter and Giles perforce had to follow.

Watching her straight back, he smiled, knowing she wanted to avoid any discussion of what had happened last night. The miles lengthened and they were alone in the barren fields, rimed and fallow, scarred by years of war and deprivation. France's farmers had suffered mightily from the long war, her men conscripted into the army, leaving the fields untilled. No wonder the general populace wanted an end to the hostilities. Pride in Napoleon's conquests had long ago diminished under the realization that the war was robbing the country of its resources. Giles thought of his own acres, peaceful in the Sussex winter, and wondered how he would feel if they were in danger. Shaking off these morbid thoughts, he galloped up to Gwyneth, who was fast outdistancing him.

"We had better turn back. I have heard that there are bands of scavengers roaming quite near to Bordeaux, and you would make a lovely prize for some brigand," he warned, drawing close to her.

Nodding, she reined in her horse. "It's hard to believe under this peaceful sky that we are at war, but I agree we must take care."

But they were too late. They had paused near a heavy copse of trees, and as they turned their horses, a group of fierce ragged men burst from the sheltering grove, halloing and frightening Giles's horse, who reared frantically at the noise.

Giles, grasping the danger, called to Gwyneth, "Quick, gallop off and I will hold them." He drew his pistol and fired at the leader, a grimy dark-visaged peasant, who fell from his horse but was quickly avenged by one of his companions, who fired in turn at Giles and hit his mount. Staggering to his feet from the fallen animal, Giles quickly reloaded his pistol as the men converged on him.

Gwyneth, realizing the danger, reined in her horse, ignoring Giles's pleas to run away, and jumped to the ground, just as Giles fell wounded from a ball in his shoulder, causing him to drop his weapon. She picked it up and stood over his body, a sickening knowledge of their probable fate almost overcoming her. Seeing a resolute lady aiming a pistol at them, the brigands stopped for a moment, one of them smiling evilly.

"*Voici une jolie femme et très farouche. Nous voulons sentir la plaisir à cette une,*" he growled, leering evilly.

Gwyneth understood what they intended, and realizing that Giles could not help her, she aimed the pistol, prepared to make a fight of it. But before she could get off a shot at the advancing menace, another man rode from the trees, screaming at the brigands. Gwyneth had a vague impression he was their leader, for he wore an officer's uniform.

"*Canailles!*" he cried to the men, who stopped and sullenly regarded him.

"*Madame,* Comte Roger de Fancher, *à vôtre service,*" he said, riding up to her as she stood, still holding the pistol, but uncertain what to expect.

"These men attacked us," she protested, determined not to be cowed.

"Regrettable, but you are safe now," the comte, a slight dark man with a dandified air, assured her. "Please do not let off your weapon. You might do some harm." He growled a command.

"My husband is hurt," she informed him, not glancing at Giles, recumbent and silent. She did not take her eyes off the so-called comte.

"I regret it exceedingly. I'm afraid my men are a little impetuous. But I will escort you back to Bordeaux. I might say you were a trifle unwise to ride so far from the protection of your army. These men are scavengers, *hélas,* and any innocent is their prey. But I would not want such a gallant lady to suffer," he insisted, oozing a Gallic charm that did not impress

Gwyneth. If he meant to help her all well and good, but she did not trust him or his command of these violent brigands.

She misjudged the comte. He was all gallantry, insisting on raising Giles, who appeared unconscious, blood streaming down his tunic.

"I think we must tie him onto a horse. You will perhaps ride behind me, since his own mount is unavailable," the comte suggested, issuing orders to his ill-tempered troop. Balked of their victims, they muttered in a mutinous fashion but evidently both feared and respected the comte.

Gwyneth, still holding the bridle of her mare with one hand and the pistol with the other, watched warily as the exchange was made. Then, gingerly, she accepted the comte's polite hand and leaped into the saddle of his horse, which he mounted behind her. Uttering a command, the comte directed the muttering cavalcade to make off toward the town walls. Gwyneth still held the pistol, which appeared to amuse her rescuer, but she was adamant. It represented her only safety.

The journey back was a slow one, and at any moment Gwyneth feared the comte would lose control of his restive men, although he displayed no such doubt. Finally, as the walls of Bordeaux appeared in the distance, he dismissed them curtly. They hesitated, but then seeing the comte would brook no disobedience, rode off, leaving her alone with her rescuer, who was leading Giles's horse and talking gaily at the same time.

"Frenchmen do not make war on lovely ladies," he promised, seeing she was still not convinced of his motives.

"Our troops occupy Bordeaux. You cannot escort

me into town. You will be taken and imprisoned,"
she warned, feeling she must make some recompense
for his good offices.

"Perhaps, but that will not be such a hardship.
At least I will get a good meal. And then I will be
exchanged, to fight again," he insisted, with no less-
ening of his spirits.

Startled by this bald acceptance, Gwyneth made no
demur. As they neared the walls, a troop of English
soldiers led by an officer galloped up to meet them.
Confused at the sight of a wounded major, an obvious
Frenchman, and a woman, they halted, gazing at the
trio in some bemusement.

But the comte was equal to the business and
explained in faultless English that he had rescued
Madame and her husband from the clutches of some
*canailles,* but not, unfortunately before the brigands
had wounded the officer. The lieutenant in charge
of the troop, little more than a boy, stood on his
dignity, much to Gwyneth's chagrin.

"You are my prisoner, sir."

"Absolutely. I am at your service as soon as we
deliver these poor people to their quarters, and you
must call a doctor," the comte insisted, taking charge
in an undeniable manner.

And so it developed that the comte rode right into
Bordeaux, not the least discomposed, still leading
Giles on her mare, with Gwyneth perched cautiously
in front of him and the troop of his enemies guarding
them. Once at their hotel, Gwyneth, helped down by
her savior, anxiously watched as some of the men
carried Giles indoors. Then, turning to the comte,
she thanked him and promised to see that he suffered
no undue hardship from his gallantry.

"I will speak to the commanding colonel and see

that you receive every consideration, sir," she said, feeling some compunction for the comte's plight after his kindness. He could so easily have abandoned her to the mercy of his men.

"Not to worry, madame. All will be well," he said blithely and rode off with his escort.

Surprisingly Giles was a docile patient and Gwyneth a devoted nurse. The wound was more severe than his earlier one, which had been aggravated by the brigand's bullet. For a time both the earl and Gwyneth wondered if he would recover, but the earl secured the services of the best French medicos and Wellington sent his own surgeon. Giles's progress was slow, but whatever he suffered, he did not complain, only becoming restless when Gwyneth was out of his sight. He seemed to take comfort in her presence and behaved with exemplary patience during his long convalescence. When he recovered somewhat, he asked her what had happened. She gave him a very edited account of her rescue, believing that the whole episode was best forgotten. But Giles pressed her for details, and she admitted that she had not galloped off to leave him to his attackers but had been prepared to face them down, even to the point of firing his abandoned pistol. He frowned at the thought of her standing over his fallen body, daring the brigands to do their worst.

"The comte's arrival was most providential," she admitted, not wanting Giles to imagine the horrors which could have awaited her if the Frenchman had not appeared.

"What has happened to him?"

"He seems to be enjoying a painless incarceration. I called on him in the prison to tender our gratitude and found him playing cards with his jailors. He had managed to take quite a bit of money off them, too," she reported with a laugh.

"He sounds a bit of a mountebank," Giles grumbled, not liking Gwyneth's approval of the comte.

Gwyneth realized his humiliation at exposing her to danger and knew he resented the enemy officer for saving her. What she did not sense was his changed attitude toward her. He had always known she was a woman of character and courage since his first glimpse of her brandishing that pistol against the invading Indians, but her defense of him, when she could have abandoned him to the brigands and ridden to safety, had made an indelible impression. He could not imagine that any of the lovely ladies he had pursued so diligently for years would have responded in such a fashion.

Lying immobile in bed gave him a great deal of time to think about his wife and their marriage. And her tireless ministrations touched him, too, forcing him to realize her other unusual qualities, not just her fierceness when challenged, but her tenderness and quiet determination to insure his recovery. Much as he might try to deny it, and he no longer wanted to do that, he found himself viewing her with new emotion. Giles was falling in love with his wife and it made him vulnerable. He felt disgust at his earlier behavior but was not ready, in his weakened state, to declare himself.

As the winter lengthened into late January, the military and political position in France altered drastically. There was no strong desire for a Bourbon restoration, and even Wellington thought "the Grand Disturber," as he called Napoleon, might be the best man to govern the country if he behaved himself. Most of his officers, including Giles, dissented, wanting the Corsican banished forever. Blücher and his German troops were advancing on Paris, but here in the south storms coming over the mountains prevented any action by Wellington until the thaw came. Soult still lingered about Toulouse, although his army was being decimated by desertion. Bordeaux had become a Royalist town, the French citizens sporting white cockades and behaving as if the war were over. But Wellington knew there were more battles ahead.

Gwyneth achieved her desire to meet the great man. One day as she was sitting by Giles's bed mending a gown, the earl tiptoed into the room, barely concealing his excitement. He glanced at his sleeping son and then whispered to Gwyenth, "Fitz Somerset is downstairs. He says Wellington has come from headquarters to review the troops, and while he is here he wants to see Giles, if he is well enough to receive him."

"Of course I'm well enough," Giles rumbled sleepily from the bed. "And stop whispering. It makes me feel like I am in a coffin already."

"Sorry, my boy. But it is a great honor. Wellington is, after all, the savior of Europe," the earl intoned, unable to restrain his enthusiasm.

"And a damned caustic brute. He will no doubt rake me over the coals for allowing those brigands to attack us," Giles insisted wryly from his wealth of experience with his commanding general.

"But you will see him?" Gwyneth said anxiously.

"If only you will soothe him. He likes the ladies, you know," Giles teased, struggling to sit up.

"He will arrive after luncheon," the earl reported and rushed off to tell Somerset that the patient would be happy to see the general.

Gwyneth was in a fever of anticipation, having

heard a variety of stories about the fabled commander. When he finally arrived, she was surprised both by his diffidence and his appearance. She had expected an arrogant, proud man who would stand on his dignity, resplendent in the lavish dress uniform of an English officer. She received a tall, beaky-nosed man, with impeccable manners and an appreciation of her as a lovely woman. He was dressed in a blue frock coat, white neckcloth, and round hat, but his sharp eyes and his air of command distinguished him.

"Well, Giles," he said, crossing to the bed where Giles was sitting up viewing his chief a bit shamefacedly. "You seem to have escaped from your own foolhardiness with the help of your wife and the enemy."

"Yes, sir. I behaved with little caution," Giles agreed.

"Your father tells me you are coming along, eager to face Soult, I suspect. We must run at him in the spring if these deuced awkward rains ever stop."

"Wellington weather, the men call it," Giles insisted boldly.

"A nuisance, but not enough to stop us," Wellington agreed.

"It was kind of you to call, sir," Giles said gratefully.

"Not at all. I had to see the troops. They're a shoddy lot, not wintering well," Wellington disapproved. Although his legendary contempt for his soldiers was often discussed, Giles thought his commander traduced. Few generals cared so much about the loss of life, and he expressed a real admiration for the infantry, the backbone of his army.

Wellington turned to Gwyneth. "It is a pleasure to meet you, Lady Fitzalen-Hill. I understand you would make a brave conscript. You are a heroine, Fitz tells me. All Bordeaux is talking about how you vanquished your husband's attackers and then charmed a French officer in bringing you both to safety.''

"Not at all, sir. I was scared to death," Gwyneth offered a bit tentatively.

Wellington let off one of his famous chortles. "We are all frightened in battle, my dear. The secret is not to show it.''

Then, bowing over her hand and leaving her flustered, he turned to Giles and admonished him. "Enough of this idling, Major. We will need you next month at Toulouse," and he took his leave.

"What did you think of the great man, Gwyneth? Was he all you expected?" Giles asked, eyeing his wife with an amused expression.

"He was much nicer than I dreamed he would be. I thought he would be very haughty and disapproving.''

"Much like your difficult husband, eh?" Giles said only half in jest. He did not quite know how to come to a rapprochement with Gwyneth.

"I must revise my opinion of you, too, I suppose. You have been an excellent patient. But I don't think the general should expect you to fight again," she protested.

"It's my job and I would not like to miss it. This battle will see the end of Napoleon and we can return to Sussex," he said vigorously.

"I want to see Paris," Gwyneth said.

"You will. I promise we will be there soon," Giles soothed, understanding her interest and willing to do all he could to accommodate her.

Within a week of Wellington's visit, perhaps inspired by it, Giles was able to rise and dress, his shoulder protected by a sling, and report to headquarters, where he was turned away as still convalescent, which disgusted him.

But Gwyneth was pleased. She greatly feared the coming seige of Toulouse and what Giles's role might be. These past long weeks had brought her to a new understanding and respect for her husband. She yearned to tell him so but was afraid of some sarcastic rebuff. And on her conscience were the London meetings with James Brush and the final farewell. Not that James was responsible for the loss of the baby, but if she had not been at the dock, the accident would not have happened, and she was convinced Giles would see it in that light and despise her. She wanted to please him, not antagonize him, and that reaction surprised her. Was she in danger of becoming a docile wife? Giles, restored to his normal good health, would return to his former ways. The intimacy of the sickroom would vanish, and once again she would be at the mercy of his casual pleasure. Could she allow that to happen?

# Chapter Nineteen

By mid-February Wellington's army was on the move, destined for Toulouse. Giles insisted on honoring his chief's request that he join the staff again, although Gwyneth thought him still suffering from his wound. In view of the coming battle, the couple had postponed any discussion of their relationship, both unwilling to commit themselves, but it was obvious to the earl, who beamed on them, that affairs between them had vastly improved. Like Gwyneth he feared the coming battle and Giles's role in it. But he felt he must act as a mediator between the pair, who came close to quarreling over Giles's decision to rejoin the army.

"I am sure, mighty Amazon that you are, that you would rush to the fray," Giles teased.

Gwyneth, who feared Giles's luck was running out, protested. She did not want to imply that he might be killed but the thought haunted her and she realized she would be unconsolable. Still, she was not ready to admit her feelings to her husband.

"Staff members are rarely in danger. All we do is dash about to one corps commander after another, delivering the great man's messages. I will be safer there than riding out of Bordeaux," he attempted to reassure her.

Gwyneth shook her head but realized she expected no less of him.

The earl, too, felt a dread of the battle but all he offered was a hope that after Napoleon's defeat Giles would consider resigning from the Army.

"I really need you at home," he pleaded, posing as an aging landlord who could barely manage his estate. Giles was not deceived.

"You are in fine fettle, Father, and you don't need me, but I will consider it," was all he promised.

The night before Giles's departure, the earl hosted a farewell dinner where they were joined by Ned and several other officers and their wives. The scene was one of rather hectic gaiety, and Gwyneth noticed that the other wives shared her apprehension but were too stoic to allow their fears to cloud the evening. After an elegant meal of trout and pheasant, followed by an intricate spun-sugar confection, a tribute to their French chef, the ladies adjourned to the Fitzalen-Hill suite, where Gwyneth poured coffee and noticed that the women felt freer to exchange confidences.

"Of course, Lady Fitzalen-Hill, you probably view the battle in a far different light, having had so many exciting adventures yourself," said one of the women, a haughty peeress whose husband commanded a regiment of hussars.

Gwyneth, who did not find Lady Somers very sympathetic, restrained her instinct to lash out and only said mildly, "I dislike war, having had some experience of it, but it's Giles's choice."

Several of the ladies had campaigned through the Peninsula and were inured to gunshot. A fetching brunette, Mrs. Rowland Masterson, hurried to soothe matters.

"Well, of course, we all want to see the end of Napoleon. For so many years he has threatened us. If I did not have every confidence in Wellington, I would be dreading this next, and I hope last, battle far more."

Gwyneth, exercising hostess prerogative, urged Mrs. Masterson to tell of some of her adventures and she obliged, making an amusing tale of her trials.

"The worst was riding a mule after Salamanca. Nasty animals and quite stubborn," Mrs. Masterson concluded. "Do you think your husband will return to Canada if Napoleon is defeated?" she asked Gwyneth.

"I hope he will retire from the Army. I am afraid that the war in Canada does not rate as a priority with the government. The best officers have refused to serve there, I understand."

Before Lady Somers could make some snide comment about conditions in Canada, the men joined them and the wine flowed freely. Gwyneth herself had more than her usual glass, and when their guests finally departed, she was feeling in a far more mellow mood.

Giles noticed her softened demeanor and was quick to take advantage of it. When they retired, he dismissed her maid, insisting he would fulfill her duties on this last night. Gwyneth giggled a bit at his deft hands on the buttons of her gown and warned him to take care. She shivered with delight as his warm hands caressed her bare back and turned to face him, blushing as she anticipated what would follow.

"You would not deny me on this our last night together for some time, Gwyneth," Giles coaxed, unfairly reminding her of what lay ahead.

"If that is what you want, Giles," she agreed softly.

"I do and I think you do, too," he said and led her to bed, where they spent a night of frantic passion, as if it were indeed their last.

The next morning Gwyneth watched as he put on his uniform, remembering another morning in London soon after their wedding when he had prepared for the war. How much had happened since then, she mused, and how their situation had changed. She could not send him off without some mention of their changed relationship.

"Do take care, Giles. Remember you have promised to show me Paris," she reminded him as his man left, having helped Giles into his uniform.

Giles crossed to her, where she was standing irresolute by the dressing table.

"You will not be rid of me easily, Gwyneth." And he took her in his arms, bestowing a passionate kiss. She responded eagerly, but her fears were evident, although she tried to put a brave face on the coming departure.

"With no tears or wailing, you make a good soldier's wife, my dear, or is it that you care so little?" Giles said a bit bitterly. Despite Gwyneth's care of him during his convalescence and the murmurs of delight she had displayed the night before in bed, he was not really convinced she cared a jot for him.

Passion could inspire emotions later denied, as he well knew.

"Of course I care, Giles. I want you to return safely. How can you doubt it?" Gwyneth replied, hurt.

But he did doubt it, although he said no more. They joined the earl for a rather subdued breakfast. Immediately after Giles rose to depart, his horse and trappings at the door of the hotel.

"Good luck, my boy," the earl said cheerfully and turned away before he could embarrass his son by an excess of feeling. Tactfully he left the pair alone. But Giles was still reluctant to make any vows of undying devotion and only gave Gwyneth a fleeting kiss in farewell.

"Behave yourself and stay away from that dratted comte," were his final words, and he was gone before Gwyneth could say more than a faint "Bless you."


The days following the army's departure from Bordeaux were tedious and frightening. Waiting for news taxed even the earl's normal good humor, and Gwyneth was morose. Only a skeleton force had been left to protect Bordeaux, but the populace did not feel endangered, convinced that this was the dying gasp of Napoleon's empire. And the Corsican would not be leading his Grande Armée against Wellington. The two giants had never opposed each other. The task of repelling the English Army had been left to Soult, whose own men had lost the taste for battle.

Gwyneth, at a loss as to how to fill her time, pursued her acquaintance with Mrs. Masterson, who optimistic facade heartened her.

"Are you worried about your husband?" Gwyneth finally blurted out, unable to restrain herself.

"Of course, but I try not to think about it. He has survived so many battles I cannot think this last one will see his death. And I have every faith in Wellington," Mary Masterson insisted cheerfully.

"I think I would rather be there, near the field, than hanging about here waiting for news," Gwyneth said.

"Well, I have been there, close to the action, and it is not reassuring with so much smoke, confusion, and turmoil. You cannot follow what is happening and the noise of the guns only adds to your fears," Mary insisted. "But you are not a timid soul as, you faced those brigands so bravely. Surely your courage is not failing you now."

Reminded that she was behaving like a ninny, Gwyneth rallied and insisted stoutly, "Of course not. But I wish it was all over." She did not confide in Mary that she also wished she had sent Giles away with more than a night of passion to remember. Absent, he appeared suddenly vital to her happiness. To herself she owned that her life would be bereft without him, and she wanted desperately to tell him so. That she loved him was an admission she hid from herself as well as she had from Giles, and now she loathed her cowardice. She dreaded exposing herself to his scorn if she told him how much she cared, although now she would even suffer that humiliation if he would return safely.

A few days later they learned that Wellington had swept the demoralized French troops from their entrenched positions but failed to follow up the victory with a strong pursuit. The anxious wives and Bordeaux garrison learned to their horror that Wellington had been wounded. A bullet had hit his sword hilt, forcing it against his side and laying open the skin. His men laid him on the ground, not knowing the extent of his wound, but it proved to be not too serious, although he could not ride for several days.

The army continued to advance slowly, reaching the Garonne River and looking ahead to Soult's fortified positions. There they remained as March ended and rumors reached them from Paris that Napoleon was dead. Castlereagh had come to Chatillon to insist on England's terms for peace. And although the rumors of Napoleon's death had proved wrong, the allies forged ahead with their demands, causing the vital Treaty of Chaumont to be signed on March 9. But the news of these intricate and finally successfully negotiations did not reach Wellington until the end of the month. The general kept telling his officers not to believe anything they heard and continued to plan for the battle of Toulouse.

Royalist sentiment increased and the allies marched into Paris on the last day of March, but not until the first week in April did the news reach Toulouse, too late to stop Wellington's assault on the town. Soult was driven from the town after a hard-fought battle during which Wellington's troops suffered 4,500 casualties, "a very severe affair," Wellington called it. He rode into Toulouse on April 12 and an hour later learned that Napoleon had abdicated. A great dinner was held in celebration.

The news of the abdication had reached Wellington from Bordeaux, where the restoration of King Louis XVIII had been hailed with great enthusiasm. But none of these climatic events roused Gwyneth and the earl to any relief. They had heard nothing

from Giles. Gwyneth's fears were heightened when
Mary Masterson appeared en route to Toulouse. Her
husband had been badly wounded in this final battle,
and her normal optimism had faltered. Gwyneth, on
hearing of the many casualties, was hard-pressed to
comfort her since she feared for Giles's safety. The
earl was all for traveling to Toulouse immediately to
discover if his son was safe, and Gwyneth could only
agree. But before they could make the arrangements
to depart, Col. Frederick Ponsonby, who had ridden
off to Toulouse, returned to Bordeaux with the casu-
alty list and called on the earl.

"Your son is safe, sir, although many good men
fell," he reported, and he handed Gwyneth a hurriedly scribbled note from Giles.

He wrote: *It's over and all is well with me. Can you
and Father join me in Toulouse? Then it is on to Paris,
for Wellington intends to lead us on a triumphal entry.*

Both the earl and Gwyneth were jubilant, even as
they realized that many families would be mourning
this last pointless effort in the twenty-two year struggle. Gwyneth retired to her room to continue packing,
Giles's note tucked into her bodice where it gave
her great comfort. He was safe, and their personal
problems suddenly appeared unimportant. That
night she slept soundly for the first time since his
departure, her dilemma resolved. She would tell Giles
of her deep feelings for him, no matter whether he
returned them or not.

The following morning as the earl was bustling
about making the arrangements for their journey,
she received an unexpected caller, Comte Roger de
Fancher.

"I could not leave Bordeaux without enquiring

about your husband, madame," he said when she received him.

"How kind, Comte. My husband survived the battle and we are about to leave for Toulouse to join him. I suppose you are going home. I cannot say I am unhappy over your country's defeat, but at least now you will be able to restore the ravages of war," she said, a bit at sea as to how to handle the man.

"Yes, Napoleon brought great glory to France but great sorrow, too. At heart I am a monarchist and hail the revival of the Bourbons," the comte admitted.

Gwyneth suspected he had trimmed his sails to the current political wind, but her own happiness made her tolerant, and she remembered how much she owed him.

"I wish you good fortune and again tender my gratitude for your brave, selfless action," she said. There was some thing about the comte that made her talk so grandiloquently despite her best efforts to speak moderately.

"I was happy to be of service to such a lovely lady. Perhaps our paths will cross again," the comte returned gallantly.

Gwyneth doubted it but made no demur. Soon after he took his leave, and she promptly forgot all about him in her eagerness to reach Giles's side.

Their journey took two days, Gwyneth chafing with impatience the whole time. Colonial Ponsonby had told the earl that Giles had taken rooms for them, and they made their way at last across the Garonne and into the bombarded city, where evidence of the battle was sobering. Finally their carriage drew up to a fine Renaissance building not far from the University, and they hurried into the hotel. They were received with a rather surprising deference. Gwyneth had feared that the citizens of Toulouse would be belligerent and sullen, but Gallic pragmatism overcame whatever sorrow their country's defeat signified.

Once established in their luxurious quarters, the earl sent a message to Giles at headquarters, and within the hour he arrived. He embraced Gwyneth heartily and clasped the earl by the shoulders, reassuring that gentleman.

"Well, I thought you would never arrive, but I see that Ponsonby gave you my message," he said, obviously in the grip of victory.

"And you suffered no damage, my boy?" the earl said, still not completely convinced of Giles's well-being.

"Of course not. We lost some men, but the Spaniards took the brunt of the casualties. Never thought they would fight so well."

"And for an unnecessary battle," Gwyneth protested, thinking of all those lost men.

"The fortunes of war, I am afraid, and also some failure of communication. But it is all over now, and we will go on to Paris as I promised," he said, giving her a warm smile.

"I want to hear all about it," the earl interrupted, ignoring Giles and Gwyneth's obvious desire to be alone.

"At dinner, Father, I promise, but for now . . ." Giles trailed off, placing an arm about Gwyneth's shoulder. "I want to enjoy my reunion with my wife."

The earl stammered, "Of course, of course," in some confusion. Reluctantly he ushered them to their bedroom, and upon closing the door, he gave a sigh of satisfaction. It would all be well between those two at last, with no war to interfere in their happiness.

The earl in many ways was a man of simple emotions. He had never completely understood his complex son, nor Gwyneth's furious reaction to Giles's delinquencies. They were both hot-blooded young people who could surely solve their differences the time-honored way. And now that process would begin, he thought with some relief, and perhaps would result in the heir he so desired.

Gwyneth had promised herself countless times that once reunited with Giles she would confess her feelings for him without any shyness. However, now that the moment had arrived, she found it would not be as easy as she had thought. Alone, without the bulwark of the earl, she remembered Giles's former sarcasm and cynicism, his inability to offer any tenderness, only passion.

Giles, sensing her withdrawal, masked his disappointment and determined to make the first move in their duel.

"As you see, I have returned to you in rude health. I missed you damnably, Gwyneth, and the night before the final assault I wondered if you would mourn me if I fell in battle. A stupid sentimentality, you might say." He desperately wanted her reassurance, and she would not fail him.

"Oh, Giles, I was terribly worried and regretted my past coolness, if that was what it was. And I have a heavy conscience," she admitted.

"What have you done?" he asked teasingly, not believing her sins could be very heinous.

"I have kept a rather troubling occurrence from you," she said, bravely meeting his eyes and amazed to see him gazing at her with a warmth that she was afraid would soon vanish from his dark eyes when he learned the truth.

"Well, I hope you are not going to confess some dalliance in London while I was miles away, bravely struggling against our enemies," he mocked.

"During the time after you left London, when I was staying with the Endicotts, I met James Brush. He had escaped from his English guards after being captured in a battle in Canada and shipped with other prisoners to England. Quite by chance we met in the street, and I prevailed upon Sir Fergus to help him find a ship bound for America. Of course, Sir Fergus did not know he was a prisoner. James represented himself as a Canadian unhappy in England and longing to return home," she explained, twisting her hands in desperation.

Giles, startled, wondered what her meeting with her former suitor had meant to her, but he was prepared to hear her out.

"Well, I don't see what else you could have done," he said calmly.

"That's generous of you, but you have not heard the worst. I went to the docks to bid him goodbye, and that is when I had the accident that caused me to lose the baby," she said miserably, waiting for the scorn and anger that Giles would let loose on her head.

"Oh, Gwyneth, what does that matter? We can have another baby if you care enough. Do you regret being forced to marry me and abandoning your Colonial? If so, you had best admit it now, because I have every intention of trying to make our marriage more than a convenient solution to what was my initial fault. We began badly, and much of the troubles we had were due to my failure to appreciate you. I admit, in the beginning, I looked upon you as just another conquest in a long list of women, but you soon disabused me of that. Perhaps my wound and the war has altered my attitude, but I find I cannot contemplate your leaving me. Did that damned fellow try to persuade you to be false to your marriage vows?'' he asked, concerned.

"Not exactly, but he wanted me to return to America with him. I never considered it. He was only a friend who needed my help. I felt I owed him that,'' Gwyneth replied, praying that Giles would understand.

"Yes, I can see you would feel that way. After all, I had given you little reason to believe you owed me loyalty,'' Giles admitted, a bit bitterly.

"I owe you more than that, and in these last weeks I have come to love you,'' Gwyneth blurted out, bracing herself for an ironic dismissal or a caustic rejoinder.

Instead Giles took her in his arms and looked deeply into her eyes, and she met his gaze bravely. "That took courage, Gwyneth, and I honor you for it. And I would be churlish not to be equally truthful with you. I cannot promise to be the gallant chevalier you deserve, but I can tell you that I love you, too. Whether that love will be enough for you, who knows. But I cannot conceive of ever finding another woman who would inspire such vows of devotion in me. You have shattered all my defenses,'' he said ruefully, as surprised as she by his admission.

"Thank you, Giles. We must both try to make this a good marriage, based on love and respect. I will do my part if you will cooperate,'' she replied, almost overcome by emotion.

Feeling they had come too near to bathos, he kissed her with a rising desire. "All I can feel this moment is a consuming wish to take you to bed and seal our bargain.''

"I want that, too," she said with the engaging honesty that he had always found so appealing. Walking to the door, Giles turned the lock decisively and then returned to her side, eager to prove his words.

# *Chapter Twenty*

Wellington rode into Paris on May 4 to the jubilant cheers of the crowd and the satisfaction of his men. Although he was hailed as the savior of Europe, had been promised a dukedom, and was the cynosure of every eye from the Duchess of Dino to the lowliest peasant, he disdained riding into the capitol as a uniformed conqueror. He wore his usual plain blue frock coat and round hat to be introduced to the German conqueror Blücher. His military career had culminated in great triumph and he had accepted the post as English ambassador to France. In his new civilian position he did not want to appear overwhelming and behaved with modest brevity.

The earl and Gwyneth had preceded Wellington and Giles into Paris, where the earl had rented a house on the Rue de Faubourg. Faced with the disbandment of the Peninsular Army, Giles had the choice of serving far from home or resigning his commission. The earl pressed hard for him to leave the Army, but Giles wavered. Discussing his options with Gwyneth in private, he admitted that he loathed the thought of returning to civilian life.

"I might get my colonelcy and the command of a regiment, but that would mean fighting in the Colonies. You must want to return home, and that might be possible if I elect to stay in the Army."

"My life is with you whatever you choose. I have no great wish to return home," she reassured him. Since their meeting in Toulouse and their passionate reconciliation, she lived in a state of constant bemusement, completely enraptured by their changed relationship. Even Paris with its myriad delights did not inspire the excitement she had expected, she was so enthralled with Giles's devotion.

"Well, like the chief, I do not want to fight in America, so I suppose I must resign. I have been a serving officer for most of my adult life, and it will seem strange to become a gentleman of leisure, busy with cows and tenants, instead of bullets and billets," he admitted ruefully.

"Will you be bored?"

"Probably, but now I have a wife to keep me busy and enslaved," he mocked, not entirely in jest.

Gwyneth was not completely convinced but accepted that he did not want to serve in America. Several letters had finally caught up with her from Canada, and she learned that the war there appeared no closer to an end, although neither side was enthusiastic about the fight.

In the meantime, Paris was thronged with English society, intent on enjoying the city they had been denied for years. The French couturiers and restauranteurs welcomed them eagerly. Adding a fillup was the presence of such august visitors as Tsar Alexander,

Francis I of Austria, and the Comte d'Artois, the younger brother of Louis XVIII, the restored Bourbon who made his delayed entrance to Paris on May 3, after being immobilized by gout. If Wellington was the hero of the hour, Talleyrand was the master intriguer. He had basely deserted Napoleon and began his clever maneuverings with the new conquerors, securing preferment and place from his former enemies. After a terror-stricken ride through France, Napoleon had been dispatched to Elba aboard an English warship and landed on the island May 4. As he rode out of Paris following an emotional farewell to his Grande Armée, he had promised to return with the violets in the spring but few paid him heed. The allies were too busy settling the fate of Europe.

Giles escorted Gwyneth to a host of celebrations, to the Comédie, to the Prince of Saxe-Coburg-Saalfeld's ball, and to Castlereagh's reception. He ordered a trunkful of new clothes for her, and proudly rode with her and his fellow officers in the Bois de Boulogne. At night his ardor increased until Gwyneth was quite overwhelmed by his lovemaking and satisfied that she had his undivided attention. But these heady days soon came to an end as Giles was ordered by Wellington to accompany him to Bordeaux where he would bid goodbye to his troops and then move on to Madrid to support King Ferdinand in his struggle with his reactionary advisors. The earl and Gwyneth remained in Paris to await his return when they would go to England in Wellington's wake.

The morning after Giles's departure, Gwyneth was idly dreaming over her morning chocolate when a servant announced she had a visitor. Not knowing whom to expect, she dressed hurriedly and entered the sitting room of her suite to find Comte Roger de Fancher awaiting her.

"I said our paths would cross again, madame," he greeted her with an effusive bow over her hand.

"So you did," Gwyneth replied weakly, not particularly eager to renew her acquaintance with this polished Frenchman.

"I saw you last evening at the theater with your charming husband," he said.

"Yes, unfortunately Giles is not here. He has accompanied Wellington on his progress to Bordeaux," Gwyneth said a bit reluctantly.

"*Hélas!* I have missed him," the comte replied, not entirely convincingly.

Gwyneth realized he had probably been forewarned of Giles's absence, and somehow this worried her. There was a nuance in his manner that troubled her. But she feigned pleasure in seeing him again and waited for the real reason for his visit. She did not think it was mere politeness.

"I thought you would have hurried home to restore your lands," she offered, hoping to bring him to the point.

"My lands were sequestered by the Corsican, but there is some hope I can retrieve the estate. I have a slight acquaintance with M. Talleyrand and he might help me, but only for a price," the comte admitted nonchalantly.

"I hope you succeed," Gwyneth said warily, beginning to suspect the reason for the comte's visit.

"It will require a large gift of francs, and unfortunately my resources are somewhat limited now," he replied with a false air of deprecation.

"How disappointing." Gwyneth would not be

drawn, although she feared he would not allow it to rest at that.

"It pains me to have to make such an appeal to a woman of your charm and ability," he oozed. But Gwyneth sensed that beneath his insouciant air menace lay barely concealed.

"If you mean what I think, Comte, I must tell you I have neither the resources nor the inclination to assist you," she countered firmly, hoping to end this unpleasant interview. "I know I owe you a great deal, but I am quite astounded that you believed I would pay your bribe for you."

"I noticed you were wearing a most expensive and beautiful diamond necklace at the theater last evening," he insisted, not at all embarrassed.

"A gift from my husband and much cherished." Gwyneth wished heartily that Giles were present or that the earl would interrupt this ugly situation. But if she were not to be rescued by her family, she must manage herself.

"I think you may be persuaded to come to my aid, madame," the comte persisted, the gloves off in their duel of words.

"I dislike your insinuation, Comte, and must request you to take your leave. I hope you manage to solve your difficulties, but it shall not be through a donation from me." Gwyneth was now thoroughly angry.

"Don't be too hasty, madame. I would loathe forcing you. But for now I will leave you to think about my demands," he replied, ruffled not a whit by her anger or her refusal.

"Goodbye, Comte," Gwyneth said firmly.

"*A bientôt*," he demurred, and bowed as he took himself away.

Left alone Gwyneth wondered if he really meant to pursue his objective, to insist she pay for his estates. And what did he mean by the suggestion that he would force her? Giles was right. The man was a mountebank, and she would have nothing more to do with him.

On reflection she thought she would not confide in the earl unless the comte renewed his applications. After all, the man could not truly believe she owed him recompense for saving her and Giles from the murderous brigands. She began to doubt his tale about the estate he had lost. More likely he was a poseur without any claim to land or status and was just trying to make a few francs for himself. Not that she thought much of Talleyrand's probity, but it was unlikely that the great conniver had indicated he could be bribed to restore the comte's heritage.

She had been thoroughly bamboozled by the Frenchman and would walk more warily in the future. After all, what could he do? Soon they would be returning to England and be beyond his machinations. But what a disappointment to learn of his duplicity. Obviously he had seen his chance to gain some advantage because of their perilous situation that day outside of Bordeaux. Well, he should not prosper at her expense, no matter how deep her gratitude toward him. Having settled this startling development to her own satisfaction, she went out to meet Mary Masterson, who had arrived in Paris with her convalescing husband, and put the comte's extortion from her mind.

Gwyneth's worst suspicions about her former rescuer would have been confirmed if she had followed him to his lodgings, a seedy apartment on the Left Bank. The comte was desperate for money and not for the purpose of retrieving his estates. He had none. Skilled at trimming his sails to the current political wind, he intended to make use of the charming Lady Fitzalen-Hill's gratitude, one way or the other. To that end he had enlisted the aid of the very brigands who had attacked her. Halted from robbing and raping her by the comte's interference, they had responded well to his plan to capitalize on her gratitude. He was not unduly disturbed by her initial refusal, which he kept to himself.

"The noble lord will be pleased to pay up when we have taken his wife," he explained to his confederates.

"We should have done the cove in when we had the chance," growled the most unsavory of the trio.

"That kind of thinking is why you will never be more than a scruffy varlet," the *soi-disant* comte answered. "I saw immediately that they were persons of quality and would repay rescuing from you dogs."

The comte had his followers firmly in hand. He had fought with them under Napoleon, doing more scavenging than actual fighting. When he saw that Napoleon's days of power were coming to an end, he had removed himself from Soult's retreating army, taking with him a few allies who would serve him well. The comte was neither a Royalist nor a dedicated follower of the Corsican, adopting himself to whatever would prove to his advantage. In this he was not unlike Talleyrand, with whom he had led Gwyneth to believe erroneously he had some association. Actually, he was the son of an agent to a former nobleman who had lost his life in the Terror. He had been educated with the noble's son, whom he both envied

and emulated. Roger de Fancher was too wily a bird
to be caught by vengeful republicans. Loyalty was not
a quality he prized. He had managed to survive by
using his wits, and they had not deserted him in this
confused period after the downfall of the Emperor.
He was determined to emerge from the affair with
gold in his pocket, and if the conquerors would not
reward him willingly, he thought he could coerce
them. Still, he was too wary to confide his ideas to the
wretched trio who looked upon him as their leader.

"For the moment we will wait and let the charming
lady reflect on the situation," he replied to their
mutterings. He knew how to control them.

Gwyneth waited impatiently for Giles's return with
Wellington while the earl made arrangements for
them to return home. Her father-in-law was so pleased
and relieved by the outcome of the war and Giles's
safety that she did not want to alarm him with her
suspicions about the spurious comte. Though she
doubted that she would hear from him, she was not
completely unprepared. In her reticule she carried
a small pistol.

Her days were filled with shopping and visits with
Mary Masterson and some other officers' wives. They
were eager to return to England, having exhausted
all that Paris could offer. Rumor had it that the Tsar
would accompany Wellington to London for a grand
reception. The Russian emperor was forming his Holy
Alliance, which the English viewed with some skepticism, but they encouraged him, for they wished to
keep the balance of Europe. Talleyrand was intriguing to wrest the best deal for himself and France,
and Metternich had decided to use his diplomatic

skills to achieve a restored position for the crumbling Austrian Empire. The earl rumbled that the peace was far more arduous than the war and wanted to put it all behind him.

Finally Giles returned, and in their ecstatic reunion Gwyneth forgot the comte's threats and basked in Giles's obvious devotion. However her interlude was rudely interrupted one afternoon as she returned to the hotel from a shopping expedition. As she entered the foyer and prepared to mount the stairs to their suite, the comte intercepted her.

"Ah, good afternoon, madame," he greeted, ignoring her frown of displeasure.

"What do you want, Comte, if that is indeed what you are. I am beginning to think you are a charlatan," she said, annoyed.

"I am wounded, madame, that you should suspect me," he replied aimiably, but with an ugly light in his eyes that he quickly hid. This high-toned English lady would not evade him.

"I am busy, Comte, and have no time for you," she insisted, wishing that either Giles or the earl would appear. Her way to the stairs was blocked by this encroaching man.

"You have given no more thought to my suggestion?"

"Of course not. It was shameless," she countered coolly.

"Perhaps, but necessary. Time is pressing, and I suspect you will soon be off to London."

Before Gwyneth could reply, Giles came down the stairs and greeted her. "There you are, Gwyneth. I just returned and was looking for you."

"You remember Comte de Fancher, Giles? Our rescuer outside of Bordeaux."

"Oh, yes, not that I actually recall much of you, sir. I was in no condition to effect an introduction," Giles agreed easily, seeing nothing untoward in the appearance of the man who had saved their lives. "I hope you are renewing our thanks to this gentleman," he said, turning to his wife.

"Yes, but I have a matter of some importance to discuss with you, Giles, that cannot wait, so I am sure the comte will excuse us," Gwyneth replied. Nodding to the comte, she took Giles's arm and pushed him toward the stairs, leaving the comte no recourse but to watch them escape. He was tempted to follow them, for he knew Gwyneth was about to confide in her husband about his appeal for money. But prudence won the day. This was not the moment to challenge the English lord.

Once in their suite Gwyneth told Giles of the imbroglio. To her surprise Giles only laughed and said, "I told you the man sounded like a mountebank and so he has proved to be."

"It's horrid. I thought he was such a charming gentleman, and now I think he is little better than a crook," she said, agitated.

"Not at all. You cannot blame the chap for trying to improve his condition. Not that he will succeed with our guineas. Forget him, Gwyneth. He was just trying it on, hoping to wrest some money from you while you still felt grateful for his saving my worthless life."

"It's not worthless, and I don't trust him. I believe he is planning some way to force us to give him the money," she replied, her brow furrowed in anxiety.

"I'm much more interested in your assertion that you do not find my life worthless than in any claims that bogus Frenchman might make. Forget him."

Then Giles took her in his arms and gave her what began as a reassuring kiss but deepened almost at once into a more passionate embrace.

Emerging blushing and shaken from the force of the response Giles could win from her, Gwyneth abandoned all thoughts of the comte and lost herself in much more cheerful imaginings.

She would not have been so insouciant if she had seen the comte angrily striding down the Rue de Faubourg. Cursing to himself at Giles's untimely interruption, he realized he had underestimated Gwyneth. She was not to be cowed by veiled threats. He would have to take some action. But it would have to be soon as they would be returning home. However, if necessary he would follow them to England and execute his plan. They would not escape him, for he was unlikely to again find such wealthy pigeons. He stopped suddenly. He must find out when they were leaving. It might be possible to intercept the lady en route to Calais. Her husband, as Wellington's aide, would probably be accompanying the great duke and not be on hand to protect her, although he would scurry to her rescue fast enough if he thought she was in danger. And once he had them both, he would easily extract a ransom from the earl. Satisfied that he had solved his immediate concerns, he slowed to a jaunty walk, dreaming of what he would do with his new prosperity.

# *Chapter Twenty-One*

Giles may have dismissed the comte as a negligible threat so that Gwyneth would not worry, but he had decided to do some investigating of the Frenchman. His experience of poseurs and charlatans was far wider than his wife's, and he feared they had not heard the last of this sham nobleman. It was apparent that the comte (Giles continued to call him that although he doubted his right to the title) had quickly assessed their worth, realizing they were of more use to him alive than dead, and so restrained his followers. The man lived by his wits and saw the opportunity to solve his financial problems. He probably suspected, too, that Napoleon's downfall was imminent and that his future lay with the occupying forces. Giles would discuss the matter with his father, whose judgment he respected, and plan how to handle the fellow. He was confident he could settle the comte.

Yet not even this momentary annoyance could cloud his satisfaction with the outcome of the war and his personal life. He continued to be fascinated with Gwyneth, both in bed and out of it. He had known many women, but few with her rare combination of honesty, courage, and zest for life. Gwyneth was no languid society beauty, but a woman with the ability to entertain him, arouse him, and inspire a strange desire to protect her, reactions he had never felt for the women who had previously engaged his interest. Giles was enough of a cynic to wonder if his present enthrallment with her would last. But even if they settled down into a steady affection supported by some offspring, he would be content. For the first time in his life he had a relationship that promised to endure. Some of his well-being could be laid to the end of the war but most of it lay in the assurance that despite all their past vicissitudes, Gwyneth had come to love him.

Not one to delay action, Giles sought out his father, who had just returned from confirming their travel arrangements, and confided his suspicions about the Frenchman.

"It's difficult to believe that the man deferred your death at the hands of his confederates in order to use your rescue to his advantage. He must be a skilled intriguer and a rare opportunist," the earl said, rather taken aback by Giles's tale.

"I do feel a certain gratitude toward him but not to the extent of paying him the outrageous sum he has asked," Giles admitted.

"No, and I have no doubt it would not be a one-time payment," the earl agreed shrewdly.

"Wellington has asked me to accompany him on the journey to England, and I can hardly refuse him. That means that you will be escorting Gwyneth home on your own. I have the greatest faith in your ability to protect her, and you will be traveling in your own coach, with your own coachman and footmen. Surely he will not try any stupid jape under those circumstances, but you are now warned if he makes an attempt to kidnap Gwyneth or some other trick."

"Yes, indeed. No need to worry. I will watch over her," the earl said stoutly.

"In the meantime, she must not be allowed out alone. When will you be leaving?" Giles asked, not completely reassured.

"The day after tomorrow. My coach and men have arrived, so that is no problem."

"Wellington plans to leave at the end of the week. He has some business to do with the allies, and must make arrangements for his new post as ambassador. I hope he has done the right thing in accepting that assignment. Somehow I feel that we have not heard the last of Napoleon. Elba is much too near the French mainland."

"He is well-guarded, but I understand that his wife and son will not be joining him in exile. I wonder if that has any significance?" the earl asked.

"I hope not. But I intend to use these last few days in investigating this comte. If I can unmask him, I might be able to secure his arrest and that would prevent him being at large to plot any deviltry."

And so Giles and the earl made their dispositions, never dreaming that any real peril could threaten Gwyneth. Once they were safely home in England, the comte's efforts would be useless. It was only during the next few days they must be vigilant. Giles did not tell Gwyneth of his fears, but he kept a close eye on her as she finished her shopping and farewell visits.

The earl's entourage was an impressive one. He and Gwyneth would ride in his coach, driven by his own coachman with two armed footmen. Another coach would follow with the luggage and Gwyneth's abigail and the earl's batman. They would leave early in the morning, but even so would have to make an overnight stop in Amiens en route to Calais. If the comte planned any mischief, it would be at the hostelry in Amiens, and the earl doubted that would be feasible. Typically he had a certain scorn for his country's erstwhile enemies and did not really believe the comte was capable of carrying out his extravagant threats. Still, he wished it were possible that Giles could be with them.

Just before he handed Gwyneth into the coach, Giles warned her to stay close to the earl, especially in Amiens. He did not want to alarm her but his recent investigations of the *soi-disant* comte had confirmed his original impression of the man.

"I will miss you damnably, Gwyneth. But I should be with you in London before too long. Do take care, and think of me," he said lightly, trying not to emphasize his concern.

"What can go wrong, Giles? I am surrounded by protectors," she reassured him, loathing their parting because she worried about Giles's fidelity, not because she thought the comte might try any last-minute chicanery. But she had not been impervious to Giles's watch over her these past few days, and she had made her own preparations. She still carried the small pistol in her reticule.

At last they were on their way, Gwyneth looking back and waving as the coach trundled along the cobblestones. Giles turned away before they were out of sight and scanned the street. Just for a moment he thought he glimpsed the slim jaunty back of the comte slipping around the hotel, but he was not certain, and when he ran to the corner, he saw nothing but a few respectable folk going about their business. Shaking his head, he decided it had been a figment of his anxiety and walked off briskly to report to headquarters.

Having provided a lavish collation for their luncheon, there was no reason to stop until they reached Amiens, so the earl relaxed as they rode through the countryside. In fact he nodded off while Gwyneth watched him with affection. Such a gallant and distinguished man, she thought, and he had been so kind to her, as if she were his own daughter. How fortunate she was to have landed on such pleasant paths. Much as she had enjoyed Paris and all the celebrations honoring the allies' victory, she would not be sorry to reach home. To her surprise she realized that was how she now regarded the mansion in Grosvenor Street and the hall in Sussex. Her life in Canada seemed distant and unimportant, for her future lay with Giles.

Settling back in the squabs she dreamt of the days ahead when he would join her and they would begin their real life together. The swaying of the coach was seductive, and she almost succumbed to the drowsiness that had overtaken the earl. They had been traveling about thirty miles, into the province of Oise, when suddenly the coach jerked to a halt, startling Gwyneth from her musings and awakening the earl. Before they could gather their wits, the door flew open, and a menacing masked man stood there holding a large pistol, pointed straight at the earl where he sat across from Gwyneth.

"Don't want no trouble, squire. Just let the lady step down," he growled in French.

Gwyneth shrank back and felt for her reticule,

which lay by her side. The earl, enraged, stuck his head out of the window, and then drew it in appalled.

"My men are covered by this *canaille's* men, and there is a great tree obstructing the road," he informed her.

"That's right, governor, but no harm intended to you or the lady if she comes quietly," the man insisted.

"What do you want? Money?" asked the earl in French, sensing that this was not just a normal highwayman's raid.

"Naw, we wants the lady and we intends to take her, either willingly or elsewise," the man said, leaning forward and extending his hand, his foul breath reeking and an evil grin showing blackened teeth.

*"Quelle sottise! Va-t'en!"* the earl commanded, and rose in his seat. But before he could make any move, the man fired his pistol and the earl fell back, blood gushing from his shoulder.

Gwyneth, enraged, fired full in the face of the man, who was unprepared for such ferocity, and he fell from the door onto the ground. Gwyneth coolly reloaded her pistol, although her hands were far from steady, and made to follow him out, but he writhed on the ground, calling to his mates, and then lay still. His companions, took one look at their colleague and decided there was no hope for him. Wondering if more shots would follow, they mounted their horses and rode off, pursued by shots from the footmen, who managed to wing one of them. That only spurred them to ride harder, and when Gwyneth stepped from the coach she saw them fast disappearing. The coachman approached her, explaining frantically that he had not seen the tree across the road until it was too late to make a diversion, and then the men appeared from behind it, leveling their weapons.

"The earl is hurt, and we must get him to a doctor,"
Gwyneth cried, not interested in what had caused this
dreadful incident. She boarded the coach and went
to the earl's side. He had managed with some difficulty to press a handkerchief to the wound,
staunching some of the bleeding, but his face was
pale and drenched with sweat.

"It's all right, my dear, just a flesh wound," he
tried to comfort her.

The next few hours were a nightmare. The coach
with the luggage and servants that had been several
miles behind the earl's vehicle finally came up and
Morley the batman was able to bind up the earl's
shoulder, providing some relief, but Gwyneth feared
he was in far more pain than he admitted. After a
hard struggle the men succeeded in removing the
tree and brush blocking the road so the coaches could
continue on their way. Gwyneth, shaken by the death
of the highwayman, averted her eyes when the men
dragged the body to the roadside. She wished he
could be given a decent burial, but the earl's injury
took precedence over all else. Also she feared if they
did not hurry on to Amiens, not only would the earl's
condition worsen, but they might be ambushed again
by the highwaymen.

Of course, she thought distractedly, they were not
highwaymen but minions of the comte, determined
to abduct her. That she had foiled them with her
shot gave her no satisfaction. The death of that man
was on her conscience, and although she had saved
herself from a nasty situation she wished she had not
killed him. But her first responsibility now was to get
the earl to a doctor, and to that end she urged the
coachman and the other servants to make haste.

After a gruelling ride, with the earl prone on the

seat across from her, bravely trying to repress his pain, the entourage arrived at the hostelry in Amiens. The earl was quickly carried to the rooms he had reserved and a physician summoned by the landlord. Gwyneth waited impatiently for the man to examine her father-in-law, fearing that his wound was more serious than he had claimed. Finally, the doctor emerged, wiping his hands on a towel, to inform her that although the earl had lost a good deal of blood, he would recover. He must rest and take nourishment to restore his health. Fortunately he was a very fit man who should suffer no lasting ill effects, the doctor assured her, and he promised to return in the morning to check on his patient. Of course they must not travel for some time to allow the earl to recuperate.

"All sorts of rabble are on the move since the war ended, trying to take advantage of the disturbed conditions. Your elegant coach was a noticeable target," he said, shaking his head. "France will be infested with these robbers if the authorities don't take a firm stand," he concluded.

Gwyneth did not disabuse him of his interpretation of the events. The prefecture's officers had listened to her tale and proved most sympathetic, impressed by the English lord and his charming daughter-in-law. Gwyneth was content to let them believe that this shocking attack had been committed by rogues seeking some gold, but she was convinced that the comte was behind it. And what would he do now that his horrid plot to abduct her and hold her for ransom had failed? She felt vulnerable in this inn and longed for Giles, but then reminding herself that she must cope alone, straightened her chin and braced herself to visit the patient.

The earl looked pale but amazingly well, considering what he had endured. He greeted her with an encouraging smile.

"What a brave girl you are. I had no idea you were carrying a pistol," he congratulated her. "Still, it was quick thinking and we had a lucky escape, entirely due to your actions. I am afraid I failed to protect you as I should have and as I assured Giles I would."

"The doctor and the prefecture's men think the attack was by highwaymen," Gwyneth said.

"It was that dratted comte. I wish you had dispatched him," the earl replied, furious at his own helplessness.

"I wonder if this failure to kidnap me has called a halt to his plans," Gwyneth murmured, not wanting to distress the earl further but yearning for some assurance that they had heard the last of this villain.

"Of course. One of his men is dead and one wounded, I understand. He will have trouble persuading them to make any further foul attempts, I am sure."

Gwyneth was not so convinced, but she did not want to worry the ill earl, and agreed that the comte would find it hard to mount another wicked scheme. Seeing that the earl needed his rest, she left him, promising to return to see that he had a proper meal. But in her bedroom, as she repaired the damages of the trip and drank a glass of wine, she continued to worry over the problem. What was the comte's reaction to the failure of his plan? Would he abandon his efforts to wrest money from them now?

Nothing was further from the comte's mind. Cursing his subordinates when they arrived at the meeting place, an abandoned farmhouse where they had hoped to incarcerate Gwyneth, he dismissed their excuses with scorn. Served him right for trusting the matter to such oafs. He paid them off and told them to make their way back to Bordeaux. Then he consoled himself with a bottle of rough red wine and brooded over his options. His money was running low, and he desperately needed the guineas that Gwyneth's husband and father-in-law possessed to enable him to live as he wished. He had taken a bold risk, but if it had come off he would be enjoying the fruits of his clever ploy instead of being reduced to pigging it in this rude hovel.

His only hope rested on the news that the earl was gravely wounded That meant a delay in the Fitzalen-Hills' arrival in England, giving him some time to consider another way of getting his hands on the money he coveted. This time he would not trust the matter to others. In London Madame would feel safe and not be on her guard, nor would she be going about with that pistol in her reticule. Who would have imagined she would have dared to fire on the men? He should have remembered her valiant stand over her husband's body that day outside of Bordeaux. Obviously he would have to take more sophisticated measures to see that she coughed up the blunt. There was a large colony of émigrés in London, with whom he had some contacts. He would journey there and see what the gods offered. There must be some way to part her from the money he thought he was owed.

# *Chapter Twenty-Two*

Gwyneth and the earl remained a week in Amiens before traveling on to Calais and boarding the packet for England. Gwyneth had wanted to stay longer, thinking the earl needed the time to convalesce, but he reminded her that Giles would be frantic, not finding them at their Grosvenor house. A message had been sent to him, but who knew if he had received it? They must hasten to reassure him. Finally Gwyneth consented, thinking that fretting would only retard her father-in-law's complete recovery.

They arrived in London on a warm June day to find the city *en fête*, celebrating the end of the long struggle with Napoleon and eager to welcome the Tsar of Russia, who was the object of much attention, as was King Frederick William of Prussia and Marshal Von Blücher. But the hero of the day was the Duke of Wellington, whom all London idolized, a situation he accepted with his usual cool aplomb.

Giles, who had shared in the hero's reception,

could not enjoy the spectacle, so worried was he about the garbled report he had heard of his father's illness. He did not know about the attack, for all the earl had managed to scrawl was that an unexpected affair had delayed their arrival in England. Giles was almost distraught when their coach pulled up in Grosvenor Street just before dinner and he saw the earl, in his arm in a sling, stumble from it. He embraced Gwyneth and plied her with questions. Horrified by their ordeal, he wanted to leave at once for the country to avoid any further attempts on his wife. But neither Gwyneth nor the earl would agree.

"We are much better off in London, not so exposed," the earl argued. "Anyway, I doubt that the fool would come across the Channel as he would be a stranger and much less able to enlist confederates to carry out his designs."

"The man is more determined than I thought. Perhaps we should pay him off, be rid of him for once and all," Giles insisted, thinking it well worth it to avoid any more trouble and insure Gwyneth's safety.

"Never," she disagreed with vehemence. "He would just come back for more. He must be apprehended and imprisoned if this persecution continues."

Giles wavered. "He probably has abandoned all thoughts of abducting you and thought up a new plan."

"Nonsense. What can he do? We have been warned and would not be caught again. Besides, I want to stay in London for all the excitement. All those lovely gowns I bought in Paris must be paraded," she appealed, believing he could not deny her this treat. "Soon you will retire to Sussex and become a landlord, and I will miss all the glamour of your being Wellington's aide."

"You don't fool me for a moment, my girl. You think because you have foiled the comte once you are more than competent to tangle with him again. This business about the festivities is just an excuse," Giles insisted, knowing his wife.

"Anyway, we have had enough journeying for the moment. In the past eighteen month, I have been from Detroit to Montreal, across the sea to London, then to Sussex and France. I need some peace," she pouted, behaving like a spoiled society miss but determined to stay in London. "And I don't think your father should dash off to Sussex just now. He needs his rest and to see a good English physician."

That was an argument Giles could not resist and so it was decided, but he continued to worry and watch, expecting trouble in some form. Although when it came, it was not at all what he might have expected.

Several nights after their arrival, Giles escorted Gwyneth to Almack's, where Wellington had promised to make an appearance. Gwyneth was glowing with happiness and looked especially charming in a gown by Picot of pale apricot tulle over satin embroidered in gold and silver, one of her Paris purchases. She also wore the diamond and ruby necklace that had attracted the comte's notice.

Just that day Giles had sold out, refusing to accept a command under Major General Robert Ross, a skilled Peninsula veteran, to fight in America. "I have had enough of war and prefer to act the role of a bucolic country gentleman," he confided ironically to his wife and father. "And the war in America will probably be over before I could win any plaudits," he scoffed. "Now that the peninsula veterans are entering the conflict, it will soon be all up with the Colonials. And I can't see that much has been accomplished."

"Since the duke has refused to serve in America, I can understand your own reluctance and applaud your decision," the earl approved and was joined gratefully by Gwyneth. If she wondered how Giles would settle to a rather tame existence as a landlord and man about town, she did not voice her fears. At least he would be safe.

Almack's, a rather dreary hall whose cachet Gwyneth did not understand, was filled with the haut monde, all intent on viewing the conquering hero. There were few uniforms among the fashionable guests, for most of the men were wearing, as was Giles, the de rigueur dress of that most proper assembly: cream satin breeches and low, buckled shoes with dark satin coats and pristine cravats. Lady Jersey took the floor with the Tsar to dance that shocking addition to the repertoire, the waltz, which had become the rage since the pair had first danced it on the Tsar's arrival in London. Others soon followed them, Giles and Gwyneth among them, for they had both learned the new steps.

It was a glittering scene, and Gwyneth gave a passing thought to her new position amid all these jewels of the *ton*. Just before eleven Wellington arrived, without his wife, and was mobbed by doting fans. Gwyneth admitted she was thrilled when the great man stopped to speak to them both, as the duke recalled their previous meeting in Bordeaux.

Her own reception by society was most gratifying, and men crowded around to claim a dance. Later, dancing with Ned Waterford, she noticed the duke was partnering a striking brunette whose lush charms and stunning sapphire gown spoke of Paris.

"Who is that beautiful woman dancing with the duke?" she asked Ned, her curiosity aroused, for the woman was an exotic contrast to the English matrons and debutantes.

"That is Heloise d'Alincourt, an émigré," he answered briefly and seemed embarrassed.

"I knew she was French," Gwyneth said, her view confirmed. "But who is she?"

"The widow of an aristo who met the guillotine. She has been here since the end of the Terror and has captured the fancy of several notable men," Ned admitted reluctantly. A loyal friend and an admirer of Gwyneth, he did not want to discuss the luscious Madame d'Alincourt further but had difficulty in evading Gwyneth's questions. At supper Gwyneth sensed that Giles, too, did not want to discuss the Frenchwoman. Pointing her out where she was sitting with Lord and Lady Castlereagh, she indicated her interest.

"What a beauty that lady is. She quite puts the rest of the company in the shade."

"She has the French élan," Giles admitted abruptly. He hoped rumors about Heloise would not reach Gwyneth's ears. Before his posting to America he had had a tempestuous affair with the lady.

"I wonder if she will be returning to France now that Napoleon has been defeated," Gwyneth suggested, for some reason not trusting Giles's reticence.

"I doubt it. She is well-established here," Giles said wryly, and turned the conversation to a discussion of Wellington.

After supper, during one of the last dances of the

evening, Gwyneth noticed Giles dancing with Madame d'Alincourt. He must know her more intimately than he had admitted, for they seemed to be enjoying themselves as old friends. Had Giles had a closer relationship with the Frenchwoman than he had wanted to confess to Gwyneth? A pang of jealousy shook her, and she answered her partner abstractedly. He happened to be Fitz Somerset, who was married to Wellington's niece.

"Do you know Madame d'Alincourt, Lord Raglan?" she asked him, annoyed at her interest but unable to restrain herself.

"Everyone knows the lovely Heloise. She has been a fixture in London society for some years," he said, hoping she would not pursue the matter. He admired Giles's Colonial wife and hoped she would not learn about her husband's notorious affair several years ago. Of course, Giles was just enjoying all the pleasures of being on the town. It was to be hoped that he had learned both discretion and fidelity since his marriage.

"She must have brought her wealth with her, for she is dressed up to the nines," Gwyneth persisted, waiting to learn more about this provocative creature who was wearing not only the latest Parisian fashion but a glittering array of diamonds.

"I suppose so," Fitz admitted, not wanting Gwyneth to suspect that the charming lady had used her charms to empty the pockets of many a young English peer, Giles among them.

Gwyneth was not so naive she did not sense that both Giles's companions in arms felt a certain reluctance in discussing Madame d'Alincourt. The gentlemen's code prevented them from mentioning the lady's amours, and quite possibly Giles had been among them. Of course, she knew he had been with many women in the past. He had never denied his interest in women, but somehow the idea of Heloise d'Alincourt as one of them disturbed her. Gwyneth was convinced that since their mutual confessions of love in France Giles had not pursued or even evidenced any interest in another woman. But now that he had left the Army, he would have to follow tamer pursuits. She wondered if boredom might not lead him to stray, and she could never countenance such an affront. But complying with Lord Raglan's reluctance to discuss the lady, she talked brightly of other matters.

"You were a great success this evening, Gwyneth. Several of my friends congratulated me on my cleverness in acquiring such a jewel of a wife," Giles teased as they prepared for bed long after midnight. "How did you like Almack's?"

"I thought it rather stuffy and remembered rather simpler dances in Canada that were more exciting."

"And where you equally starred as a belle. What a challenge you are, Gwyneth. I never know quite where I am with you," Giles replied, not entirely in jest.

"Good. A little mystery is enticing," Gwyneth mocked.

"Well, there is nothing mysterious about your appeal for me. Let us put it to the test once again," he insisted and, taking her in his arms, began a steady assault on her senses. Gwyneth soon forgot all suspicions of Madame d'Alincourt as their passion rose and was satisfied.

However, she would have been more than a little apprehensive if she had known of the direction of

Heloise's thoughts that same evening following her dance with Giles. Heloise was an accomplished courtesan who had used her numerous charms to attract wealthy men to her side. She had managed to hang on to a vestige of respectability, but there were several staid drawing rooms in London where she was not welcome. She knew that the patronesses of Almack's had been more than reluctant to grant her admittance to that sedate assembly, but Lady Jersey, whose own morals were sketchy, had been prevailed to sponsor her. An opportunist and intriguer, Heloise rarely allowed her emotions to interfere with her pragmatic interests in securing her comfortable lifestyle.

But Giles was an exception. She had bid him goodbye with an assumed insouciance, but she had missed him dreadfully. Now she would like to renew their earlier affair. The temporary inconvenience of his wife did not worry her. With practical good sense she realized that men of his stamp had to marry, establish their nurseries, provide for the next generation. That did not preclude romantic diversions outside the bonds of matrimony. Of course, he must have been greatly attracted to his little Colonial, but he would soon be bored with her and look for a romantic adventure. Heloise would definitely be available. Not only was Giles a fascinating lover but a generous one, a combination she rarely experienced, and she would not allow him to escape this time.

Unlike many women of her type, Heloise did not rely on her sensuality and talent in the bedroom to attract her lovers. Well-educated and knowledgeable in both politics and the arts, she was shrewd and intelligent, able to talk entertainingly on a host of subjects. She had parlayed her various skills into a career the most expert *demimondaine* would not scorn.

Realizing that she had only herself to depend upon and knowing the transitory appeal of sexual pleasures, she had learned to flatter, cajole, and entertain, fascinating her lovers both in bed and in conversation. In Giles she had found not only the ultimate protector but a man who appreciated her other qualities. Remembering their past relationship, she settled back against a mound of lacy pillows and planned the best approach to him. A blatant invitation would not do. She must design some more subtle ploy.

Roger de Fancher had decided that he, too, must employ more subtle means to thwart Giles if he were to succeed in his attempt to lure a sizeable gift from that obdurate nobleman. Arriving in London some days after the Fitzalen-Hills, he contacted some indigent émigrés whom he thought might be of use to him. Despite the hospitality they had received, for the most part these exiles had no love for their hosts. They yearned to regain their lost position and sequestered estates. And they were not above using any method available to attain those ends.

The comte had devised a plan that he thought might gain him what he desired. There were several émigrés who might help him, but what he really sought was an attractive Frenchwoman with entree to the *ton*. And more importantly, one who would cooperate because it was to her advantage.

After careful investigation he had heard of Heloise d'Alincourt, who had gained a certain reputation among her compatriots. Patience was not one of the comte's assets but in this case he exercised it with commendable artistry. Finally, he was prepared to act and prevailed upon a distinguished matron whom he had charmed with his bogus tales of deprivation and his harsh treatment by the Revolution's leaders. Madame Marie de Bocquer was a lonely widow who had endured much before she escaped to London in a fishing trawler, and had seen most of her family and friends fall victim to the guillotine. The comte with his practiced address and sympathetic manner played her with great expertise, and she was not impervious to his flattery and the comfort he offered. It was Madame de Bocquer who told him of Heloise, sniffing somewhat in disgust at that lady's ability to make her way in a hostile world.

"You must remember her, Comte," she said as the two shared a glass of wine, brought by the comte, in her humble rooms off Wigmore Street.

"The name does seem familiar," he agreed cautiously.

"She is notorious for her amours and gulling the English lords to provide her with the money she needs. For some reason our late Queen, poor Marie Antoinette, found her amusing and they became quite intimate in the last days," she confided with barely concealed spite. As a member of the ancient regime, she despised such opportunists.

"What happened to Monsieur d'Alincourt?" the comte asked, suggesting by his tone that he had doubts of that gentleman's existence.

"She had married him at sixteen, an arranged union, I understand. She must be in her late thirties now. He owned impressive estates in Provence, which led to his arrest as a supporter of the monarchy. He died, as so many others, as a royalist, but she managed to escape with the help of the Queen's friend, Count Axel Fersen." She referred, of course, to the Swedish diplomat that many believed was the Queen's lover.

"A clever and fortunate lady," the comte suggested, concealing his delight. Madame d'Alincourt was just the woman he wanted, but he must tread warily. "And I suppose she managed to ensnare some English lord the minute she arrived here."

"So I understand," Madame de Bocquer sniffed. But the wine had loosened her tongue, and she went on to regale the comte with a list of Heloise's conquests, including Viscount Fitzalen-Hill.

"I cannot understand why so many of London's most distinguished matrons have accepted her," his confidante continued at the end of her recital.

"Perhaps their husbands left them no choice," the comte offered.

"No decent woman should countenance her, but we know the English are barbarians," Madam de Bocquer complained, despite the fact that several of these same ladies had been most kind to her.

The comte had learned what he needed to know and before long left his disgruntled informant. An arriviste he might be, but he was clever enough not to abandon her entirely, and the poor neglected woman looked forward to many cozy chats with the charming comte, never suspecting he was bogus.


Gwyneth was enjoying London's various fetes in honor of the victorious duke and his fellow officers. Giles was absent a great deal, renewing acquaintances with old comrade, and attending the duke, who mourned his resignation but was assured that he could count on Giles if he needed him in the unlikely event that England would go to war again, a disaster Wellington hoped to avoid by his diplomacy.

Gwyneth, who had heard a great deal of gossip

during her forays into London society, wondered if Giles's frequent absences meant that he had renewed his relationship with Madame d'Alincourt. Her own meeting with that lady had done nothing to reassure her. They encountered each other at a ball given by Lord and Lady Melbourne, who were recently returned from Ireland. It was a rakish affair, for the notorious Caroline Lamb, Lady Melbourne, had not abandoned her pursuit of Byron, her former lover, but instead besieged him with attention. The scandal was the talk of London. Caro Lamb had made a confidante of Heloise, who was most sympathetic to her trials, while warning her of her husband's fast-vanishing patience. Naturally, Heloise was at the ball, and Gwyneth prevailed upon Ned Waterford to introduce them.

"Delighted," purred Heloise at the introduction. She was looking most ravishing in a gold tissue gown that did little to mask her figure. Gwyneth felt the veriest dowd in her Paris gown of embroidered cream silk, but she managed a smile for the lady.

Heloise, who had her own reasons for cultivating this Canadian upstart, said sympathetically, "We must become friends since we are both, in a sense, exiles from our countries. England must be such a dramatic change from Canada."

Gwyneth, who did not in the least want to be friends with the lady, wondered if that was a veiled insult at her background, but made no demur. Before she could come to the real business that had impelled her to seek out Heloise, Giles interrupted them with a fierce frown at the embarrassed Ned.

"Good evening, Heloise. I see you have met my wife." His tone held a warning Heloise was only too willing to accept.

"*Charmante,*" she agreed, not making any effort to

flirt with Giles. She intended to cultivate the little colonial and evidenced no interest in Giles.

"I believe the next dance is ours, my dear," Giles insisted, turning to Gwyneth with what she thought was an endeavor to interrupt her talk with Heloise.

"Yes, but I hope we can prevail on Madame d'Alincourt to call upon us. We are at home on Wednesday afternoons," Gwyneth said blithely and swanned off on Giles's arm, leaving the discomfited Ned and the urbane lady alone.

"Giles's wife is a darling. I am very fond of her. And he is quite enamored," Ned blundered into speech, reddening at the thought of what he might have begun.

"Yes, indeed. Somehow I never thought Giles would settle down. War must have altered his propensities," Heloise said easily, and before Ned could protest she had wandered off in her turn with a doting young Guardsman.

Giles was too adroit to make any reference to Heloise, and if he was concerned at the meeting of his former mistress and wife, he showed no sign of it. He appeared entirely indifferent to the lady, but Gwyneth's suspicions were aroused. She despised herself for her jealousy, since she remembered how easily Giles had accepted her explanations about her meeting with James Brush. But somehow she could not easily supress her doubts.

# Chapter Twenty-Three

Heloise cultivated few of her fellow émigrés, having decided long ago that their use to her was limited. Only the English aristocrats could provide her with the position and wealth that were vital to her comfortable survival in London. However, she had a grudging admiration for Madame de Bocquer, who, although she posessed no title and lived miserably, commanded a certain respect. The elderly widow had standards Heloise had long since abandoned along with her virtue, but she recognized Madame's worth and would often confide in her, knowing her secrets would be safe with this honorable woman. So when Madame requested that Heloise call upon her to meet a fellow exile, she reluctantly consented. She knew just what to expect, some desiccated bitter old man who mourned the passing of the Capets and railed against Napoleon. She had little patience with those of her countrymen who lived in the past. *Carpe diem* was her motto and not one that many émigrés seemed able to adopt.

Still, she felt she could not refuse Madame de Bocquer and agreed to call upon her on the designated day.

To her surprise she was introduced to Roger de Fancher. The comte, determined to enlist this charming lady in his cause, had prepared carefully for the meeting. He had learned quite a bit about the courtesan and recognized in her an opportunist as skilled as himself in parlaying a few assets into a comfortable situation. He bowed gallantly over her hand and expressed his delight at the meeting.

"How kind of you to spare the time to see me. I know you must have many friends who press you for your company. You have the reputation as a reigning goddess in this *farouche* English society," he said, adopting a subservient air.

"Not at all. I am vastly fond of Madame de Bocquer and would always honor an invitation from her," Heloise replied graciously. Her own assessment of the comte was not far different than his had been of her. She recognized a smooth imposter, for she doubted very much that he had any claim to the title he espoused. A warm-hearted woman when her own interests were not at risk, she wondered how Madame de Bocquer had been gulled by the man, but decided the poor soul was lonely. The attentions of a charming young man who claimed to be of a society in which Madame had been so comfortable in happier days would naturally attract her. But what was his object in cultivating Madame, who was hardly in a position to assist him in whatever ploy he had designed? Heloise would see to it that he did not take advantage of their hostess.

"Comte de Fancher has suffered as we all have from the Revolution and only recently was able to make his way safely to London. Of course now that the war is over he hopes to regain his estates which were sequestered during the late troubles," Madame explained.

"And where are your estates?" Heloise asked abruptly.

"In the south of France," the comte answered vaguely, hoping this charming lady was less astute than she was attractive.

Heloise sensed that he did not want to pursue the matter and obliged by turning to Madame and inquiring as to her well-being. The comte, following her lead, exerted all his considerable charm, and the tea party progressed in an amicable way until the end. He chose his moment well—as Heloise prepared to take her leave.

"Perhaps I might escort you home, Madame d'Alincourt," he suggested effacingly.

Heloise had been waiting for just such a suggestion. She understood the comte wanted to get her alone, and she was not averse to discovering what he intended.

"That would be kind, thank you."

With many professions of thanks and a promise to see Madame de Bocquer before long, the pair took their leave.

Having secured a hackney and handing her into it, the comte chatted easily about fashion and the peculiar habits of the English as the carriage made its way through the crowded streets to Heloise's small house on Wellbeck Street.

"Alas, it is not a fashionable address," she apologized as they drew up in front of her residence. "But it is all I can afford in my straits."

Since the comte's own address was even less chic,

he made no comment but a soft murmur of understanding, and embarked, reaching up to assist her.

"Perhaps if you are not engaged, you might spare
me a few moments as there is a matter I wish to discuss
with you," he offered, ready for a rebuff.

But Heloise's curiosity was aroused. She had
expected some such attempt from the comte and
wondered just what his motive could be. Undoubtedly
he had arranged the meeting through Madame de
Bocquer and was losing no time in capitalizing on
their acquaintance.

"Of course. I have quite a nice wine you might
enjoy. Do come in and we will discuss whatever you
want," she said with a frankness that rather startled
him. He must be on his guard with this woman. She
had a certain astute knowledge of men and affairs
he could use to his advantage, but he must also tread
with great care.

A trim little maid relieved them of their hats and
gloves. He followed Heloise into her small but elegant
drawing room, noticing the signs of affluence in the
silk draperies and Persian rug.

Once seated with the promised wine, an expensive
vintage the comte recognized and for which he was
grateful, he edged cautiously toward his objective.

"I understand you have an entree into the most
reputable of London salons. Naturally, such a lovely
lady with your myriad talents would enjoy much
acclaim," he flattered.

"I have been here some years and have carved out
a comfortable niche for myself, Comte, but what can
I do for you? Much as I enjoy your compliments and
clever repartee, I sense you arranged this meeting
for a reason," Heloise replied, becoming tired of the
subterfuge.

"I think it is rather what we might do for each other. I suspect we both have an interest in a certain gentleman who has just returned from France, a nobleman who acquitted himself with gallantry as a member of the great duke's staff," the comte said, not ready to make a more blatant approach.

"Ah, I see. You have some interest in Lord Fitzalen-Hill," Heloise said, cutting off any intricate explanations by the comte. "And why would you think I have any relationship with the noble lord?"

"I understand several years ago you were very close."

"You have wasted little time in pursuing the usual rumors, I see. But yes, at one time Giles and I were quite intimate," Heloise admitted, amused. What business did this poseur have with Giles, and could she use him to her own ends?

"I suppose the affair broke off when he went abroad to fight in Canada and then married that rather unsuitable Colonial," the comte suggested, revealing he was well up on Giles's career.

"Quite right, and before you go further, I will tell you I would not be unwilling to resume our affair," Heloise said boldly. "But I cannot fathom how that would benefit you, or why I should enlist your cooperation."

"I will tell you, Madame, and we will combine to win both our desires."

After a half an hour the comte left, profuse in his admiration, and Heloise settled back to review what he had told her. As she had thought, the man was a meretricious charlatan, although he never confessed to adopting a bogus title, but he did tell her of his intention to wrest money from Giles and how he could help her attain her own wish, to ensnare that lord once again. She had given him no definite promise of cooperation. He suggested her initial move might be to cultivate the Canadian wife. She would set about that with no delay, as it suited her own plans.


Gwyneth had, in truth, established quite a little salon of her own. Giles's fellow officers found her drawing room a relief from the usual starchy receptions given by many of London's *ton*, and gathered eagerly in Grosvenor Street, where they could relive their battles and enjoy a good glass of wine. Having been endorsed by Lady Jersey, Gwyneth was achieving without much effort a certain cachet that many long-established hostesses envied. Giles congratulated her on her success, proud that his wife had been accepted by his friends. But often he did not attend these galas himself and Gwyneth could not help but wonder how he was spending his time. She hoped it was not with the fascinating Heloise.

Giles sensed a certain coolness in his wife and was baffled by it. He had never thought she might doubt his fidelity, for he never doubted it himself, being more than content with what she offered. He had never dreamt that she could be so satisfying, so receptive in bed, and so entertaining out of it. He had no reason to stray, and his absences were entirely due to Wellington's calls on his time.

Wellington, like Giles, was facing the difficult transition from military to civilian life. He had accepted the post of ambassador to France, where patient diplomacy and tact would prove abler weapons than decisive and brilliant direction of brigades. Wellington knew that his former allies on the battlefield would be much less amenable to his orders or suggestions now than when Napoleon threatened. Old rivalries, jealousies and statesmen's self-esteem all influenced the peace process.

All in all Wellington must step warily, and he wanted trusted men by his side, men whose reliability had been tested in battle. Giles was one of those men, and Wellington urged him to come with him to Paris. Giles hesitated. His father claimed to need him, and he thought Gwyneth preferred Sussex to the diplomatic life. But he was prepared to give as much of his time as the duke requested in London, hoping he was of some use. His own inclination was to stay in England, but he could hardly dismiss his commander's pleas summarily. He had told Gwyneth some of his dilemma, and she appeared to understand that his responsibilities to Wellington kept him occupied. She loathed the role of a suspicious wife, but London society was filled with examples of straying husbands, and she was not completely reassured, especially when Heloise d'Alincourt appeared on the scene.

As Heloise dressed for Gwyneth's Wednesday at-home, she wondered just why she was acceding to the comte's request. She was not a vindictive woman, and what little she had seen of Gywneth she liked. She was not convinced that it was to her advantage to aid the comte, and she was quite sure he had not told her the truth about his claim on the Fitzalen-Hills. He insisted they had promised to help him with a generous gift of money and an intercession with the French government to restore his estates. If he had an estate, it was probably no more than a barn in Provence, if that. When she had finally refused his effort to enlist her in his scheme, he had turned quite ugly, pointing out that he had means to compel her.

Somehow he had discovered that during her exile she had betrayed the English by sending information, gleaned mostly in the bedroom from incautious lovers, to Fouche, the dreaded head of Napoleon's secret police. When she explained that she had done it not for personal gain but to insure the safety of a beloved niece, her only surviving relative, from the guillotine, the comte had not been impressed. He warned her that if he revealed the information to the authorities she risked imprisonment or at the least deportation, and that did not suit her, well-established as she was in England. She felt she had no choice but to follow his instructions, although every instinct rebelled.

Gwyneth was not completely surprised when Heloise called in Grosvenor Street, looking quite ravishing in a scarlet redingote faced in cream and a rakish shako on her head. She greeted her politely and thanked her for coming.

"There is no need for me to make any introduction to my guests, I am sure," she said. "I suppose you know most of them better than I do."

"Ah, no, Lady Fitzalen-Hill. I understand you have had a grand success in society and that the *ton* flocks to your door," Heloise flattered extravagantly. "But I do seem to see a great many familiar faces."

As the Frenchwoman said this, several members of Parliament approached Heloise and greeted her fulsomely, to be followed by Princess Esterhazy, the wife of the Austrian Ambassador and, rumor had it, mistress of Metternich. Obviously Madame d'Alincourt had the entree to the pinnacles of society, for, even if some starchy dowagers disapproved of her, their husbands enjoyed her company.

Giles happened to be present, and Gwyneth tried not to appear too interested in the meeting between Heloise and her husband. But Heloise was too clever to force herself on Giles immediately, if, indeed that was her purpose in accepting Gwyneth's impulsive invitation. She exerted her charm on the gentlemen who surrounded her and made no effort to engage Giles in a tête-à-tête. Skillfully she maneuvered her entourage into a corner by one of the garden windows, near where Giles was chatting with Lord Palmerston. The older gentleman was one of her admirers, and he looked up and saw her, a smile breaking over his austere face.

"Ah, Madame, what a pleasant surprise. Our host did not tell me you would be present today," he said, indicating Giles, who had no recourse but to join the group around Heloise, who made way deferentially for Lord Palmerston.

"*Bonjour,* my lord," Heloise greeted Lord Palmerston with a warm smile, and then turned to Giles. "I decided to accept your wife's kind invitation and here I am," she said innocently.

Giles cast a glance across the room at Gwyneth, who had been cornered by Lady Bessborough, a voluble talker, and appeared not to notice them.

"It's always pleasant to see you, Madame d'Alincourt," he said briefly, while inwardly wondering what she meant by this visit. The last thing he wanted was for Heloise to cultivate Gwyneth, and that might be what she had in mind. Of all his mistresses Heloise had proven to be the most provocative, for she had talents beyond the scope of most courtesans. He had become involved with her despite knowing she would cost him a pretty penny and had been relieved when the war interrupted their relationship. She was too sophisticated to be demanding and too expert in the arts of love to bore him, but he had never trusted her. And he greatly feared that her attempt at reestablishing an acquaintance would only lead to trouble. After a few casual words, he left her with Lord Palmerston and drifted across the room to where his father was talking with Lord Sidmouth, the Home Secretary, about agricultural distress in the Midlands.

Within a few minutes Heloise had taken her leave. She was satisfied that she had made an impact on Giles and was rather amused at his light rebuff. She had a very good idea of what he was thinking but she was prepared to allow him some license. She doubted that he was still attracted to her, for the gossips implied he was totally enamored with his wife and had abandoned all his past flirtations. But she was not discouraged. She had several weapons in her armory and Giles represented a challenge, not entirely inspired by the comte's insistence on her cooperation in his designs.

Somewhat reassured by Giles's indifference to Madame d'Alincourt, Gwyneth relaxed but later that evening could not resist questioning him about the lady.

"I wonder how old she is?" she asked him as they prepared for bed.

"In her thirties, but very well preserved," Giles mocked. He thought Gwyneth was unduly interested in the lady and wondered what she had heard.

"More than preserved, Giles, absolutely stunning. She puts us all in the shade."

"Not you, my dear. You have qualities Heloise d'Alincourt never possessed. Don't be gulled by that stylish facade, her stock in trade. She is an intriguant that puts even Sally Jersey to the rout."

"Don't you like her?" Gwyneth asked innocently.

"At one time I more than liked her, but don't get maggots in your head. That was long before I met a fierce Colonial who entrapped me," he teased, hoping to distract her.

"Oh, dear, I do hope I will not always be stumbling over your past loves and having to protect you from their efforts to win you back," Gwyneth answered wryly.

"Not to worry. I haven't the time. Between you and Wellington I am thoroughly exhausted."

"But not too tired to go to sleep, I hope," Gwyneth smiled at him with a wicked glint in her eye.

"Never that," Giles promised, and for the moment Gwyneth's suspicions of the experienced and fascinating Madame d'Alincourt were put to rest as more exciting endeavors took precedence.

# Chapter Twenty-Four

Preoccupied with each other, their plans for the future, and the London celebrations honoring the defeat of Napoleon, Gwyneth and Giles were convinced that the comte had disappeared from their lives. Certainly they saw no sign of him as they went about their various duties and pleasures.

Any daily surveillance of the Grosvenor mansion would have been noticed, and the comte was not so foolish as to attempt it. Neither was he so foolish as to think that Heloise d'Alincourt could be enlisted in his plan to kidnap the Fitzalen-Hills. All he wanted from her at the moment was a report of their activities, and she seemed willing to supply this information, for a price. The comte was well-aware that Heloise had her own motives, and with his experience of women, he mistakenly believed she was inspired by revenge against Giles for deserting her. In that supposition he badly misjudged his ally. What he did not realize was that Heloise did not believe a word of

A RAKE'S JOURNEY 291

his far-fetched story but had her own reasons for cultivating Lord Fitzalen-Hill. She hoped to cause a rift between Gwyneth and Giles which would enable her to regain her lucrative position as his mistress. Perhaps the bogus comte would be of some use to her in this scheme. Not for one moment did she consider conspiring in any dangerous, illegal, or suspect behavior that would rebound to her disgrace. In some ways she admired the comte's effrontery and ambitions, but she was not prepared to risk her own position to help him.

He had made a habit of calling upon her in mid-morning, tactfully allowing time for her to repair whatever the night's excesses had brought. It was not part of his plan to encounter any of her lovers, so the later hours of the morning seemed the most convenient and reliable time for his visits. But he was becoming impatient with his lack of progress and had determined to persuade Heloise that further exertions were necessary.

"Good morning, madame," he greeted her as she came into the small morning room, looking quite rested and attractive. But beneath the cleverly applied cosmetic aids, the comte thought he saw the beginning signs of age that she could not keep at bay forever. She must be well into her thirties and could not have many years left in which to parlay her talents and beauty into the comfortable income she craved. But he would never refer to such an indignity.

"How are you, Comte? Still determined to force the Fitzalen-Hills into coughing up the guineas?" she mocked, intent on reminding him theirs was not a sociable arrangement.

"With your help, madame, I am sure I can accomplish it while you attain your heart's desire," he said grandiloquently.

"You have been most cooperative with your reports on the Fitzalen-Hills' movements. But I feel I cannot delay much longer."

"No," Heloise agreed. "I heard from the viscountess that they will be leaving for Sussex soon. Whatever nastiness you have in store for them will be much more difficult there," she said, a smile robbing her words of some of their sting.

"You traduce me, madame. I am only trying to settle accounts," the comte replied, looking grieved. Then he abandoned any further posing and settled down to the business of the day.

"Have you established yourself so well with the household that an invitation from you would be accepted?" he asked.

"An invitation to which one, Lord or Lady Fitzalen-Hill?" Heloise asked.

"Well, preferably, Lord Fitzalen-Hill. It would be most helpful if he would renew his former relationship with you. And you would not be averse to that," the comte suggested slyly.

"No, I wouldn't," Heloise admitted frankly, "but I don't think it's possible. He is quite in love with his wife, and of the two she is the friendlier, with that rather engaging candor one can expect from Colonials. Doubtless she has heard of our former affair but discounts its importance, and she is right to do so."

"Well, that rather alters my thoughts, but I think I can still contrive to gain my purpose," the comte assured her and then gave her some orders in honeyed tones that did not deceive Heloise. If she refused to cooperate or betrayed him, she would find herself in an unhappy situation with the authorities. Even if she managed to talk her way out of any accusation of treasonable activity, her reputation would suffer and she would be forced to seek sanctuary in France, where her opportunities were limited. She must agree to what he ordered. She sensed that beneath his suave compliments and flattering deference lay a brutal and dangerous bourgeois who would stop at nothing to achieve his avaricious desire. Though she knew she was most likely wasting her time in trying to lure Giles into an affair, she wondered if she could outwit the comte and secure her own safety by pretending to go along with him and find some way to warn the Fitzalen-Hills. It was a course filled with peril, but she might find it to her advantage. However, none of the thoughts racing through her mind were revealed in the bland well-schooled face she turned to the comte as he revealed his nefarious design.

"You seem to have provided for every contingency, Comte," she praised him, secretly aghast at his audacity.

"Perhaps, but your role is most important, madame, so do not fail me, and do not take too long in carrying out my instructions," he warned in a manner she found intimidating.

But she appeared to accept his implied threat casually. "I will be seeing the Fitzalen- Hills tonight at a dinner party and can set the scene," she promised.

His purpose accomplished, the comte bowed and prepared to leave but not without a final word. "Do not disappoint me, madame, or I might have to disappoint you," he said cryptically and hurried away, leaving Heloise with dark thoughts and prey to all sorts of fears and indecision.

There must be some way out of her dilemma that would thwart the comte, protect her from his revenge, and insure the gratitude of the Fitzalen-Hills. But how was she to arrange this pleasing denouement without putting herself in jeopardy? Of course, she could go to the Fitzalen-Hills and confess that the comte had tried to enlist her in a dastardly scheme to wring money from them. But the comte had cleverly not told her the exact details of his plot. Her part was only to lure either Gwyneth or Giles to her house, and then he would direct events. If the Fitzalen-Hills turned up with an escort, intent on apprehending the comte, she was convinced he would escape that fate by meeting them with bland assurances that Heloise had mistaken his friendly endeavors to press his demands. There was no proof but her word, and he could deny it all, leaving the authorities no recourse but to let him go. Then she would be in a dreadful situation, prey to his revenge. No, there must be another way. She carefully weighed her options. To inform the Fitzalen-Hills and secure their gratitude or to go along with the comte, protect herself from arrest or deportation, and insure her position. Was it possible to emerge from this business unscathed?

Arriving at Lady Bessborough's home that evening for dinner, Heloise appeared even more ravishing than usual, in a daring gown of silver tissue accented by a large and expensive set of rubies. She was escorted by Lord Alvanley, a notable bon vivant and bachelor whose reputation as a wit and sportsman was unrivaled. A connoisseur of food, wine, and women, his appearance lent a cachet to any occasion.

"Between us, my dear Heloise, we will insure that Lady Bessborough's dinner will be *une pièce à succès*. Beauty and the beast, eh?" he quipped.

"You flatter me, my lord, and traduce yourself," Heloise purred. Her cultivation of Lord Alvanley had been a master stroke, for his endorsement opened many doors to her, and she was genuinely fond of the portly peer.

Lady Bessborough, mother of two of Wellington's most highly regarded officers, took a keen interest in military affairs. She thought it a pity that Wellington had resigned from the Army to become an ambassador, and spoke her mind plainly. Giles, fond of the voluble lady, tried to defend his chief but laughingly agreed that the duke's talents were more fitted to the battlefield than the salons of Paris.

"He should have gone to America and settled the Colonials," his hostess insisted, a martial light in her eye.

"I believe that small conflict is winding down. No sense in sending in the heavy guns when a few grapeshots will do the job," Frederick Ponsonby, Lady Bessborough's son, protested. Ponsonby had behaved with great valor during the Peninsular campaigns, and Wellington had mentioned him often in dispatches.

"You fought in Canada, did you not, Giles?" Ponsonby asked.

"Yes, and was thoroughly routed by a charming Canadian," Giles quipped, referring to Gwyneth, who smiled in appreciation of her husband's reference to their meeting, but was not about to allow him too much license.

"As I remember it, we had several rather spirited passages at arms before the final victory," she reported, earning laughter and a rueful agreement from Giles. No longer in awe of the high sticklers in London's closed society, she found that they rather enjoyed a woman who spoke her mind. She scorned the methods used by practiced flirts and watched Heloise exert her charms with a certain distaste, but then reproved herself. Who was she to criticize? In her impregnable position as Giles's wife, a respected member of a society whose rules she sometimes found hypocritical and rigid, she had not had to make her way as had Heloise. Despite her knowledge of Giles's past affair with the Frenchwoman, she did not dislike her. She found her intriguing but also rather pathetic. With all the arrogance of youth, she was convinced that finding herself in a like position she would not have insured her survival by Heloise's methods.

Later in the drawing room where the women had retired to leave the gentlemen to their port and war stories, she sought out Heloise, aware that several of the starchier guests tended to ignore her.

"I do admire your gown, madame. You manage to make the rest of us look like dowds," Gwyneth complimented her as they sat on a settee somewhat removed from the rest of the company.

Heloise thanked her prettily while thinking that Gwyneth was, in truth, unusual. Any other woman in her position would have treated Heloise with haughty disdain. She loathed having to embroil this lovely innocent in the comte's schemes, but she had long ago learned she could not afford charitable gestures if they threatened her own well-being.

"Lady Fitzalen-Hill, I do hope we can be friends. I fear many English ladies of high rank view me with suspicion," Heloise said, sighing a bit as if to signify she did not understand this attitude.

"Of course, madame, and do call me Gwyneth. I have not yet accustomed myself to Lady Fitzalen-Hill, stupid I know, but we are much more informal in the Colonies."

"How kind and do reciprocate. My name is Heloise. I have always hated it, but it was my godmother's. Poor lady, she died during the Terror, but I was quite fond of her." Heloise often made these small references to her situation, not so much seeking sympathy as reminding London's doyennes that they had not suffered any such experiences. The haut monde here, as in France, vastly feared the rabble and the import of Revolutionary ideas that might imperil their own status. Then realizing that she had secured Gwyneth's compassion, she capitalized on the moment.

"I am having a small rout on Friday afternoon, a quite spontaneous party. I know you and Giles are besieged with invitations, but I would be so honored if you could come," she said, careful not to be too pressing. If Gwyneth refused, she would have to fall back on a less attractive alternative.

"I cannot, of course, speak for Giles. He seems to be heavily occupied at the Foreign Office these days, but I will certainly manage to attend your rout. Thank you for inviting me," Gwyneth accepted.

Heloise smiled and thanked her. She could not but think that this little Colonial could give a lesson in manners to some of London's high steppers, whose arrogance often led them to outright rudeness and, equally annoying, a certain indifference to anyone's convenience but their own. Heloise thought again how much she hated deceiving Gwyneth and wished there was some way to warn her of the comte's chicaneries. But nobility would not protect her own rather perilous situation, and she had best remember that.

Before too long the gentlemen joined them, and

there was no more opportunity for any exchange between Heloise and Gwyneth. Nor did Giles make any attempt to approach her. Heloise smiled. He was unnecessarily wary. She had almost abandoned any effort to renew their former affair. In view of the comte's plans, it would not only be unsuitable but rash. Well, she had accomplished her mission for this evening. She had done all she could for the comte. Now she must look to her own survival. And she settled back to listen to the rather overblown soprano who was entertaining the company with a selection of arias.

Riding back to Grosvenor Street after the dinner party, Gwyneth hesitated to broach Heloise's invitation. For some reason she felt Giles would not be receptive, and she wished now she had not succumbed so easily herself. A momentary pity for the émigrée had overcome her common sense. Surely no good would come of them spending any time in Heloise's company. Well, she could always send a note pleading a prior engagement for them both. Snuggling down beside Giles in the coach, she thought how fortunate she was to have won Giles's love and respect after their miserable beginnings. Now all that was needed to seal her happiness was to become pregnant. Actually, she wondered why it was proving so difficult when that first time aboard ship had been enough. She giggled thinking of that tempestuous occasion.

"And what are you laughing at? Not me, I hope?" Giles asked her indulgently.

"I was remembering that storm aboard ship when I behaved so disgracefully. But look what my reward was."

"Me?" Giles mocked, but then took her in his arms

and kissed her soundly. "You are a minx, but I have won my just desserts."

Since Gwyneth could only agree with those sentiments, she gave herself up to the delights of Giles's caresses, and all thoughts of Heloise d'Alincourt were banished.

# *Chapter Twenty-Five*

However, the next morning Gwyneth did remember Heloise's invitation and mentioned it to her husband.

"I really don't want to go, Gwyneth," he said rather
sharply.

Gwyneth, tempted to ask why, bit her tongue. Giles,
noticing that she seemed somewhat annoyed at his
abrupt refusal, hurried to explain.

"It's not that I fear exposing myself to her charms,
but I rather dislike her blatant cultivation of you.
Heloise may be charming, but she is a conniver and
must have some reason for these tenders of friendship. And I don't think she believes for one minute
I have any interest in renewing our long-ago relationship," he said frankly, determined to get this whole
business out into the open. "You know, Gwyneth, the
French are devious and practical at the same time, a
nasty combination that makes them difficult to deal
with. Look at Talleyrand."

"Well, I doubt that Heloise is any Talleyrand, and what harm can it do to attend her party?" Gwyneth persisted stubbornly.

"None, I suppose. We will compromise. You go and make my excuses. Say I was delayed at the Foreign Office and might join you later. I don't trust Heloise. Thank goodness we are going down to Sussex next week."

"Yes, I have had quite enough of London. All right. I will make a brief appearance and assure her you are in great demand by high and mighty ministers," she teased, and they left it at that.

The next few days were troubling ones for Heloise. She had accomplished what the comte had ordered but felt most uncomfortable about it. And she had not contrived a way to thwart the comte, save the Fitzalen-Hills from what she was convinced was a dangerous plot, and insure that she herself escaped any repercussions.

The comte had paid her a visit to insure that all was in train for the Friday rendezvous. Heloise made one last effort to dissuade him.

"I doubt you can bring off your rather primitive plan, sir. It will be quite obvious to the Fitzalen-Hills that I am not giving a party when they see no carriages on the street."

"They will not realize that until it is too late, and they might just think they are early arrivals." The comte believed he had provided for every contingency, but he had underestimated Heloise. He thought she was so frightened of losing her secure life that she had completely submitted to his domination and threats. That she thought him distasteful, he found amusing, rather enjoying his control over this high-toned lady. But to his surprise she suddenly made certain demands of her own that he was in no position to refuse, having gone this far.

"I will not take part in this charade. I have done what you insisted, lured your victims to my house so that you could carry out your abduction, if that is what you have in mind. But I will not receive them and behave as if I were your partner in this regrettable plot," Heloise insisted.

"You forget, madame, I have the means to coerce you," the comte said as if her objections were hardly worth discussing.

"No, you forget, Comte, that if I am in your power, you are equally in mine," Heloise warned.

"Oh, I don't think so, madame. I have proof of your treasonable behavior."

"I wonder if the proof is not a figment of your imagination. I might still put it to the test," she replied coolly.

"Why are we quarreling, madame? Surely we both have a great deal at stake here. To humor your delicacy I will not insist that you be present on Friday. But do not entertain any wild ideas about betraying me to the Fitzalen-Hills," he said in an ugly tone.

She shrugged her shoulders and turned away, hoping he had not noticed her alarm at his reference to her warning his victims. That was just what she had in mind, although she had not quite figured out how to effect it without putting herself in jeopardy. But she was determined to do it and in the meantime deceive the comte. Both Heloise and Roger de Fancher were adept at concealing their real motives, although Heloise perhaps had a slight advantage he did not enjoy. She understood the world which he

was trying to enter and could judge the reactions of
the actors in their drama far better. It was just as well
he did not perceive this or he might have reconsid-
ered his scheme. He believed his other attempts had
failed because he had trusted their execution to dolts.
Now he would personally control events, and all
would turn out as he had planned.


On the Friday in question neither the earl nor Giles
were home for luncheon, so Gwyneth dined alone
on a tray in her bedroom. She had spent the morning
writing a long letter to her sister Delia, whose prior
letter concerned the coming relief of Detroit and
a reunion with her husband. Delia appeared quite
uninterested in her sister's travels and marriage, perhaps because she sensed their ways had diverged drastically. But Gwyneth did not resent this failing on
Delia's part. She understood it and sympathized with
her sister's unhappy position. Her own life had
altered so dramatically since leaving Detroit, she
sometimes wondered if she had dreamt all her adventures.

But she had not imagined the outcome of marriage,
a blissful aspect she did not deceive herself could
continue at such a passionate pace. But she was convinced that Giles's attitude, whether because of his
wounds and the war, or some late realization that his
life needed stability and warmth, had changed. She
was such a sentimentalist, she chided herself,
believing that she might be responsible for this
change, even though he assured her countless times
that she was.

And here she sat, comfortably contemplating
attending a rout given by his former mistress. What

a sophisticate she had become! She laughed at herself and rose to ring for Mary to assist her in dressing for the party.

The comte arrived at Heloise's house just as she, too, was finishing her luncheon. She did not offer him any, which did not improve his humor.

"I agree, madame, that you need not be present in the salon when the Fitzalen-Hills arrive, but do not leave the house. I have with me some confederates, rather rough men, who would be forced to restrain you if you tried. But I am sure you would not, even at this late hour, attempt any bêtise."

Heloise showed no alarm, only shrugged her shoulders, and said indifferently, "I am in your hands for the moment, sir."

The comte frowned. He did not like her tone or her words. Nothing must go awry at the last moment. He had too much invested in this affair, and he must succeed.

"Perhaps I may be allowed to retire to my boudoir, Heloise said." You may post one of your thugs outside the door. My maid has been instructed to take the guests into the drawing room, where she assumes I will be awaiting them. There is no reason for her to know more."

"Of course not, madame. Very wise," the comte agreed, thinking he had intimidated his ally enough and must treat her with at least some civility. "I have regretted embroiling you in this business, madame, but I really had no choice," he explained as if apologizing. The comte always believed he could charm any woman out of the sullens.

* * *

Gwyneth arrived before Madame d'Alincourt's house promptly at four o'clock. She had not yet adopted the fashionable habit of late attendance but was somewhat surprised not to see other carriages letting off guests. She told the coachman to return for her in an hour and a half, thinking that sufficient time to pay her respects. As she mounted the steps, a sudden distaste for the occasion overcame her. She had stubbornly insisted on accepting this invitation, despite Giles's objections, and now she felt he might be in the right of it. She should not have come. Well, there was no use for it. She must just do the civil and escape as soon as she could.

At her knock she was admitted by a smartly attired maid, a girl with a sly expression and bold eyes, who looked approvingly at Gwyneth's modish walking gown of sprigged silk, and took her straw bonnet and gloves.

"Just this way, milady," she said and ushered her toward the closed doors of the drawing room, throwing them opening and announcing, "Lady Fitzalen-Hill."

Somehow Gwyneth was not completely taken aback to discover the drawing room was empty, no sign of her hostess. But from one of the wing-backed chairs beside the fireplace, a familiar figure arose at her entrance.

"Good afternoon, Lady Fitzalen-Hill. We meet again, as you see," Comte Roger de Fancher said in that smooth, suave voice Gwyneth remembered well.

* * *

While Heloise and Gwyneth had been having their luncheons at their separate establishments, a Runner at the desk of the Bow Street magistrate's office received an odd anonymous communication. Reluctantly he abandoned his pie and pint and took the message into Sir Nathaniel Conant's office.

"Thought you ought to take a gander at this, governor," the man said and handed his chief the heavy cream stationery. "It was delivered just now by a neat little maid, looked a superior type."

"You should have detained her," said Sir Nathaniel.

"Couldn't do that, gov. She hadn't done nothing."

Sir Nathaniel opened the letter reluctantly. He sensed trouble and he wanted to leave for his luncheon.

> *To the Magistrate:*
> *If you will visit the house with the green door*
>    *on Wellbeck Street at four o'clock today, you will*
>       *prevent the abduction of Lord and Lady Fitzalen-*
>       *Hill by a false Frenchman.*
>                              *A Concerned Citizen*

"Probably a hum, but best not to chance it. Fitzalen-Hill is the Earl of Selkirk's son and has just returned from France where he was on Wellington's staff," the magistrate informed his underling, who did not seem impressed. The Runners rarely became involved with the *ton*. Occasionally they would be hired to chase a thieving servant, but most of their work lay among the flash houses, where cutthroats and purse snatchers dwelt. Only recently had Bow Street installed a force of detectives to augment the Runners.

"Best to send Sayers and Thompson," Sir Nathaniel, ordered, referring to two of his best plain-clothesmen. "I think they would be wise to call on Lord Fitzalen-Hill first to see if this is all some monstrous joke. Young bucks often think up japes like this, but we must be sure there is no truth in the tale." Sir Nathaniel thought he would eat a hurried lunch and return here to control events if they warranted it. He did not want to offend the Earl of Selkirk or his heir, both of whom had friends in powerful places as well as being aristocrats of the first stare.

So Thomas Sayers, a burly but mild-mannered man, and his partner, thin, rangy Bill Thompson, both bowler-hatted and carrying their, truncheons, set off well before the appointed hour to call at Grosvenor Street. With them went three Runners, who would obey their instructions. All of them felt some reluctance to invade nobs' territory, but Sir Nathaniel had made his orders clear: if Lord Fitzalen-Hill were not at home, they were to discover his direction, and if that proved impossible, to call on the house with the green door at Wellbeck Street and interview the head of the household.

In Heloise's drawing room Gwyneth faced the bogus comte with a coolness she was far from feeling. "You do not seem surprised to see me, Lady Fitzalen-Hill. Can it be that you were expecting me?" the comte said with a disingenuous air. He had his victim at his mercy, and he rather enjoyed drawing out the business since he knew he would be victorious in the end. He had not forgotten Gwyneth's scornful dismissal of him at their last meeting, nor her shot on the road to Amiens. She would pay for those indignities.

"Well, Comte, you do seem to turn up like the bad penny," Gwyneth replied nonchalantly, although she was far from feeling at ease.

The comte greeted this sally with a tight smile, and crossed to the wall where he gave a hard tug to the bell pull. Milady would be singing a different tune before long.

"Would it be maladroit of me to ask where my hostess is?" Gwyneth asked, sitting down calmly in a bergère chair. Looking about she decided that Heloise's taste in decor, as in dress, could not be faulted. The appointments were fresh and elegant, combining soft shades of rose and leaf green, and the furniture well-tooled Sheraton.

"She has been delayed and asked me to give you tea," the comte replied, taking a chair facing her. For a moment watching his victim, who did not appear in the least discomfited, he wondered if she were carrying her little pistol in that beaded reticule by her side. But no, he scoffed, a fashionable lady would not set out on an afternoon call with a weapon. But Gwyneth's air of patient distaste irritated him. She would regret her casual treatment of him.

The bold-faced maid appeared with a tray which she deposited on a nearby table and left the room without a word. Before Gwyneth could make any move to play hostess, the comte had lifted the Sèvres teapot and poured two cups of tea. He crossed to Gwyneth and offered her one. All unsuspecting, Gwyneth accepted and took a comforting sip, prepared to hear whatever the comte had decided to say. Her expression revealed nothing but a recognition of a tedious duty that must be performed before she could take her leave.

The comte said, "You have not changed your mind

about providing me with some token of your gratitude for my rescue of you and your husband that day in Bordeaux?" His grandiloquent style Gwyneth found faintly ridiculous when the man was trying to blackmail her.

"No, Comte, I haven't," she replied firmly, but having swallowed her tea rather quickly now began to feel uncomfortably hot. Of course, it was a warm day, and Heloise had not allowed any windows to be opened. It was very stuffy in here. The comte's face swam eerily before her, a sly expression of evil shadowing his usual smooth guise.

He watched closely as she slipped rapidly into unconsciousness. It was a powerful and quick-acting opiate, and before long Gwyneth had slumped sideways in her seat, her breath rising and falling softly.

Giving a grunt of satisfaction, the comte rose and took one of her hands, which was unresponding. Yes, she had gone off nicely. Turning, he walked to the door, opened it and nodded to an accomplice who stood waiting.

"She will give no trouble for a few hours. Have you the carriage outside?"

"Yes, governor. All ready," the man growled.

"Well, take a look to see we are unobserved. It's a quiet street. We will have to be sure there are no watchers, but we can always say she is my sister who has suffered a spell and we are taking her to the physician if anyone would be so bold as to enquire. But the English are a stolid lot and probably won't even notice," the comte sneered. So near his objective he was preparing for anything, although he believed he had already triumphed. That uppish Madame d'Alincourt was secluded in her room, under guard. She was no threat. He had had her under observation all day, and she had made no move to divulge his plans. Now he could convey this fine lady to the hiding place where she would remain until the ransom was paid. The comte and his confederate lifted Gwyneth's slight form and carried her across the hall. The comte peered out the door.

"Where is the carriage?" he cried in alarm. But before he could take any action, the door was kicked open by a hard boot and three men rushed into the hall. The comte's paid thug, taking one look, dropped Gwyneth heavily and made to run toward the servants' quarters and the back door, but was brought down smartly by a hefty Runner, who planted a large foot on his body. In the meantime Sayers and Thompson had manhandled the astounded comte, and handed Gwyneth to Giles, who grasped his wife and turned a steely eye on the comte.

"What have you done, you devil?" he asked in tones that frightened the comte more than the restraining arms of the Runners. Prudently he said nothing.

"Doped her, it looks like, my lord, and was trying to abduct her," Sayers answered, prodding the comte with his truncheon while his colleague took out a pair of handcuffs and manacled the comte's hands.

"I'll kill him," Giles threatened, thoroughly aroused and eager for revenge as he looked at Gwyneth's pale face and felt the imperceptible fluttering of her heart beneath his hands.

"No need, sir. Abduction is a capital crime. He'll swing for it, never fear," said Thompson cheerfully.

The comte gasped and sputtered, "I don't know what you mean. The lady took ill as we were having tea, and I was just carrying her to a physician."

"Don't believe him, sirs," muttered the man who lay beneath the Runner's boot. "He meant to take her off and keep her until the guineas were paid.'' The man, realizing his own peril, was trying to mitigate his crime by placing the blame on the comte in the usual fashion of thieves who fall out.

The Runners, under the direction of Sayers and Thompson, made a thorough search of the house, capturing two more thugs, one outside of Heloise's boudoir and another in the kitchen. They offered no opposition. Whatever Heloise heard or thought of the movements, she made no appearance. Her explanations would come later.

Giles, who had followed the Bow Street Runners to the house in his own vehicle, wanted only to get Gwyneth home, and placed her tenderly on the squabs, barely waiting to see that the comte and his confederates were bundled off under the careful guidance of the Runners. He promised to call on the station in Bow Street later and press his charges, but it was obvious that there would be no release for any of these base conspirators. His first instinct was to carry Gwyneth to safety.

# *Epilogue*

The warm sun shining from a cloudless sky touched Gwyneth with soothing comfort as she sat with Giles and the earl on the terrace of Selkirk Hall. It was some days after her horrid encounter with the comte, and she had completely recovered her spirits, although she admitted she had quite lost her fancy for tea. She had awoken from the effects of the sedative in her own bed in Grosvenor Square, with a bad headache, to find the earl sitting by her side.

"Giles went off to Bow Street to make sure that villain was charged," he explained. "How are you feeling, my dear?"

"My head aches and I can't seem to focus my eyes properly, but I am sure I will feel better soon," Gwyneth admitted.

"The doctor says you will have no ill effects once the opiate has worn off, but it was a dreadful ordeal for you," he said, shaking his head. "We should have expected some move from that false Frenchman.

Never trusted the French, all charm and no substance."

"Poor Heloise," Gwyneth said now, remembering that lady's part in the deception.

"I don't see how you can possibly feel any sympathy for her," Giles protested, not willing to abandon his own anger toward Madame d'Alincourt, although she had made a piteous plea for forgiveness.

"Oh, the poor thing. She has no husband to protect her, and the comte was blackmailing her, too, so she had to appear to cooperate with him. After all, she did send the warning letter to Bow Street," Gwyneth insisted, feeling some compassion for Heloise.

Giles felt so such emotion. He had endured a very heated interview with the lady during which he had forced from her a somewhat edited account of her involvement.

"Well, she ended up without you, Giles, and might even have to give up her comfortable situation in England and return to France," Gwyneth offered teasingly. She knew Giles felt some guilt that Gwyneth had ever been exposed to Heloise in the first place.

"Heloise will survive. She always manages to find a protector, and she has several good friends in high places. I doubt very much if she will suffer as she deserves." Giles would not forget Gwyneth's near brush with tragedy, nor how he had felt on seeing her white face and limp form that afternoon.

"I've never understood how you arrived so providentially," Gwyneth questioned, until now not really interested in anything but the knowledge that she was safe from any more attempts by the wretched comte to capture her.

"Well, Heloise had cleverly decided to thwart the comte, but naturally wanted to insure her own safety.

Instead of doing the courageous and sensible thing, warning us personally, she dispatched her personal maid to Bow Street with that damned mysterious message."

"Be fair, Giles," the earl interrupted temperately. "She was in some danger herself. The Frenchman had men watching her, and it would have gone badly with her if she had tried to send us a message and been caught by him. Really most astute of her to send her maid out with a shopping basket. The fools never suspected her real errand."

"Yet she knew that the comte was sitting in her drawing room like some fat spider waiting to lure Gwyneth into his net. Even if he had not informed her that he meant to abduct you, she must have known he meant no good."

"But how did you come so quickly on the scene?"

"Sir Nathaniel Conant, the magistrate, insisted the Runners call at Grosvenor Street to find me, and Hoskins told them I was at the Foreign Office. They interrupted me in a very trying discussion about Canada and showed me the note. As soon as I saw the mention of the house in Wellbeck Street with the green door, I knew Heloise was at the back on the whole unsavory business. You might remember I told you not to accept that invitation."

"Nothing is more tedious than a man who preens when he is right," Gwyneth complained but with a twinkle in her eye. "But I admit I would have been most happy to see you, that is if I had been conscious."

"All very well, my girl, to laugh now, but I was never so frightened as I was that afternoon. It will teach you the worth of obeying your husband."

"We'll see." Gwyneth was not so subdued by her

experience that she was eager to give in to Giles on all counts.

The earl, sensing that they were about to have one of their famous passages at arms and knowing it would all end with passionate kisses, excused himself and left them to their brangling.

Gwyneth watched him affectionately as he crossed the lawn on his way to the stables and a comforting chat with his head groom.

"Your father is such a darling, so kind and tactful."

"Unlike his son," Giles admitted ruefully. He knew how much Gwyneth admired his father and for those very qualities he seemed not to have inherited.

"You have other assets, and unfortunately I find them so enticing that I fall under your spell and become most weak-willed," Gwyneth said.

"Stubborn and shrewish," Giles countered, but robbed his words of an animus by bending over her chair and giving her a sound kiss.

"Despite poor Heloise's conduct, I still think she was very clever. Perhaps I will ask her to be godmother to the heir."

Giles opened his mouth to protest but then Gwyneth's real meaning shocked him into sputtering, "What do you mean? Are you pregnant?"

"Yes, I think so, and this time I will make no forays into dangerous situations," Gwyneth promised.

"I will see to that," Giles asserted himself, and in the months ahead he did, without too much opposition from his spirited wife.

*Author's Note*

The occupation of Detroit by the English from August 12, 1812, until September 14, 1813, has not received much attention from historians of the War of 1812. However, the fort was the pivotal post for the English control of western Canada, as well as evidence to the Indians that the English had not abandoned them. Isaac Brock, Henry Proctor, Thomas McKee, and Sir George Prevost are not fictional characters. All of them played a vital part in the struggle for Canada. Once Commodore Oliver Perry defeated the English in Lake Erie, the English forces had to abandon Detroit and any hope of holding the western part of North America.

But the war decided little, despite President Madison's claim that the Americans had insured the "freedom of the seas." New England almost seceded from the union over Madison's intransigence. The English had abandoned the hated Orders in Council which boycotted American trade before the war even began, and once Napoleon was defeated the impressment of seamen abated. All the war settled was that Canada refused to be annexed by the United States, although ever since it has been tied strongly to the nation to the south by its economy.

The only liberty taken with the historical facts is that Bordeaux was captured by Wellington some months after the scenes in the novel. Actually, it fell to the duke following the battle for Toulouse, but aside from this one premature arrangement of historical fact, the events of the novel are accurate.

# ZEBRA REGENCIES
# ARE
# THE TALK OF THE TON!

**A REFORMED RAKE** (4499, $3.99)
by Jeanne Savery

After governess Harriet Cole helped her young charge flee to France—and the designs of a despicable suitor, more trouble soon arrived in the person of a London rake. Sir Frederick Carrington insisted on providing safe escort back to England. Harriet deemed Carrington more dangerous than any band of brigands, but secretly relished matching wits with him. But after being taken in his arms for a tender kiss, she found herself wondering—*could* a lady find love with an irresistible rogue?

**A SCANDALOUS PROPOSAL** (4504, $4.99)
by Teresa DesJardien

After only two weeks into the London season, Lady Pamela Premington has already received her first offer of marriage. If only it hadn't come from the *ton's* most notorious rake, Lord Marchmont. Pamela had already set her sights on the distinguished Lieutenant Penford, who had the heroism and honor that made him the ideal match. Now she had to keep from falling under the spell of the seductive Lord so she could pursue the man more worthy of her love. Or was he?

**A LADY'S CHAMPION** (4535, $3.99)
by Janice Bennett

Miss Daphne, art mistress of the Selwood Academy for Young Ladies, greeted the notion of ghosts haunting the academy with skepticism. However, to avoid rumors frightening off students, she found herself turning to Mr. Adrian Carstairs, sent by her uncle to be her "protector" against the "ghosts." Although, Daphne would accept no interference in her life, she *would* accept aid in exposing any spectral spirits. What she never expected was for Adrian to expose the secret wishes of her hidden heart . . .

**CHARITY'S GAMBIT** (4537, $3.99)
by Marcy Stewart

Charity Abercrombie reluctantly embarks on a London season in hopes of making a suitable match. However she cannot forget the mysterious Dominic Castille—and the kiss they shared—when he fell from a tree as she strolled through the woods. Charity does not know that the dark and dashing captain harbors a dangerous secret that will ensnare them both in its web—leaving Charity to risk certain ruin and losing the man she so passionately loves . . .

*Available wherever paperbacks are sold, or order direct from the Publisher. Send cover price plus 50¢ per copy for mailing and handling to Penguin USA, P.O. Box 999, c/o Dept. 17109, Bergenfield, NJ 07621. Residents of New York and Tennessee must include sales tax. DO NOT SEND CASH.*